Eternal Allies
in the
Epoch of Time

STEVE MEOLA

Copyright © 2017 Steve Meola.

All rights reserved. No part of this book may be used or reproduced by any means, graphic, electronic, or mechanical, including photocopying, recording, taping or by any information storage retrieval system without the written permission of the author except in the case of brief quotations embodied in critical articles and reviews.

Archway Publishing books may be ordered through booksellers or by contacting:

Archway Publishing
1663 Liberty Drive
Bloomington, IN 47403
www.archwaypublishing.com
1 (888) 242-5904

Because of the dynamic nature of the Internet, any web addresses or links contained in this book may have changed since publication and may no longer be valid. The views expressed in this work are solely those of the author and do not necessarily reflect the views of the publisher, and the publisher hereby disclaims any responsibility for them.

Any people depicted in stock imagery provided by Thinkstock are models, and such images are being used for illustrative purposes only. Certain stock imagery © Thinkstock.

ISBN: 978-1-4808-4317-2 (sc)
ISBN: 978-1-4808-4318-9 (hc)
ISBN: 978-1-4808-4319-6 (e)

Library of Congress Control Number: 2017901109

Print information available on the last page.

Archway Publishing rev. date: 1/26/2017

Contents

Chapter 1 1
Chapter 2 8
Chapter 3 22
Chapter 4 33
Chapter 5 41
Chapter 6 54
Chapter 7 64
Chapter 8 76
Chapter 9 87
Chapter 10 114
Chapter 11 127
Chapter 12 143
Chapter 13 168
Chapter 14 181
Chapter 15 192

Epilogue 197

For J.

Chapter 1

Saturday, November 10, 1984, 3:45 p.m.

It had been several days since I put my head down for some much-needed rest. I couldn't stop myself from this obsession. I had been pushing myself to the point of complete exhaustion and obsessing over my idea of constructing a time viewer. Anyway, that's what I thought it would do when it was completed: see into the past, or maybe the future. At least that is what the visions in my head told me. My hands were raw from manually twisting the copper wire into neat, tightly bound bundles for installation into the archway. The living room archway provided the perfect space for the coils of wire. I tried many different configurations of twisting the wire to produce the highest amount of magnetic force; the greater the magnetism, the greater my chances of success. With each twist of the wire, my hands produced a new blister, and now some of them were starting to crack and bleed. Reaching for another Band-Aid and applying it to the new blister, I continued to work unabated and uninterrupted, pushing forward at a fever pitch, feeling an urgency I did not understand to get this device operating.

I sat back against the wall for a moment and relaxed my hands from around the wire twister, looking at my hands; blood was seeping through the bandages. I let the twister fall to my side and watched as it hit the floor beside me. I saw it hit the floor, but the sound it made did not register in my brain until a few seconds later. I seemed to be out of sync with my surroundings, in a constant state of focused fogginess. Does that even make sense? I lifted my head and let it rest against the wall. I let my eyes close for a second and started to drift off to sleep, fighting it every step of the way.

My mind was trying to make sense of the concept of viewing objects, and even people, from the past. My thoughts were constantly moving in and out of reality, with one part of me screaming to give this up and enjoy the peace and quiet and the other side fighting just as hard, pushing me to move forward. Not only was this a crazy idea, but also the closer I got to its completion, the more I felt it might be something that might actually work.

I fell into a deeper sleep, and my brain started to work even harder. I saw formulas and schematic drawings floating in front of me, almost as if I was being programmed from some unknown outside source. I couldn't shake the constant bombardment of new data into my brain; sleeping only seemed to speed up the process. After a nap, I usually felt even more restless and unsure. Most of the time after waking up, I found myself covered in sweat, so much so that a shower and a change of clothes would be needed. Still, with everything going on within me and around me, I continued to move forward, always forward.

It was only three months ago when I first had the idea of a time viewer. I was standing outside in the back yard, grilling up a couple of burgers for Marie and me. I wanted to try out my new homemade barbecue and was keeping my fingers crossed that the thing would hold together after heat was applied to it. I had cemented together stones I found in the yard into something I could grill on. Stepping back and looking at it, moving my head side to side, I noticed that it was a little lopsided, but at least it worked. While standing there, staring into the smoke, watching the 100 percent beef patties sizzle over the open flame, I had a vision—not just any vision, but a clear, vivid projection beamed directly into my brain.

I saw in my mind's eye a machine of some kind that opened a portal into another time. I saw this as clearly as my own reflection in a mirror. I saw people standing on both sides of this machine, conversing with one another. I clearly identified that they were speaking over the distance of many decades. I had a vision of a schematic drawing that laid out the specifications in detail as to its construction and operation. Not only did I have a vision, but also for some reason, this thought was etched into my mind, and it consumed me totally. All this while grilling up some burgers! I found it hard to think about anything else or anyone else, for that matter. The only person who could break this spell was Marie, and only when she was physically next to me did I have any relief from this—shall we say—torture.

My head fell forward and snapped me out of the sleep I was experiencing. Extremely groggy, I looked over at the wall clock and noticed three hours had passed. It was now 6:47 p.m., and I still had much to do. I shook off the dizziness, took a couple of deep breaths, and returned to my project. I placed my earphones over my head and played some relaxing music to help me concentrate. The doorbell rang a few times before I realized someone was on the back porch. I dropped the tool in my hand and made a mad dash for the kitchen door, stumbling over my own feet in the process. I lifted the curtain on the window to see who it was on the other side.

Marie was standing there, holding bags filled with groceries. "Are you going to let me in or just stand there staring at me?" she said with a huge smile.

I opened the door and immediately grabbed one of the overstuffed bags in her hands. Marie instantly noticed the condition of my hands as I gripped the bag.

She only looked for a second and then shot her attention back to me, saying, "Thank you."

"No problem," I said. "Sorry, I was working on my project."

"You're always working on that thing."

"I know; sorry, I didn't hear you ringing with my earphones on."

"Did you forget I was coming over?" she asked with a little chuckle in her voice.

"I did not forget," I said in the most convincing voice I could muster. "In fact, I have the kitchen all set up for you; see? Everything is ready."

I looked around the kitchen and, to my own surprise, saw that it was indeed already set up and ready for her to make dinner, but I could not remember doing it. *Great,* I thought, *now I'm doing things and not remembering!*

We placed the food on the kitchen table, and Marie walked into the bedroom and removed her coat and shoes, making herself at home.

She returned after a few minutes, gave me a kiss, and said, "You've made a lot of progress on that thing you're working on."

"I still have a good deal to do; winding the wire around the kitchen door frame is harder than I thought."

"Yes, I can see by the bandages all over your hands that you've been very busy. Are you done for the night, or do you still have more to do?" she asked.

"I just have to put away my tools, and I will be back to help you prepare dinner."

"I'll get things started," she said with a wink, and with that, she began unpacking the bags.

I walked into the bedroom and began collecting my tools, which were scattered all over the floor. As I bent over to pick up my soldering iron, I had a vision. I had been trying to increase the amount of magnetic force my coil could produce, but no matter how many times I wrapped the fine wire around the core, it registered the same reading. The thought I had was to create several layers of individual coils instead of one single coil. It made sense in my head, but I wasn't sure how to go about it.

Marie appeared in the doorway and asked, "Are you coming?"

I sprang up and put the last of the tools away. "Sorry," I said as we walked back to the kitchen, "I was just thinking about how to wire up the coil."

"No problem. Here, you can cut these." She handed me two onions and two green bell peppers.

I quickly washed my hands, placed fresh bandages over the blisters, and began cutting the vegetables into fine cubes and putting them aside.

She was already busy preparing the chicken to be baked. Cooking with Marie was one of the few things that relaxed me. My thoughts were focused on the food and the savory aromas filling the air. We worked together quickly, and in no time, we had everything in the oven. The aroma of the chicken filled the house and mixed with the smell of the homemade tomato sauce.

"While we wait for the chicken, let's get comfy," Marie said as she took my hand and led me to the living room. "I hope there is a good movie on."

"Well, you have thirteen channels to choose from," I reminded her.

After a few turns of the knob, we settled on Channel 13 to watch an old black-and-white movie starring Humphrey Bogart.

Before the movie had ended, the chicken was ready to come out of the oven. I put a pot of water on for the pasta, lit the burner, and began to set the table.

"What this place needs is a woman's touch," Marie said, pulling a tablecloth from one of her bags.

"How much stuff is in there?" I asked her as I leaned over and looked into the now-empty bag.

She moved the table settings aside. "Here, help me spread this."

I grabbed one end of the white table cloth, and Marie took the other, and we spread it over the table, smoothing out the creases and wrinkles and then replacing the dishes and silverware to their respective positions. It gave the room a little warmth and made the bare features of the table even more inviting.

Marie stepped back to admire her work; it didn't look half-bad.

As soon as the water began to boil, I placed the homemade pasta into the pot.

"This will only take a few minutes," I said, giving the tomato sauce another stir.

Marie pulled out yet another surprise from the bottomless pit of shopping bags. "I got one of each," she said, placing two bottles of wine on the table.

The pasta was ready, and I drained the water from the pot, added

Marie's homemade sauce, and mixed them together. Then I pulled the chicken from the oven and let it sit a few minutes before cutting into it.

Everything looked perfect, including Marie, who was now trying to open a bottle of wine with my cheesy cork screw.

"I'm going to buy you real cork screw as soon as dinner is over," she said, giving the handle another turn. "This is impossible," she said with a look of despair. "Can you help me?"

I reached over and pushed the cork into the bottle.

"Why did you do that? I almost had it."

"Trust me, it's the only way to do it with that piece of shit."

We sat down to eat; as Marie served the food, I poured the wine. She adjusted her chair and looked up at the glaring florescent light flooding the room.

"Wait a minute," she said as she got up and walked into the bedroom.

When she came back, she was holding two candles. She grabbed two small plates and then melted the bottoms of the candles over a flame on the stove. She placed the melted end of the candle on the plate, where it hardened in place. She then brought them over to the table, placed them in the center, and relit the wicks.

"This will give us a little atmosphere," she said, turning off the lights.

Marie returned to the table, sat down, and gave me a quick glance before lifting her glass in my direction, giving me a hint that she wanted to toast our evening together. I lifted my glass to meet hers, and they clinked together.

"Here's to us," she said, and I repeated, "Here's to us," and then we took a sip of wine and began to eat.

Marie was a fine cook, and the meal was excellent. After we ate and cleaned up the dishes, we retired to the living room to watch a little more television. After a good meal and good wine and a good woman at my side, content and comfortable, it wasn't long before I fell asleep.

Around eleven o'clock, it began to snow, and the ground outside began to turn white. I was the first to wake up; I walked over to the window, lifted the curtain, and watched the snow falling ever so lightly, attaching itself to whatever it came in contact with. I loved how snow could turn any dull-looking street into a winter wonderland. It was very quiet outside; there wasn't a soul in sight. I opened the window and breathed in the cold, crisp air. I filled my lungs several times and then exhaled, satisfied with the effect it gave me on my brain. I turned around and noticed Marie still lying on her side; her eyes were open and she was looking out the window.

"Pretty," is all she said and then gave me a smile.

"Yes, very pretty," I replied, smiling back at her.

I stood up and walked over to her and then knelt down and touched her face.

"Yes, very pretty indeed," I whispered and then kissed her lightly on her lips.

Marie sat up and gave me a hug that almost cut off the circulation to my head.

A tear formed in one eye, which she brushed away as she said abruptly, "I have to go."

"Stay with me tonight," I said, taking her hand and kissing it lightly.

"The weather is getting bad; I should get home before the roads become too slick."

"It makes more sense for you to stay the night and leave in the morning, after the sun is up and the roads are cleared."

"I haven't brought anything to change into, or to sleep in, for that matter."

I pulled her closer and kissed her forehead and then the tip of her nose.

"You make a good argument," she said, as she returned the kisses.

She knew that she was losing the fight; we retired into my bedroom, where we both fell asleep.

Chapter 2

Marie was up early and was busy looking for articles of her clothes. "I didn't want to wake you," she said after she noticed I was up.

"That's okay; I wasn't really sleeping."

"You don't sleep much when I'm here, do you?"

"Not really."

"What do you do when I'm sleeping?"

"Sometimes, I just watch you sleep; you are like an angel, you know."

"I don't think I like the idea of you watching me while I sleep. It kind of makes me nervous."

"Why is that?"

"I don't know, you should be sleeping and not watching me sleep. It's just a little strange."

"Sorry, I just like to look at you, and when you are sleeping, you look so peaceful and a pleasure to watch. It actually relaxes me. Does that make any sense?"

"I'm not sure; I'll have to give it some thought."

With that, Marie collected the remainder of her clothes and made her way to the bathroom to wash up and get ready to leave.

"I'm not crazy about putting on the same clothes I wore yesterday," she said while closing the bathroom door.

I sat up in bed and looked over to the doorway facing the kitchen, noticing the bundles of wires surrounding the large wooden frame. *If only I can generate enough power,* I thought, *I can increase the output of magnetic field to the point where time itself will be effected.* Closing my eyes again, I could see as clear as day the schematics that I would use to build my time viewer. The next phase was now in focus. My goal was to be able to see into the past using my device and read the residual effects that people or objects left behind. Well, that was my theory, anyway.

Marie returned, all freshened up and beautiful as ever; she bent down to give me a kiss. I grabbed her and pulled her down to me and planted one on her.

"Don't start something you can't finish," she said with a smile.

With that, I smiled back and released her from my arms. I stood up, walked over to the window, and looked outside. Whatever snow fell on the street overnight had already melted. Marie would have no trouble getting home.

She stood up, put on her coat and shoes, and turned to me with her arms open. "Well …," she began.

I gave her a big hug and thanked her for a wonderful, romantic evening.

She returned the hug and looked at me with some sadness in her eyes; something seemed to be troubling her.

"Are you okay?" I asked.

"I'm fine; I just have something in my eye," she said, clearing her throat.

She began to reply but stopped; looking up at me, she smiled and said, "I have to go," and with that, she threw her arms around my neck and kissed me hard on the lips.

Her face was wet from a tear that had formed; I could feel it on my cheek. She turned and let herself out the front door. I thought to myself that our parting seemed a little emotional but passed it off as nothing serious. I watched from the window as Marie walked over to her car and stopped for a second just before putting her key in the lock; she turned and looked up at the window, perhaps rethinking her decision to leave, and then got into her car and drove away.

I washed up, ate some breakfast, and then sat down to sketch out my ideas for new the coil configuration. I worked hard throughout the day and into the night and the following day, as well. I was able to rewire the entire device and was about to test it when the phone rang. I was almost delirious from the lack of sleep and answered the phone.

It was my father, who told me he had decided to sell the house that I was living in. He

had purchased the house from his sisters and brothers some years ago, after the death of my grandfather. He just wanted to let me know so I would have time to make other arrangements. *Hmm*, I thought, *other arrangements! That's just perfect. Where am I going to go?* I refocused my attention on the mass of wires hanging from the wooden molding of the kitchen door frame.

I spent the day reinstalling the wooden molding, thus hiding the wires from sight. I had run the wires to the breaker box but did not yet connect them. There were still some tests I needed to conduct to make sure it was safe to turn on, but even then, I did not know if it would it work or would it just sit there and catch fire.

A week went by, and then another while I went about my daily routine. I went to work, came home, and then repeated the sequence. With each day that passed, I developed another excuse not to test the coil. Before I knew it, I was packing my things and getting ready to move into the new apartment I had found. I tried calling Marie to tell her where I was moving, but the operator said that her phone had been disconnected.

It had been weeks since I last spoke to her. After one last look around, I loaded the remainder of my things into my car, left the keys on the front porch, and drove away to start another chapter of my life. I decided to make a detour before driving over to my new apartment in Bloomfield. I drove past Marie's place and noticed her car parked in the driveway.

I was tempted to pull over and knock on her door but decided that I would leave her a note with my new phone number and just see what happens. All I managed to do today was cloud my head further with the thought of her going off with that other guy and getting married. Some little part of my brain would not accept the reality of the situation and for some reason kept me moving further and further away from her. I drove to my new apartment and moved into the new place.

It was just starting to get dark; the air was cold, and it was at this point that my mind started to wander back to Marie and all the fun we had shared together over the years. I sat on the floor with only a blanket and pillow to separate me from the cold wood. I shifted myself, put my head down on the pillow, and just stared at the ceiling. I closed my eyes and drifted off the sleep.

When morning came, I turned side to side, trying to find a spot on my body that didn't hurt from sleeping on the floor. I sat up slowly and looked around my small one-room apartment; everything was still in boxes and resting the floor. I pulled myself up, stretched my arms and legs, and gave out a yawn that sounded more like a dying cat. I walked over to one of the boxes and pulled out my notes and drawings for the magnetic coil. I glanced at the drawing of the visualization output reader and realized that I had not taken into account the secondary receiver coil.

This was a huge flaw in my design, and only now, after leaving the Newark house, did I understand the complexity of the situation. If only I could have taken the entire device with me to continue my work, but the location was absolutely critical. The exact spot where the coil was installed in the Newark house had a unique quality, as my early magnetic readings revealed. This exact spot in particular had a high electromagnetic force; after months of investigation, I could not determine how this was possible.

There was absolutely nothing in the vicinity that would give off such a reading. It seemed to be picking up a ghost reading. This was my interpretation, of course. I was picking up something, but what? My device would be able to amplify the faint but detectable electromagnetic readings. If my calculations were correct, I should be able to create a visual representation using the magnetic field and in turn see what (or who) was creating this phenomenon.

Every living thing on the planet gives off some degree of

electromagnetic force. This force is detectable with specialized and ultrasensitive devices. The problem is that once the object is removed from the field of view, the reading slowly disappears. My viewing coil would magnify the sensitivity to the point where it could see electromagnetic readings from the past. It would be able to determine what made the reading and thus reconstruct it into visual form. My theory was that if a person had walked though this doorway sometime in the past, I should be able to sense that person and create a visual representation. I had tried hundreds of other locations and found that only this spot worked.

With a new design in mind, I began drawing the secondary coil. I knew that I would never be able to test it unless I was to somehow move back into the Newark house. For now, I would have to settle for a design in theory only. I spent the rest of the day with my head in my hands, trying to solve the problem of primary and secondary coil collaboration. The device would not work if one of the sections was not functioning properly.

The day turned into night as I continued working on the problem. About 9:30, I realized that I had not eaten all day. I was feeling a little weak and could not focus my eyes. I decided to call it a night and treat myself to a hot shower and head out for a bite to eat. I needed to clear my head, and the possibility of the fresh air and a warm meal may present a new perspective to my problem.

As I stepped out of the shower, I realized that my phone was ringing. I had it set so low that it was almost undetectable. Leaving wet footprints from the shower to the phone, I picked it up.

"Hey."

"Marie, is that you?"

"Yes; are you alone?"

"Yes, I'm alone; I was just getting ready to head out for a bite to eat. Care to join me?"

"I would love to. Where are you?"

"I'll pick you up on my way out, and we can have dinner together. Are you home?"

"Yes. How much time do I have to get ready?"

"I should be there in about forty-five minutes."

"I'll meet you outside; I'll be standing next to my car, okay?"

"I'll see you soon," I said and hung up the phone.

Between the hot shower and the call from Marie, I felt a renewed sense of energy building inside of me. Just the sound of this woman's voice always had such a calming effect on me. It was a shame that someone else was enjoying her many attributes instead of me.

I started to get dressed but had a hard time finding my clothes in the pile of boxes. I did manage to put something together but wasn't sure if the colors matched; I wasn't even sure if I cared. The thought now was to see Marie; everything else was secondary. I finished tying my shoes and began searching for my car keys. *I really have to put this place in order,* I thought to myself as I lifted yet another box to discover my keys underneath. I grabbed them and flew out the door like a man on a mission. It wasn't long before I was pulling up to Marie's place, and true to her word, she was standing there, next to her car. It was another cold evening, and her coat did not seem to be offering her enough protection.

I got out of my car and began to walk around to the passenger side to open her door, but she raced forward and said, "I got this," and let herself in.

I got back into the car and was met with a huge, chilly kiss.

"Oh, my God, it's cold out there," she said as we pulled away. "So where are we going?"

"I thought we'd go to the Nevada Diner, if that's okay."

"Sounds good, let's go," and with that, Marie sat back in her seat and briskly rubbed her hands together, putting them to her mouth and using her warm breath to remove the sting of cold. "Ah, heat," she said as she put both hands in front of the blowers on the dash.

"How long were you out there?" I asked.

"Only about five minutes, but it felt longer."

After a few minutes, the car's heater did its job, and Marie started to feel normal again. "So what have you been doing with yourself?"

"I've been w—"

And before I could complete the sentence, she finished it for me: "Working on your project."

"Yes, I was working on my project. So how are you?" I asked.

"I'm good, and you?"

"I'm okay, I guess." I looked over in her direction and noticed that she was smiling. "You look happy," I said with some degree of a question in my voice.

"I'm happy to see you," she said, with the emphasis on "you," putting her hand on my lap.

"Well, I'm happy that you're happy to see me."

And in turn, Marie replied, "Well, I'm happy that you're happy that I'm happy to see you."

At this point, we both started to laugh, and the laughter continued through dinner. We always had such a nice time together; every date with her, I remembered, was always next to perfection. She had a way of putting you at ease and letting you just be yourself, whatever that may be.

We finished our meal, and she suggested we go back to have some tea at my new place. I told her that I wasn't really ready for company, but just one look at her dreamy brown eyes made the words "Come over" fall out of my mouth. I don't know what it is about her that melts my heart and sends me into another dimension, where time and space give way to a place where only the two of us exist.

I pulled into the long driveway, making sure I did not block any of the other cars. Marie and I raced from the car up the stairs to my door, where I fumbled for my keys. The light above the door was out, so it was hard to see, but I managed to get it open, and being that we were both leaning on the door, we partially fell inside. After a very brief tour of the room, Marie removed her coat and placed it over the back of a chair.

"This is small even for you, but at the same time, it looks cozy," she said, walking over to the kitchen area. "Where's your teapot?"

"I'm not sure; I think it's in this box over here," I said, lifting the cover and pulling out several other items before finding the teapot. "Here it is," I said, as if finding buried treasure.

I handed it to Marie, and she filled the pot with water and then placed it on the tiny two-burner stove. With a turn of the knob, the flame was on, and then I was set to the task of finding tea bags. I figured it would make sense, putting the tea bags with the teapot, but as I emptied the box of all its contents, I realized that I wasn't as smart with the packing as I imagined myself to be.

"Here they are," Marie exclaimed, as if discovering an important clue in a cold case file. "Now we can have tea and warm up."

"You mind if I try and straighten up a bit?"

"Go right ahead," she said as she took another look around. "Where's your —"

"Bathroom?" I finished.

"Yes, how did you —?"

"Just a guess," I said. "It's over there." I pointed to what looked like a built-out closet.

"I'll be right back," she said as she took her huge purse with her. "Oh, keep an eye on the water for me."

"No problem," I responded with a sense of purpose, as I headed toward the stove. Keeping one eye on the kettle and the other on the mound of boxes, I began to organize the clutter in the middle of the room.

After some time and considerable thought and planning, I managed to make some sense of the mess of boxes; taking decisive action, I pushed everything into one corner. I picked up the blanket and pillows from the floor and placed them neatly on top of the pile of boxes. Stepping back and surveying my hard work, I thought it actually made the room look somewhat bigger.

Just then, the teapot began to whistle. I turned it off and found the two mugs that Marie had put out for us, with the tea bags inside. I poured the water and allowed the tea to steep.

"I smell tea," Marie said as she emerged from the bathroom.

"What?" she said, looking at me with the kettle still in my hand. "I changed into something a little more comfy, do you mind?"

Still looking in her direction, I said, "No, not at all."

Marie had changed into a pair of sweatpants and an oversized football shirt. Man, this woman could put on a potato sack and make it look sexy. She threw her clothes into her purse and placed it on top of the new pile of boxes, which actually came in handy to get the other clutter off the floor.

We sat down on my only two chairs and had our tea. I switched on my little TV, and we moved ourselves to the floor, where I propped up what pillows and blankets I had, giving us a cushy place to spread out.

"I like rustic," Marie said with a smile. "First thing you need to do is get a bed."

I looked around my little apartment, trying to figure out where I would put a bed if I had one, then saying to Marie, "I know; it hurts to sleep on a hard floor, and it gets cold at night."

We snuggled up close together and finished our tea. "It is a little cold," she said.

"Yes, it is," I said, not taking the hint from Marie to pull her closer and share our body heat. After a while, I figured it out and added, "I'm sorry, where are my manners?" I pulled her closer to me, and she rested her head on my chest.

Her hair was soft and silky, and it gave off the pleasing aroma of something light and sweet but not overpowering. I always enjoyed playing with her hair, feeling it fall through my fingers; in many ways, it seemed to relax her.

"This is nice," she said as she slipped one arm around me and rested her hand on my stomach.

She exhaled slowly, and I could feel her warm breath on my chest. I began to rub her shoulder slowly and then moved my arm down her back.

"Ummm," she said as she lifted her head slightly and gazed into my eyes.

I could feel my body warming up, and the room itself began to melt away. Looking into her eyes, I slipped down to meet her at eye level and kissed her lightly on her lips.

I cupped her face into my hands and took a mental picture. "You are so beautiful," I said and kissed her again and again.

Marie responded with kisses of her own, as she maneuvered into a more comfortable position. I began to lose myself in time and space; all of the problems I was facing faded away as I took her into my arms.

I began kissing her, with tiny little pecks from her head down to her neck, stopping to inhale her sweet aroma. Her skin was so soft that it made me want to touch it all the time. I inhaled again, and her essence filled my senses, transporting me to another place.

"Ummm," Marie sighed again.

We shifted ourselves again to where we could watch the little TV flicker away, giving off a sort of electronic candlelight and setting the mood. We started to reminisce about days together not so long ago and how we always seem to have a wonderful time together. We laughed and giggled like children as we remembered some of the crazy things I did while working at the pizzeria in Clifton back in 1980.

"I remember you used to catch flies with your hand."

"Yes, and I would put them into plastic bags and freeze them."

"That was a little strange; why did you do that again?"

"I just wanted to see if they would come back to life after they defrosted."

"Huh," Marie replied, as she reached over to touch my forehead and feel for a temperature.

We continued to exchange stories and memories, as we sometimes do until we started to get sleepy.

Marie positioned her head on my chest and let out a sigh. "You have a strong heartbeat," she said, nestling herself even closer. Her scent filled the air and transformed my dingy little apartment into a home.

It wasn't long before Marie drifted off to sleep. I just watched her sleeping for a long time. She reminded me of an angel when she slept; she looked so peaceful and content. Watching her made me feel peaceful and content as well, and I began to drift off to sleep too.

The next morning came, and Marie was already busy, washing up and brushing her teeth and getting dressed. I opened my eyes and noticed the faint glint of sunlight peeking through a crack in the window shade, causing me to blink several times to focus. I took notice of Marie, moving around the room like a woman who had a laundry list of items she was trying to take care of.

"Hey there, good morning," she said and bent down and kissed me.

"Good morning; what time is it?"

"It's almost seven."

"What?"

"Are you hungry? I'm hungry."

"I have nothing here; let me wash up and change, and we can go out for breakfast, okay?"

"That sounds like a plan. I'll just make some tea while you get ready."

"Just give me a few minutes; this floor is tough on my back."

"Yeah, I know what you mean; took me awhile to pick myself up this morning."

Marie put on some water for tea, sat down on the blanket, and switched on the TV. "Got to know what's happening in the world," she said.

I moved slowly into the bathroom and took a quick shower and got myself together. After fifteen minutes, I was ready to go. Marie stood up and grabbed her coat and shoes, and I did the same.

We went out the door, and I decided to go to the Nevada Diner in Bloomfield; they always had good food there, and I knew we were both hungry for a well-cooked breakfast. As soon as we were seated, we ordered coffee. Marie picked up a menu and paged through it for something tasty. I already knew what I wanted and just sat there, waiting for the coffee to be served. The waitress arrived with our coffee and asked if we had decided what we wanted. Marie ordered a western omelet with a tomato salsa and rye toast dry. I asked for a Swiss cheese omelet and a toasted corn muffin.

During breakfast, Marie's mood changed slightly, and I noticed her staring out the window a few times, as if preoccupied with something.

"Anything on your mind?" I asked.

"Sorry."

"What are you thinking about?"

"Oh, nothing. I was just daydreaming, I guess. Why do you ask?"

"It's just that I always see you with a smile and feeling happy, but today, you seem like you have something troubling you."

"Oh sweetie, nothing I can't handle, nothing for you to worry about."

I sat there across the table from her, watching as she replied. Her eyes never met mine, and that made me a little unsettled.

Afterwards, I took Marie home and pulled up in her driveway. She sat in my car for a minute or so, not moving or saying a word.

Then she turned to me, looked into my eyes, and touched my hand with hers. "I, um, I had a great time with you last night."

"So did —"

"Shh, I just wanted to tell you that," she said with some degree of sadness in her voice.

"Anything wrong?" I asked her.

"Nothing, nothing at all when it comes to you; everything is just perfect." With that, she reached over and kissed me, got out of the car, and made her way to her apartment.

I sat there for a few minutes and watched her go inside. I caught myself thinking out loud, asking why she still bothered with me when she had this other guy who wanted to marry her. As if having a conversation with another person, I answered out loud, "Because she loves you, dummy!"

I took a deep breath, put the car into drive, and headed home, all the while thinking that this may have been the last time we would ever be together. I think that a lot, you know. I'm just not sure why I don't do something about it. No other woman had ever made me feel more like a man than she did, yet I hesitate. I hold back. I just don't understand why.

I arrived at my apartment, parked the car, and sat for a minute or two, thinking about the night with Marie. Clearing my head, I realized that I should get to the task of unpacking and getting myself settled. I went inside and dove right into the boxes. Time passed quickly as one box after another was emptied.

It was just about six o'clock when the phone rang. I followed the cord until I found the phone under some newspapers on the floor. I picked it up and said hello. I heard a voice that sounded familiar.

"I just have to warn you not to complete the project; it will be disastrous," the voice said in a low and almost growling tone.

"Who is this?" I asked.

After a few seconds of silence, the line went dead, and I was left standing there with my mouth open. My mind began to race, as I struggled to make sense of the call. Outside of Marie and myself, who knew about my project? Who outside of Marie had my new phone number? I hadn't given it out to anyone else.

I stood there, staring at the phone, half-expecting it ring again, with the other person saying they were only joking, but it did not. I walked over to my little kitchen table, where my notes and plans rested, and just stared at them with concern. *I could really be on to something here,* I thought. What would be the harm of detecting people's images from the past? Besides, there was no finishing the project now; I did not have access to the location any more. I thought it pointless to continue working on the plans and started to gather the papers together in order to store them away, but something caught my eye. I sat down, pulled a lamp off the floor, and placed it on the table for a better view.

The primary and secondary coils needed a way to communicate together, some way of regulating the collector or receiver coil and another way of controlling the discharge or display coil. After all this time, I finally realized that without some way to control the flow of collected energy, the discharge would be dangerous, the way a capacitor discharges its stored-up charge. The magnetic field surrounding the device should insulate the process, just like the earth's magnetic field protects against gamma rays from the sun penetrating through and destroying all life on the planet. The complexity of the problem seemed to be bigger than I imagined, but time was on my side, and the fact remained that the application could not be applied because of my circumstances. For now, it would remain a work in progress.

I gathered up the drawings and notes, rolled them together into a cylinder, and placed a rubber band around it to secure it. I put the plans off to the side until I could figure out what to do about the control portion of the project.

Realizing I needed some sleep, I moved over to the temporary bed on the floor, put my head down on the pillow, and stretched out. It was quiet in the apartment, and the thought of the previous night was still on my mind. It was then that I recognized the scent on the pillows and pulled one into my face and inhaled. Marie's scent was on them, and I couldn't get enough, as I took in another breath and then placed the pillow under my head. I felt myself drifting off to sleep, with all the day's events passing in front of me, one by one. Still, there was something at the edge of my mind, something about control, something …

Chapter 3

Weeks passed, and I had no contact with Marie whatsoever. I kept myself busy with work and the occasional reconfiguration of a section of my imaging device. It all looked good on paper, but would it work? At this point, I had no way of knowing for sure, and looking forward, it didn't seem that I would ever get the chance to test my theory. Feeling defeated before I had even begun, I again returned the drawings to the corner of my room. I decided to turn on the television and treat my brain to something that did not require much thought. I switched the TV to Channel 5 and started to watch a program about computers in the home. Can you imagine every person being able to afford a computer for their home? What would they do with them, anyway?

I turned to Channel 7 and started watching a movie about a lost dog. *Well*, I thought to myself, *it's better than nothing*, and walked over to my new foldout sofa bed and sat down. I watched the movie, but my mind was constantly wandering, first to my device and then to Marie and back again. I couldn't seem to stay focused on any one thing long enough to make any progress. I guess I can apply that reasoning to Marie and me, as well. Just then, I realized the amount of time that had passed since I last saw her; I decided to take a chance and give her a call.

Marie's phone rang for five minutes before I decided to hang up. I figured that I would try again later in the day. If only she had an answering machine, I could leave her a message and then she could get back to me, but I knew she didn't have one, so I had to settle for hit-or-miss. I began to feel restless and wanted some stimulation, so

I got myself together and went for a drive. I wasn't out long when I noticed that my car was taking me past my former residence in Newark. I didn't even realize I was heading toward the house until I was right up in front of it.

I stopped, pulled over, got out of the car, and walked over to the front stoop. I put my hand on the brick front. This action reconnected me in some way to the old place, and I began to remember many interesting nights that were spent here. Many of them included Marie and me. I looked up at one of the first-floor windows and noticed an old man looking down at me. I could see from the look in his eyes that he thought I was up to no good. I stared back at the man and looked at him intently; with a squint in my eyes, I thought he looked familiar. The man stood there motionless, with his eyes fixed solely on me and on my every move. He stared at me until I removed my hand from the stoop; I returned to my car and drove out of sight.

Again, I found myself driving aimlessly toward nothing in particular. I then decided to visit my parents in Nutley. The drive from Newark to Nutley took about twenty minutes, and before I knew it, I was ringing the bell.

My mother came to the door and said, with a smile, "Hey, it's Doug." She let me in.

Instinctively, I migrated into the kitchen and opened the refrigerator to see what goodies were available for consumption. Mom always had plenty of leftovers waiting to be discovered. I found a plate of cold fried chicken, pulled it out, and placed it on the table. I then poured myself a glass of milk and sat down for a quick snack.

My mother and father came out to the kitchen to join me, and we all sat around the table, catching up with conversation. I asked my father about the new owners of the Newark house and when they moved in.

My father gave me a confused look and said, "The new owners have not taken possession yet; the house is still empty, something about their bank loan. I'm not really sure."

I said with a degree of certainty in my voice that I was there today and saw a man in the window, looking right at me.

"That's impossible," Dad said. "I have not turned over the keys yet, and I made sure it was locked up tight when I left there just yesterday."

I sat for a moment or two, thinking that maybe my mind was playing tricks on me, but the old man in the window looked so real. He seemed angry that I was there, touching his front stoop.

Again, I sat and thought and then remembered the phone call some weeks ago, when a man called and warned me not to finish my project. This was getting a little strange, and I asked my father if I could borrow the keys and check the place out for myself.

"If it will make you feel better, here," he said, passing a set of the keys over to me.

I fumbled the keys for a minute or two, playing with them in my hand. I thought for a second of handing them back to my father and forgetting about the whole thing, but I gripped them tightly and placed them securely into my pocket.

I finished my snack and felt a sense of urgency building inside of as I made ready to leave. "I'll be back shortly," I said as I headed out the door.

I could not understand what I thought I had seen. The fact that I was second-guessing myself left me feeling uneasy and insecure. I had to make sure the house was empty; I wanted to prove to myself that it was all in my head. When I reached the Newark house, it was just starting to get dark. I pulled up to the front of the house and climbed out of the car.

I walked up to the small gate, opened it, and then closed it behind me. I continued to walk along the side of the house to the rear, where I would take the stairs to the second-floor porch and enter the house that way. This was always the way I came in and out when I lived here, so it felt quite normal. After reaching the kitchen door, I inserted the key, gave it a turn, and opened it slowly. I stepped inside the kitchen and took a look around but left the door wide open, just in case I needed a quick exit.

I expected to see complete emptiness, wall-to-wall nothing, and that is what I witnessed. Nothing seemed out of the ordinary, as I passed from one room to the other. I walked over to the front window, where I thought I had seen the old man staring at me earlier that day, and pulled back the curtain, only to find nothing but a dirty window pane. I was about to turn around when I saw something out of the corner of my eye. There was something metallic lying on the floor next to the door that led to the upper floor. I walked over, picked it up, and examined it. It appeared to be a flat piece of aluminum, the size of a business card. Inscribed on it were several groups of numbers.

I wasn't sure what to think but placed it in my pocket and opened the door to the upper level. I moved toward the staircase, and just as I started to climb up, I heard a noise. It was the sound of someone talking, and it was coming from the upper level. I began to climb the stairs, and with each creaky step up, the voice I was hearing became louder and louder.

I reached the top step and stood just outside the door to the attic. I did not move any farther but strained to hear if there were any signs of movement or voices. As I stood there, I heard a clicking sound and then nothing at all. The attic was dark, and I knew the only light fixture was inside the first room. I did not think that someone would have moved it from its location, so I stepped into the first room, turned to the left, reached out, and touched the lamp base.

I followed the base with my hand to the top bowl, where the pull cord was located, and gave it a tug. Nothing; the light did not work, and then, thinking that maybe I didn't pull it hard enough, I tried it again. This time, the incandescent bulb clicked on and flooded the attic with a wash of dull yellow light.

At first glance, everything appeared normal, but then, I heard that voice again. This time, it was clear and audible, and I recognized the person who was speaking: It was me. It reminded me of one of the recordings I made some years ago, when I used to keep track of my thoughts about electromagnetism and other things that interested me. I moved slowly and cautiously into the second room; the voice sounded like it was right there in front of me. I looked around but found nothing. Then, I noticed something at the opening of the third room.

Just to the left of the doorway on the floor was a tape recorder, still plugged into the wall; inside the compartment was a cassette tape caught in a loop. The voice said, "Whatever you do, don't finish the project." It was my voice for sure, but it seemed aged in some way. I hit the Stop button, and the tape popped out of the recorder. I reached for it and held it to the light for a better look.

I could see that the tape was, in fact, made to repeat a message over and over again. The hair on my arms stood at attention as I struggled to grasp the situation. Who or what was trying to get my attention, and why were they warning me not to finish my project?

I gave the three rooms one final sweep, just to make sure that nothing was overlooked. After I was sure that the entire floor was clear, I took the tape recorder, put the cassette into my pocket, and headed back down to the main level. I descended the stairs slowly and cautiously looked back over my shoulder a couple of times. I walked past the window where I thought I saw the man earlier and reached over to pull the curtain back into its proper place, but before I could swing it over, I noticed something strange on the window that had not been there before. The window appeared slightly moist, as if someone was breathing on it, and if that wasn't strange enough, there was something written in the moisture. It appeared to be the symbol for infinity.

What the hell was going on here? I was the only one in this house; I was sure of it. How could this happen without my knowledge? I looked around the main floor again and called out a faint, "Hello, is anyone here?"

There was, of course, no reply. I continued to walk toward my point of entry in the kitchen. As I came up to the archway that separated the kitchen from what used to be my bedroom, I encountered a shadowy figure in the shape of a man. It appeared briefly and then was gone, and what followed struck me dumfounded. The unmistakable smell of ozone filled my nostrils. Ozone, a colorless toxic gas with a pungent odor and powerful oxidizing properties, is formed by the sudden release of high electrical discharges. A large amount of energy is required to produce ozone, such as a lightning strike.

The smell of ozone quickly dissipated, and it left me standing motionless for another minute or two. Remembering that my coil bundle was still packed away behind the thick molding of the archway, I reached out and placed my hand along the molding and traced the entire perimeter. It was cold to the touch and did not appear to represent any immediate danger. Still, I had been subject to strange phenomena over the past few months, ever since I redesigned the coil bundle, but I never even had the opportunity to test it. I thought for a moment and tried to convince myself that it was all in my mind and that everything was a result of a lack of sleep or stress at work and even my relationship with Marie, something, anything, but not the fact that I may be going crazy. I brushed off the thought of going crazy and settled for the notion that I would eventually figure out what was going on. Maybe there was a ghost in the house; that at least would explain some things, but would it really? I took one last look around the kitchen before closing and locking the door behind me.

The ride back to my parents' house was brief, and as soon as I arrived, I found both my mother and father waiting for me at the door.

"Well?" my father asked with one eyebrow slightly elevated.

"Well what?" I replied.

"Did you see anyone in the house?"

"No, I did not; you were right, it was empty, and there were no signs that anyone had been inside. Everything was just as I had left it when I moved out."

"That's a relief," he exclaimed.

I handed the keys to him, said my good-byes, and returned to my car. Well, I did need a little stimulation; I guess I should be careful what I wished for in the future. Hmmm. "In the future"; something about that phrase weighed heavily inside my brain. Again, I brushed it off instead of overthinking the situation. What I needed now was some rest and a chance to recharge.

It wasn't long before I found myself back at my little apartment. I immediately emptied my pockets of the items I recovered from the Newark house. I placed the small piece of metal, the cassette, and tape recorder on the kitchen table. I stared at the metal strip intently and then picked it up for another look. Its edges were not entirely smooth, and a closer examination with a magnifying glass revealed tiny peaks and valleys, like you would see on a regular key, but much less prominent. The tiny serrations were only visible on three sides of the metal strip. The numbers stamped into the metal made absolutely no sense to me. There were three sets of numbers; each group had eleven numbers within it. The first set started with a 3 and the next set started with a 6, and the last set began with a 9. What this represented was totally unknown to me. It may be nothing at all, maybe a part to a kid's toy or to a mechanical device of some sort. Whatever it was, I decided to hold onto it for now.

I placed the small metal strip down on the table once again and picked up the cassette. Other than the obvious alteration, the thing appeared to be perfectly normal. I plugged in the player, put the cassette into it, and pushed Play. I wanted to turn up the volume and listen more carefully to the message. I waited a few seconds for the message to begin, but for some reason, it would not play. My first thought was that maybe I had damaged the volume control on the player in some way and could not hear it. I ejected the tape and placed another one in its place. I closed the cover and pushed Play again, and the heavy sound of music filled the room.

It was a song from Meatloaf's *Bat Out of Hell*. I turned it off and switched the tapes again and pushed the Play button once again, and still nothing; no sound at all. I looked down at the tape itself and could see the tiny wheels spinning in unison. I sat back in my chair and again thought that maybe I had imagined the entire thing. Maybe there was a ghost in that house, or maybe I somehow erased the tape while in transport.

Just then it hit me: erased? Hmmm, I wondered, as I picked up the tiny piece of metal and brought it over to the stove. As soon as it made contact with the metal surface, it magnetically attached itself. The magnetic force that this small piece of metal contained was astonishing, and removing it was quite difficult. That would explain why the tape was erased: The strong magnetic force wiped it clean. I was unconsciously destroying the evidence of my own sanity. This raised the question: Did I actually hear what I thought I heard? Was I going crazy?

With my brain spinning in circles, I decided to stop thinking so much; I gathered everything together and put it into a box next to my plans for the imaging coil. I didn't want to consider it any longer. After everything was out of sight, I felt somewhat relieved. I walked over to the phone, picked it up, and started to dial Marie's number, but then I changed my mind and put it down. It wasn't unusual for Marie and I not to see each other for weeks or even months at a time, and I didn't want her to think my only reason for calling her was to release stress. Besides, I knew she had other people in her life right now. I'd just be getting in the way.

That thought of getting in the way with Marie and her life outside our little world caused me to pause and reflect on what the hell I was doing. I knew I loved this woman, and I loved every single second we were together. I knew that she was intelligent and sexy and beautiful and so many other attributes that are hard to find, all wrapped up in one woman, yet there she was, and here I was, and there you had it. I felt strongly that we were meant to be together; every part of me was in agreement, yet some force unseen was keeping us apart. Oh, we got together on occasion and caught up quickly on events in our lives, and then it was like no time had passed at all. We just continued where we left off. One thing I was thinking about lately was the fact that Marie and I never discussed in any real detail our feelings for each other. We talked about everything under the sun, but when it came to us, we were silent. Why was that, do you think? We made such a great couple; why couldn't we move on to the next level? Why did I let this other guy continue to exist in her life?

I sat at the table with my head in my hands, pining away over Marie and the relationship we had settled into. I had to stop kicking myself over this, I thought, and walked over to the television and switched it on. *Pride of the Yankees*, one of my favorite movies of all time, was playing on Channel 13. This caused me to sit down instantly and stare at the tiny screen. For the next hour, I was at peace in my head, and it gave me a chance to catch my breath, so to speak. After the movie was over, I once again picked up the phone and called Marie; the operator answered and said that the line was disconnected. Again with a disconnected phone line; hmmm, maybe she didn't pay her phone bill or something? I put the phone down, and a thought occurred to me: Maybe she would call me eventually, and then we would get together again.

Then a strange feeling came over me, a small pain in my chest, followed by a doubt in my mind. I wondered if she had run off with that other guy, left me without saying good-bye, but I knew she would never do that. She was always too concerned about hurting other people's feelings to just run out and not say anything. The thoughts in my head continued until I just had to drive over to Marie's place to see what was up. I didn't like just showing up unannounced, but I felt like I had no choice.

All the way over to Marie's apartment, I found myself talking out loud; I actually held a conversation with myself. I was running scenarios through my head to see which one would hurt least, but whatever way I sliced it, it still ended sadly. I pulled up in front of her apartment and got out of my car. I looked up at the top floor, where her apartment was, but there were no lights inside, and her car was not in the driveway. I decided to leave her a note on her door, asking her to call me, so I scribbled something down and walked up the steps to her door.

Before I could leave the note, I noticed a small envelope wedged into the window pane; on the front, it read "Doug." My first thought was that this was my Dear John letter (or Dear Doug letter, as was appropriate in this case). My heart sank deep into my chest as I removed the envelope from the pane. I put it in my pocket, right next to my own note, and headed back home. I didn't want to read it until later; I didn't want to see the words "Good-bye." I just didn't want to think about it.

I drove around the main avenue of Nutley for an hour, going back and forth, over and over again, before heading home. I put off reading Marie's letter as long as I could stand it. After I got back to my apartment, I sat down at my little kitchen table, opened the envelope, and removed the pages. It began "Dear Doug"; my heart sank deep into my chest, and breathing became a little difficult. I continued reading: "Knowing you as I do, I figured that you would eventually come to see me and find this letter. This is not the way I wanted to say good-bye. I tried several times to tell you when we were last together, but the words would not come. We had such a wonderful time together, and I just couldn't stand to see your face after I had told you that Brian and I were going to become officially engaged. I feel that I must let you know that I wish it was you that I was getting married to.

"I have tried over the years not to let you into my heart, because your heart and mind were in so many places at the same time. I didn't think that you were ready for this type of commitment. I may be wrong in assuming that your obsession for science and that project of yours kept you far enough away from me so that we could never progress as a couple. I want you to know that even though this is supposed to be a happy time for me, I can't help but feel I have lost my best friend/lover, and it makes me very sad. You will always have a special place in my heart. I tried not to, but I can't help the fact that I fell in love with you. There, I said it; now you know. Good-bye, Doug. I will truly miss you! Marie."

I carefully placed the pages back into the envelope and put it off to the side. The totality of the letter started to sink in. I could feel my eyes begin to swell, and tears rolled down both cheeks. It felt like my little world was falling apart. I wasn't sure how long I sat there, crying like a baby and wishing that I never knew anything about electromagnetism. I guess I always thought that we would just be there, whenever either one of us wanted to get together. I took her for granted, and I never knew her true feelings for me; that is, until now. I searched my own heart and discovered that I loved her, as well. I guess it was not meant to be. I hoped she would be happy. I wished I could have told her good-bye, but then again, that may have been worse. I don't know.

Feeling an overwhelming surge of anger, I stood up abruptly, forced my chair back into the wall, and then watched as it toppled over. I felt another surge of anger envelop me as I reached over to the corner, where I had stored my notes and drawings for my project. I picked everything up off the floor and haphazardly stuffed it into a box. I taped the box shut with one roll of tape and then another. I threw the box into a corner and made it my goal never to open it up again. I was finished with it.

Chapter 4

The years passed, one after the other; seasons changed, and time worked its way into my body. I was no longer a young man with dreams of becoming famous for discovering a way to see into the past. I had given up that life many years ago. I had since married and had a daughter which my wife and I named Ariana and then divorced and was now getting ready to move into another house. I read online about a month ago that the old Newark house was up for sale. The thought of moving back there brought back memories of a much better time. The price was something I could definitely afford, and it was available for immediate occupancy. I called the Realtor who had listed the house and made an appointment to see it right away.

I met the agent at the house; upon seeing me, he extended his hand and introduced himself. "Hello, Mr. Lupo, I'm Robert Morrison, your agent from Shultz Realty."

"Nice to meet you," I said, and I took hold of his hand and gave it the appropriate squeeze.

"Are you ready to see the home?" he asked with some degree of excitement in his voice.

"Yes, I am. I was hoping that we could get started right away."

"No problem, sir," Robert said as he turned to open the key box on the front door knob. He fumbled with the combination a few times before getting it right, opened the box, and removed the keys to the house.

"You're my first customer," he said with a squeaky voice.

"First customer today?" I asked.

"No, first customer ever," was his response.

Robert was very young and very eager, and I could tell that this sale would mean a lot for him. Still, I wanted to negotiate a lower price, and I had the feeling that he would be the right person for that.

"Do you know this area at all, Mr. Lupo?"

"Yes, I do; as a matter of fact, I used to live in this house when I was younger."

"Oh? How long ago was that?"

"Well, let me see now, it's been about twenty-eight years since I last set foot in this house."

"Twenty-eight years? Wow, that's quite a while ago," exclaimed Robert.

"Yes, it is, quite a long time."

Robert managed to unlock the front door; we stepped into the small foyer, and then he opened the secondary door, and we stepped into the house. We were instantly met with the stale odor of mildew, which seemed to waft into our faces. There were cobwebs hanging down from the light fixture in the main entrance, just in front of the staircase. There was an even layer of dust on the floors, which displayed no human activity in quite some time. Ours were the only footprints on the floor.

Robert gestured with his hand that I should take a look around. "I'll be right here for questions should you need me," he said, as if hesitant to move any farther into the house.

"That's okay, Robert. I still remember my way around. I'll take myself on a tour. But Robert?"

"Yes, sir?"

"Tell me something. I'm a bit curious."

"Sure, sir, what are you curious about?"

"Correct me if I am wrong, but when a Realtor lists a home for sale, don't they at least inspect the house first?"

"Typically, yes we do," Robert said.

"Then tell me why this home was not even given a look-see?"

"I don't really know, sir," he said, with a hint of embarrassment in his voice.

"Did you list this home, Robert?" I asked firmly.

"Yes, sir, I did."

"Is this the first time you have ever been inside this house?"

"Um —" He thought for a moment considering his words. "Yes, sir, this is my first time."

"I see, and is there any reason why you did not inspect this house first before listing it?"

"Well, to tell you the truth, Mr. Lupo, this listing was given to me."

"Who gave it to you?"

"One of the senior agents, sir," he said with a shaky voice.

"Did the senior agent tell you why he was giving you a listing instead of keeping it for himself?"

"He did not say, sir."

"Weren't you at least a little curious why he would hand off a home for you to sell?"

Robert appeared to be getting more agitated with each new question. "I thought he just wanted to help me get the experience of selling a home." He continued, "I did ask around the office and heard some disturbing things."

"Oh? Like what?"

Robert took a few seconds to collect his thoughts and then said, "I was told the house was haunted."

Without flinching, I asked him, "Did you hear anything else?"

"Yes, sir, but I don't think I should tell you, because you may not want to buy it if you knew."

"I don't think there is anything you can say that would turn me off to the idea of buying this home," I said firmly.

"The previous owner lived in this home for over twenty-five years, and one day, he just went missing."

"Is that so?"

"Yes, sir; they never found him, and according to the other agents in my office, there have been reports from the neighbors that on occasion, they have seen a man in one of the windows."

Just then, I remembered my own experience some twenty-eight years ago, when I thought I saw a man staring at me from the first-floor window.

"Robert," I asked, "are you scared to be in this house?"

"I think maybe I am, a little, sir," he said, still standing in the doorway and looking around, half-expecting to see an apparition manifest itself right then and there.

"Okay, then, you stay here. I will go through the home and inspect it, and then I can give you any details you may need to know."

"That sounds real good, Mr. Lupo. Thank you!"

I left Robert standing in his spot and began walking through each room of the house. One of the first things I noticed was that the floors were never touched, and by never touched, I mean never cleaned. There was a layer of food particles scattered over the kitchen floor. The bathroom was extremely dirty, with dark rings around the drains of the tub and the wash basin. The toilet had no water in it at all, and the smell of sewer gas was making its way to my nostrils. I reached down and gave it a flush, but nothing happened. I leaned down and opened the water valve behind the toilet and instantly heard the water rush into the tank. After a minute or so, I gave the flush another try, and it worked. I ran the water in the sink and the tub without any difficulty. I tried the hot water, but that didn't work, and I just assumed that the hot water tank was simply switched off. I moved back into the kitchen and tried the water in the sink, and it worked. I checked the rear porch area and then proceeded up to the second level.

I passed Robert, still standing in the exact spot. There was plenty of sunlight washing over every inch of wall, so it made it much easier to see if anything was out of place.

"I'll be upstairs for a few minutes," I said to Robert.

"I'll be right here," is all that was returned.

I climbed the stairs, and as I did so, I was reminded of each creaky step. I made it to the top and walked into the first room and then the second and finally the third. Everything appeared to be normal. Aside for a little cleaning and painting, there wasn't much else to do.

I returned to Robert and asked him to join me in the back yard of the property, where an old tool shed was still standing, saying, "I want to check out the tool shed, do you mind?"

"Not at all, let's go," he said with an enthusiastic burst of energy. He was actually relieved to be going outside.

We walked out the front entrance and went around to the back yard. We continued to walk across the overgrown grass toward the metal shed in the rear of the yard. I led the way, and Robert followed closely, nearly bumping into me a few times. We passed the old wooden shed that my grandfather built many years and was still standing. I could hear Robert taking deep breaths as we went along, probably in a sigh of relief after leaving the house. We reached the metal tool shed, and I tried sliding the flimsy metal door open; it was difficult but eventually gave way. The tool shed at first glance appeared empty, but then an object caught my attention. In the far right corner of the shed was an old wooden box, no bigger than a loaf of bread. I pulled the box out of the shed and placed it in the direct sunlight for a clearer view.

Robert's attention was now focused on the box with me. I open the box and found a small scroll that was tied with a black ribbon. It reminded me of a tiny graduation diploma. I removed the ribbon and open the scroll. Robert's head was just over my shoulder; he peered intently, as he was taken over by his curiosity.

"What is it, Mr. Lupo?"

"Not sure yet." And then I read what was written on the page: "DO NOT FINISH THE PROJECT!"

Robert gave out a "Hmmm" and then turned his head, now completely uninterested in what he saw. I on the other hand was reminded of the warning messages many years ago. Something or someone was trying to tell me not to finish the project, but I didn't have a project. I never got any further than installing the coil in the wood molding to the kitchen. I never even turned it on, or did I? I placed the scroll back into the box and closed the cover. I took the box with me, as Robert and I walked back toward the front of the house.

"Well, Mr. Lupo, I guess you are not interested in the house?"

"I didn't say that, Robert. I think I would be interested if we can do much better on the price."

"I'm sure we can work something out, sir."

"Good. Let's discuss the details at your office, okay?"

"That sounds real good, sir," Robert exclaimed. "I'll lock up and we can go," he said with obvious anticipation in his voice.

"This could be your first sale," I said, whetting his appetite further.

Robert finished locking the doors and placed the key back into the combination lock box. He practically sprinted to his car and called out to me to follow him to his office. I climbed into my car and stared up at the house, which seemed to take on an eerie glow in the midday sunlight, then the next thing I knew, I was shaking hands and signing papers.

There was quite a bit of interest with some of the other agents over the sale of this particular home. One by one, they strode by the desk to get a look at the person who was foolish (or crazy) enough to buy a haunted house. I knew what they were thinking but didn't care. I knew that all of these strange occurrences could be explained by a fair degree of logical deduction and scientific reasoning (then again, maybe not).

It wasn't long before I found myself unpacking the last of my boxes at the Newark house. I would refer to this house as my home from now on, I thought to myself. The last box looked like it had gone through a war. It was yellowed and broken in several places. There were massive amounts of wide cellophane tape wrapped around and around the cover and base. I remembered what it contained and placed it on the kitchen table and just stared at it for a few minutes. The last time this box was opened, Marie had just walked out of my life. I picked it up and then put it back down, trying to decide whether to open it or not. After another minute or so, I took a knife and opened the box. Inside,

I found my old plans, sketches, specs, and a cassette with a cassette player and a small piece of metal.

Suddenly, I had a flashback and remembered the circumstances of when everything came to be: the strange written messages and the message that was recorded on the tape. As I was looking over the items in the box, my mind started to wander, and all the years that preceded the idea of the time viewer suddenly flooded my thoughts. Just then, I was startled by the annoying sound of rear doorbell.

I've got to do something about that thing, I thought to myself. *It scared the shit out of me.* I walked over to the door and, without even looking to see who it was, opened it.

Robert had stopped by to give me a large envelope, containing all the original sale documents and a few other items that were part of a file that had been kept at his office for years.

"Hey, Mr. Lupo," Robert said as he extended his hand. "How are you doing, sir?"

"I'm good, Robert; please come in."

"I can't stay, sir. I just wanted to drop off these documents to you personally and thank you for helping me make my first sale."

"It was no trouble, Robert; to tell you the truth, the house kind of sold itself."

Robert had a puzzled look on his face and replied, "Not sure why it would be so appealing, sir, if you don't mind me saying."

"My reasons are purely personal, Robert, somewhat sentimental, you know what I mean?"

"Yes, sir, I do," he said while handing me the large envelope. "If you have any questions about any of the documents, please call me." With that, Robert extended his hand again and said, "Good luck, sir, and thank you again."

As fast as Robert came, he left even faster. I had a feeling that he was still very uncomfortable about being too close to this old house. I took the envelope, placed it on the table, and decided to read it over later, when I was settled in for the night. I took the box containing the coil project documents and brought them up to the second floor, where I had set up a drafting table. I decided I needed a place where I could spread out and think.

I placed the box on the floor next to the drafting table and sat down in my cushy, imitation leather chair. I kicked at the floor and sent myself swirling around in circles, like a little kid in Daddy's big office chair.

I tilted my head back, and my mind started to wander back to the days when Marie and I were still together. *God, I still miss her*, I thought, as my head continued to spin round and round.

Just then, I had a revelation and stopped spinning. If I were to successfully put my device into operation, I would be able to see her again. Granted, the images would be quite old and, as far as I knew, blurry as well. I wasn't even sure that it would work at all, but it restored in me a new sense of urgency and a reason to continue my work. I was excited at the prospect; finding something new within something old made all the difference in my attitude. I continued to work hard to get the old place into shape and to set up a workshop where I could really let myself go and get the creative juices flowing again.

I wanted to lose myself in my work, and I wanted nothing to get in my way. I wanted this idea of a time viewer to work. I needed this idea to materialize into a working machine. I wanted to see Marie again, even if it was only her image on a screen. Sure, it would be easier to pop in a VHS tape and watch an old video of us together, but I didn't have one. Marie never let me take her picture or film her. She would always say she didn't like the way she looked in pictures. I could kick myself now for not doing it anyway. I decided to move my base of operations into the basement apartment, which I filled with equipment, wires, computers, and finally a cooling system, which was necessary to regulate the temperature in the space due to the excessive heat given off by this equipment. The windows in the basement apartment were tiny and unmovable, so the cooling system was indeed necessary.

Chapter 5

While sitting in my usual seat in my kitchen this morning I attempted, as I do every day to enjoy a nice cup of hot tea. I placed a single tea bag into my favorite cup, slightly chipped at the top. Removing the screaming kettle from the stove, I poured the hot water into the cup with a shaky hand, then returned the kettle to its usual place on the stove. I watched as the steam let out little puffs of clouds into the air. Mesmerized by the display, my mind began to wander into yet another daydream. This has become something of the norm for me. It has become difficult to hang onto a one single thought for any length of time. My mind has become scattered and inconsistent, unfocused and ruefully unwilling to cooperate with the rest of me.

I snapped back and took the cup into my hands, sipping my tea slowly and trying not to burn the tip of my tongue. I remembered how Marie would remind me to use caution before drinking something hot. She would tell me I had an asbestos mouth. "Doesn't that burn your tongue?" she would ask. I would let out a slight puff of steam and reply, "Nah."

I sat in my usual chair, staring out the rear window into the back yard; my mind began to wander as I recalled the event once again. Why couldn't I have one day of peace, one day to forget what happened? She was still a relatively young woman, with many productive years ahead of her. We had planned so many things together; the world was still new to us and waiting to be explored. I'm cursed to live out the rest of my days alone and in constant torment unless I corrected the past and repaired the future.

I was not a young man anymore, I kept reminding myself, and I didn't know how long I would be alive in this self-made prison that I had single-handedly created. No matter what I did or how I manipulated the past, it always had the same outcome: She died! When I was a young man, I thought I knew everything. I thought that no matter what, I would be able to figure out how to repair the damage to the timeline. How could I have been so careless, so selfish, and so conceited in that notion? All I had managed to do, without doubt, was simply ruin our lives.

Another sip of tea brought me back, and the fogginess lifted just long enough for yet another thought to enter my cloudy mind. What might I try next? I came to the conclusion that I must involve my younger self in order to team up and properly reset the past. The concentration and planning was overwhelming, frustrating, and tiring to me. I needed the help that youth and a fresh mind could offer. I needed to incorporate the vitality of who I used to be with the experience I had gained over the years. I updated my notes in the log book, and my current calculations showed there could be a light at the end of this long tunnel.

I fully understood that if I was ever successful at restoring the past, I may in fact vanish from existence. For all I knew, I may not even be alive in the original timeline. It would be a small price to pay to give Marie back what I stole from her so many years ago. Another sip of tea and another thought came to mind to scribble down. I swirled the last bit of tea in my cup and swallowed it like a shot of stimulating whisky. I put the cup aside, finished jotting down my next plan, and closed the log book. It had grown to humongous proportions over the years, so much so that I could hardly lift it anymore.

Placing my hands on top of the book, I noticed just how wrinkled and spotted they had become. The arthritis in my fingers made it difficult to grasp certain things. Even the simple task of putting on my clothes was a challenge. Buttons were the biggest problem, so I usually wore loose pullovers. Lifting my hands to my face and turning them, front to back and then back to front, cemented the image of their age deeper into my brain.

I pushed myself away from the table and moved over to the sink, where I washed my tea cup and placed it on the drain board. I took notice of its twin, still in its place, right alongside mine. I had not touched it since the day she was taken from my life. From time to time, I would dust off the top of it. I had resigned to the notion that she would once again drink her tea from her own cup, or I would die trying. I had repeated these words over the years numerous times, so for now, it stayed right where she placed it years ago.

After drying my hands, I turned and picked up the cumbersome log book and made my way to the bedroom; following my daily routine, I dressed and prepared myself for yet another trip back in time. I had devised my next plan of action, knowing that this may be my last attempt. My strength was nearly gone, and my mind was weaker still. I gathered a few personal items from a box at the foot of my bed and placed them side by side on the bed next to the log book, making sure everything was accounted for. I reached down and picked up an old photo of Marie when she was very young and stared at it longingly. This was the only photo I had ever taken of her.

She would forever be just like this to me. She would never get any older, and she would remain just as I saw her in the photo. I opened a drawer to my nightstand, placed the photo inside, and closed it. With no other preparations to make and some time to kill, I decided to take in some fresh air and visit my garden.

I slowly walked to the kitchen through the archway, which contained the coil to the time device. Thoughts of its construction flashed into my memory. I recognized the all-too-familiar hum and vibration as the device slowly charged and was made ready for my time trip later today. I placed my hand on the thick wooden trim as I passed by, feeling the vibration pass through my fingers, connecting me to it in a deeply personal way.

I walked through the kitchen and went out the door to the back yard. The steps leading down to the patio were very steep and had become harder to maneuver in the last few years. I carefully descended the steps, pausing periodically to regain my balance. Reaching the bottom, I turned to my left and walked past the flowers and vines into the vegetable garden. The air had a distinct aroma of fresh basil and cilantro and other fragrant herbs. Thank God that my sense of smell had not diminished over the years, like my other senses. I inhaled deeply, bent down as carefully as I could to one of my plants, and removed two bright red tomatoes. Putting them to my nose, I could smell their sweetness. Then taking out a small pocket knife, I cut into one and placed a wedge into my mouth. The juice dripped down the sides of my mouth as I bit down. Wiping away the juice with my sleeve, I thought that it tasted absolutely wonderful.

My garden had become a way for me to rejuvenate and refresh myself, toiling for endless hours, not realizing the passage of time. It was my only means of regaining clarity, at least long enough to get through another day of planning how to reset the past. Years ago, I relied on Marie to keep me grounded and healthy and encourage me to not give up in the pursuit of repairing our future life together. I looked around the yard, observing all that I had done over the years. Some of the apple and cherry trees planted with Marie so many years ago were still healthy and bearing fruit, serving as a constant reminder of my feelings for her.

It was funny how I could remember with vivid detail certain days with her and yet not remember what I had for dinner the previous evening. Oh, what I would give to be able to share this experience with her, seeing and enjoying the fruits of our labor. She should have been here with me to enjoy all of this. She was a huge fan of the garden; she especially enjoyed the tomatoes and made wonderful salads for dinner several nights a week. We never lacked when it came to eating fresh and healthy. Marie would always say that we needed to stay alive for as long as possible, so we could enjoy as much time together as we could.

I gathered the strength to stand, brushed a small tear from my eye, and cleared my thoughts. I knew all too well that dwelling on her memory would only bring me more pain, yet at the same time, it had been my motivation to get out of bed every morning, to press on, and to work myself to the point of passing out each day. Once again, I shook it off and continued to pick a few more vegetables to set aside for this evening's dinner.

I knew I would be hungry when I returned from my trip into the past. I set two places, as I did every night, with the anticipation that today would be the day everything would return to normal. She would once again be seated next to me, sharing a fresh salad and engaging in conversation about whatever struck her fancy.

I continued to move slowly through my garden, taking notice of all the various types of vegetables whose growth had exploded over the past few weeks due to the abundance of much-needed rain. Summers here in Newark, New Jersey, tended to be hotter and dryer than in the rest of the state. Winters as well tended to be a little colder and snowier and harder to navigate through while driving, although I didn't do that anymore. Still, this had been home for us for a very long time. Looking around, I imagined the things that were and all the things that are, simultaneously. It was sometimes undistinguishable and confusing to me, and other times, it was hurtful and damaging to the unfortunate reality I had come to know as my life without her.

Ghostly figures rushed in and out of my view, as if trying to find their proper place in time. They always had a confused look on their faces; many times, they appeared angry as they stopped for a second or two to look at me with some type of recognition and then flew off and disappeared. This look of anger, I had come to realize, was no more than their way of trying to fix something that they had no idea how it became broken. There are so many timelines and so many weary confused, frustrated people, trying to make sense of it all. I created all of this misery for all of them, and I was solely responsible for screwing up their lives.

I finished gathering what I wanted from the garden and started making my way back to the steps leading up to the kitchen entrance. I stopped at the foot and stared at the height, taking a breath and grabbing hold of the handrail with one hand, putting all my effort into the first step. After that, I'd work on the next step and then the next until I made it to the top. In my mind, I thought that it was no different than scaling a pyramid. Years ago, I never had to give it a second thought, but now, it had become a plan of action and required much thought just to accomplish the task. Ah, the second step was completed, and then the third. I figured I could take a break on every fourth step and still make it to the top in ten minutes or so. Reaching the fourth step, I took my first break and held on to the handrail with both hands to balance myself until I was ready to move again.

Turning to continue, I lifted my leg and placed my foot firmly on the next step. I began lifting myself forward when a cool breeze washed over me. I stopped and looked up to the remainder of the steps. The cool air had a pleasant aroma to it, like flowers or a hit of perfume. I breathed in the fragrance and thought it very familiar, as I waited for my mind to catch up with the rest of me. *Yes*, I thought, *I know that smell, I'm sure of it.* I pulled myself up another step and then another, taking a breath in between each one. Just then, I was interrupted by yet another cool breeze, but this time, it was much denser and seemed to hang in front of me. It gave me chills, and I could feel goose bumps running up and down my body.

I tried pushing my way through this wall of cool air, but I could not breach it. My first thought was that my strength was depleted and that I needed another break, but then I realized it was something else. The dense air in front of me began to take on substance and developed into a form, resembling a woman. Obviously, this was one of my daydreaming incidents, I thought to myself, so I just went with it. The figure in front of me became increasingly solid and took the shape of someone I knew very well. Even if I failed to recognize the face, I would always remember her smell. After a few more seconds, there she was, standing there with her familiar smile and holding out her hand.

I had to admit that this was one of the most elaborate daydreams I ever had. I began talking to myself in an attempt to try and snap out of it. Then again, why would I want to snap out of it? I was actually enjoying the entire experience. The ghostly figure of Marie gestured with her hand as if to say, "Let me help carry that load for you." I reached out to her with my sack of vegetables, and she took it and motioned for me to continue up the stairs. Without any further thought, I climbed the remainder of the steps without any difficulty. Marie followed behind me, and we entered the door into the kitchen.

We walked over to the kitchen table, and she placed the bundle down on it. The vegetables spilled out of the sack and rolled onto the table, spreading themselves out into a heart-shaped pattern before coming to rest. I closed my eyes and took another breath, trying again to clear the fogginess from my brain, wondering just how this could possibly be.

I opened my eyes again and looked directly at Marie, who was standing there in the same dress she was wearing the last time I saw her alive. She smiled again, moved closer to me, and began to speak.

"You have gotten so old," she said, putting her cool hand on the side of my face.

I felt her soft fingers touching me, and then I backed away slightly in disbelief.

"Am I dead?" I asked.

"Not yet," Marie replied, moving closer to me again.

"Are you dead?" I asked Marie.

"You're funny; of course not, how can I touch you if I were dead?" she joked.

"Then what is going on?" I asked. "How can you be here, talking to me like this?"

"You really don't remember, do you?" Marie asked.

"Remember what?" I asked her in a serious voice.

"You set this up a long time ago for me to be here to talk to you when the time was right."

"When the time was right for what?" I asked.

"Before you would make your trip through your time machine to see your younger self," she said, with sadness in her voice.

"So this will be one of my last trips, after all?" I asked. "I must be getting close to the finish. Why did I arrange for you to be here before I left?"

"You wanted to see me one last time, so you would remember my face and my smell before you got to where you were going to end up."

"Where am I going to end up?"

"You told me about a place where we would have to find each other all over again."

"What kind of place did I say it would be?"

"The only thing you said was it was a place where the heart takes over for the brain and that what we carry around inside of us will be needed as reference and guidance."

"That doesn't give me much to go on; what you are describing sounds a little like a fairy tale."

"I thought so as well, but you were extremely serious about it."

"One thing I have come to realize is I should believe what you tell me, no matter how crazy it sounds." Marie walked over to the window facing the back yard and looked out toward the garden.

"I remember when we planted most of those trees except for the large cherry tree planted by your grandfather right smack in the middle of the yard. I remember when you would water them every day."

"The garden looks amazing," she said, turning with a smile. "Have you made preparations for tonight's jump?"

"I have everything ready that I can think of."

"Did you update your log book?"

"Yes, that is also ready to go," I replied.

"You warned me not to tell you anything about what will happen over the next few jumps, in fear that it might change your plan in some way," Marie said sadly. "But I can say that whatever you do will eventually work out."

Standing there, I realized that I had not taken my eyes off her once since we entered the house. Some part of me did not want this bittersweet daydream to end.

"How long will you be here?" I asked Marie.

"I will be here until you leave on your trip tonight, and you will never see me again; well, not like this, anyway," she said with a slight chuckle.

"Is there anything else I need to prepare?"

"The only thing I can tell you is just go with your feelings and do what you need to do, no matter what." Looking at me again, Marie commented sadly on how old I had become and how the years of torment had left their mark on my body.

"I should have never built this fucking machine," I said, shaking a fist in the air.

"We did have some wonderful adventures with that crazy machine of yours," Marie said with appreciation in her voice.

"Yes, but at what cost? Look at me, all wrinkled and one foot in the grave. What do I have to show for my life? What am I going to leave behind to say who I was and what I thought and who I loved? Who will remember me? Who will care? I wanted a life together with you, and look at what I did in return. I stole your future and ruined our second chance at being happy."

"Now don't get yourself upset," Marie said in her best uplifting voice. "It's almost over."

"I guess you're right. I should concentrate on what's happening right now."

"Yes, good idea," she said. "Let's concentrate on right now."

Then she took my hand and led me to the living room, where we could sit and talk for a while.

"We have at least four hours to spend together before we have to say good-bye, so why waste them feeling sorry about the past?" Marie said. "Let's talk about all the fun things we did years ago and whip up those memories, shall we?"

"Sounds like a great idea. I can use a little time to relax before taking my trip."

We spent the next several hours engaged in conversation and reminiscing about our past together. For her, it was only a few hours ago, but for me, it had been many decades. I was reminded about what a rich and rewarding life we had shared. That is, until that day when she was struck by a car and killed, by someone who should have never been alive in the first place. I mentioned the accident, but Marie had no recollection of it at all. This was because I had sent her back to see me right before it happened, so in her timeline, this had not yet taken place.

I chose this day of all other days to send her back to see me. This day had overwhelming importance, because it may be my last attempt to fix all of this. I had told her several times about the car accident over the years, but I guess she chose to believe that either her fate would somehow miraculously change the outcome or I would figure out how to stop it before it took place. She always remained confident of my abilities and never let herself become depressed or worried to the point where enjoying our life together would be compromised. She was my strength and my motivation to better myself; in short, she made me want to be a better man. As it turned out, I could not stop the car from hitting her, and she died in my arms, right there in the street.

The paramedics were able to revive her during the trip to the hospital, but she died a second time at the hospital. Time travel had been both a blessing and a curse for us, but if I were given the chance to do it over again, I would choose to never harbor a single thought about the subject.

I sat for a moment and realized that my life had been given meaning because of her and what we meant to each other. She had been in my thoughts daily for as long as I could remember. No matter what happened to me now, at least we had this life, however abbreviated or altered. Marie reminded me that I gave her something to live for all those years ago. According to her, I brought happiness and adventure and unconditional love back into her life, and for this, she would always be grateful.

"I don't mind telling you, I'm feeling kind of mushy right now."

"Me too, sweetie," Marie said, looking at her watch. "You should be getting ready soon."

"Some part of me wants to stay in this chair and just keep talking to you, but I know I have to go."

"Unfortunately, I have to go, too. I have a car accident waiting for me later today," she said, with a hint of sarcasm but also a glimmer of hope in her voice.

I knew that she was just plain scared, and this was her way of dealing with it, by acting a little silly and throwing off the notion of what would actually happen.

"Somehow, I know with 100 percent certainty that you will make this right again," she said. "I don't want to die. I have too much to live for now," she added, giving me one of her classic winks. "We have too much to live for together."

"I agree with all my heart. Don't worry. I will fix this."

"You know, now that I think about it, I have not felt one single ache or pain in my body since you arrived here today," I said. "You always knew just what to do to calm me down and ease my worries and take away any aches and pains. I want the missing years back that we were supposed to have. I am grateful for your visit with me today; it has re-energized me."

"I'm glad, sweetie; you needed a break," she said with a tear appearing on her cheek. "Do what you have to do and finish this," she added, sobbing.

I walked over to her, lifted her face ever so gently, and told her that I was going to set everything right again.

"I know you will," she said, wiping away her tears. "Just do one thing for me, will you?"

"Sure, anything," I replied.

"Don't be too hard on yourself when you meet yourself today, which is your younger self, I mean," she joked, trying to change the mood.

"Why? Did my younger self complain about meeting his older self?" Now I was doing it.

"It's just that you both are so stubborn in your ways," she said, patting my cheek.

"I promise not to be too hard on him."

"Thank you," she said and touched my face again feeling the

coolness and softness of it. "Oh, I almost forgot to tell you something very important." She waited to see if I could guess what that would be.

"You love me?" I said.

"Yes, I love you," she said.

Just then, I heard an annoying sound like a ... shit, my alarm clock. I hit the off button and struggled to get out of bed. I had forgotten that I lay down to take a nap before the time jump. Shit, it was only a dream. That really sucked. I wiped the crap out of my eyes, slowly swung my legs over the side of the bed, and placed my feet on the floor. I stretched and heard cracking coming from every part of my body. *I'm surprised that my skin can hold these old bones together,* I thought to myself. *Anyway, I have to get ready.*

The power-up cycle for the jump was nearly complete at 99.99 percent; it would only be a matter of minutes before it reached 100 percent. I sprinkled a little water on my face and washed away what was left of the sleepies. I was now fully awake and feeling quite refreshed. *That was some nap,* I thought to myself. I was feeling very energetic. My mind was clear and my plan firm. I was ready to go. The readout on the remote read "100 percent Ready." The date and time set, I took a look around the room to make sure I had everything. I picked up the heavy log book, held it tight to my chest, and pushed the engage button.

The machine came to life. The vibration and familiar sound filled the air. The floor under my feet vibrated so much that it actually had a massaging effect on me. The archway glowed, and the distorted surroundings of the walls and furniture began to reconfigure themselves. I held my breath, stepped into the archway, and began the transport back to July 7, 2014, at 4 p.m.

The effect of the machine on my body was something I had gotten used to over the years. I had developed a sort of immunity to its temporary side effects. One thing I did notice on this trip was that the magnetic pulling and pushing actually made my old body feel energized and refreshed. *Hmmm,* I thought, *if nothing else, I can market this to the geriatric community as a sort of rejuvenation machine.*

After several more seconds, the machine finished its process, and my view of the kitchen became clear. All the old furniture I had was in place. Looking around the kitchen, I noticed the rear window into the yard; it appeared absent of life without my garden to make it feel homier. Realizing that I still had a few minutes to prepare before meeting my younger self, I reviewed the last few pages of my log book, just to keep it all fresh in my mind. My younger self was very opinionated and a little hard-headed. He would want to do things his own way, and I would have to steer every decision he makes, without him knowing what I was doing. I knew how to get his attention and keep him focused; I would be forced to make him aware of Marie's tragic end as soon as possible. Just like me, he had a very soft spot for her in his heart and would do whatever it took to keep her safe.

I didn't want my resolve to appear weak in any way. He must be made to understand that the plan needed to be followed without question. Knowing myself as I did, this would be difficult, having him follow my instructions without questioning every little nuance of the plan and making his own alterations that could ultimately lead to further disaster. In any case, I would be there to make sure everything stayed on track.

Checking the time on my remote, I saw it was 4:13 p.m. He would be here shortly. The archway began to vibrate. I stood off to the side, out of his view, until the process was nearly completed. I knew that he would not attempt to step through the archway if he saw me, because if he did, we would meet head-on; he needed to think I was just a vision, instead of tangible. He did not need to know that I was physically here, in the next room. I'd just leave him with that thought; he would find out at some point in the future, and by then, it would be too late to do anything about it. I watched as everything blurred and then returned to normal. The machine finished its cycle. It was now show time.

Chapter 6

July 7, 2014, and another year had passed. I was finally ready for my first test-run of the coil. I had spent the last few months insulating the device as well as every single wire that ran through the house, all the way to the step-up transformers and capacitors that were now part of the basement apartment. The house was divided into a two-family home during the 1930s. The last time a tenant occupied the basement apartment was in the early 1990s, when the elderly couple renting it became too ill to take care of themselves and were taken to a hospice by some family members. I was now checking my program sequence on the computer. I wanted to check and double-check for any errors that might have eluded me previously.

When I was sure everything was in place, I took hold of my remote control and stood in front of the archway, facing the kitchen. The time was four o'clock, and the sun was blazing through the shades and curtains; the thought occurred to me that this was as good a time as any to test the device. I had made many excuses over the past few months not to turn it on, partly because I did not want to accept failure and partly because I did not want to blow myself up.

At 4:03 p.m., I pushed the engage button on my remote and winced at the idea that it might in fact blow up and set the house on fire. The device began to make a very low hum. Slowly, the hum grew louder, and I could feel the vibration through the floor and through my body.

I was standing at least six feet away from the device and noticed the hairs on my arm were standing straight up. I also felt the hair on my head was also at full attention. I put it off as static electricity and continued to observe the opening to the kitchen. There was a crackling sound, like an electrical short circuit, but I could not see anything out of place.

I continued to watch intently as the fixtures in the kitchen began to dissolve into a blur of colors. All the other rooms around me were unaffected and undisturbed by what was happening through the archway. I checked my watch and noticed that three minutes had passed; I made a note to that effect in my log. My eyes were once again fixed on the archway; the blur of colors were now becoming sharper and in better focus.

At this point, I saw something moving toward the other side of the archway. Whatever it was stopped just on the other side of the arch. I continued to watch closely, making mental notes so I would not miss a single thing. What happened next startled me to the point of almost losing consciousness.

A voice was emanating from the other side of the arch. It was not clear and sounded garbled, as if someone were trying to speak through a glass of water. Slowly, the sound sharpened, and so did the image I was viewing. I shook my head in disbelief as I quickly made a note in my log: "4:14 p.m. first contact." I stopped myself and asked the question, "Contact?"

The voice became louder, and now the image was crystal-clear. I was utterly amazed at what I was viewing. There in front of me was the image of a man.

I recognized the face immediately, but it appeared old and weathered, with wrinkles on the forehead and baggy sacks under the eyes. The man was almost entirely bald, and whatever hair was still visible on his head was pure white. He had on what looked like a beige sweat shirt and baggy khaki pants.

The old man on the other side stared at me, crunched his lips together, and then spoke: "I warned you not to finish the project; it was you who trapped me here, and I have been unable to return."

I stood there, motionless, with my mouth wide open, staring back at the old man. I searched my brain for something to say in return, but nothing developed.

"We have a lot of work to do," the man said, and then the viewer disengaged. The man disappeared.

It took me several minutes to collect myself and try and make sense of what I saw. There was no longer any doubt. I was not crazy, and I did see that same old man in the window many years ago. That man who I recognized, even though he was much older now, was me.

After my initial shock at seeing myself as an old man, I instinctively wrote down my observations in my trusty log book. Then, as if I had just woke from a bad dream, I ran down to the basement to check my controls. I was not sure why the device malfunctioned and wanted to subject it to a complete diagnostic. I reached the control center, where I found the computer program still running its prearranged sequence. The electrical circuits were still engaged; I was puzzled. I half-thought to just turn the thing off when I heard a loud thud above me. I raced back upstairs to the archway again and saw a large brown book, sitting on the floor on my side of the archway.

It was quite worn; both the binding and pages appeared faded and wrinkled. "Here, everything you ever wanted to know about time travel but were afraid to ask," the voice rang out, clear as a bell.

I knew who was speaking, and I knew if I answered, I would literally be talking to myself. Just then, I had a flashback to a much earlier time when I was a boy at home, and my mother would tell me to stop talking to myself.

"Mom would be quite amazed at this," I said aloud. "What do you want me to do with this?" I asked.

The older me walked back into view and said, "Study everything in that book; everything that went wrong with the project is all there."

"What went wrong?" I asked.

"Just study it and we will talk again," and then the viewer went blank again. The normal image of the kitchen was once again in plain sight. I picked up the very large and heavy binder and opened it to the first page. It began, "July 7, 2014 at approximately 4:03 p.m., I pushed the engage button on the remote."

The room began to spin out of control, and my legs gave out underneath me, as I was unable to support myself. Everything turned black, as I hit the floor, falling face-first into my own log book.

I was not sure how long I lay there on the floor, with my face buried in my own notes. I opened my eyes and tried to focus and then sat up. I looked around the room, which was now my living room, and then looked toward the kitchen. I checked my watch and found that I had only been out for a few minutes. Everything appeared normal, just as it was before my test of the viewer; everything was the same, except for the addition of the log book.

After a minute or two, I pulled the binder close to me so I could get a better look at it; like someone who wanted know the end of the story first, I turned to the back of the log book and searched for the last entry.

I scanned the last page intently, and there in the center of the page, I read, "January 18, 2036. I have tried several times to make contact with the younger version of myself. I was able to escape briefly from my confines by building up enough energy to allow me access into the past for only several minutes at a time. For reasons I do not understand, it requires more energy for me to move forward in time than it does going backward, so much more in fact that it takes nearly eight months just to collect it.

"It appears that my plan to get myself on track to repair the damage that was done was successful. I knew that after being told not to do something that I would eventually do the opposite. Timing is absolutely essential, and I had to stop the progress of the device until we were both ready, both meaning the younger version and the older version of myself. Now with everything in place, we must repair the past."

I was at a loss to understand what could have happened, when all I wanted to do was view past images of people who were in close proximity to the viewing device. How could something possibly have gone wrong?

I knew the only thing I had going for me now was reading the history of what led up to the malfunction. I put on a pot of coffee, sat down at the kitchen table, and settled in for some serious reading. I sat there in the kitchen for eleven hours, reading until my eyes were too dry to open. Feeling the effects of a lack of sleep and now coming down from the caffeine buzz, I was ready to pass out. I climbed into bed and was asleep in seconds.

The next morning came and went, and when I eventually woke up, it was nearly six o'clock in the evening. My head still abuzz from the previous day's activities, I was able to shake it off and managed to get myself together. I crawled out of bed, took a long hot shower, and revived myself. I ate a good meal and changed into some comfortable clothes.

I resumed reading the log book and found out some very interesting things. First of all, my viewing project took a turn somewhere in the middle and became something else. What I could determine from the notes is that a hole in time and space had opened, and through it, one could step into the past and actually interact with it. I found the whole thing extraordinary; I could not believe it, but then I remembered my encounter the day before with my older self. I continued reading well into the night, until I found what I was looking for. On the top of page 1136, I read, "October 16, 2022 11:36 pm. My attempts to retrieve Marie from the time machine were unsuccessful.

"All avenues of access to the point of entry have failed. I had developed a series of guide lines or instructions, if you wish. These guide lines were to be followed to the letter, and Marie was in complete understanding as to the consequences if any of the instructions were not implicitly followed. I lost contact with her only minutes before we were to re-enter the machine to return to our time. Something happened, and now I have discovered what it was."

The entry in the log book went on to say that Marie was in her car, on her way back to the house, and was only a few blocks away when she was struck by another vehicle. The accident placed her in a coma, and she remained on life support for several weeks. What I could not determine from my notes was the outcome of what happened to her. I turned page after page until I came across a newspaper clipping from December 26, 2022; it read, "Car accident victim dies from complications."

I sat back in my chair and stared at the ceiling in disbelief. How could this have happened? What did I do that brought this on? My emotions boiled over, and anger filled my body as I threw my arms into the air and shouted, "Nooo!" I collapsed into a fetal position on the floor, grasping wildly at nothing until blanking out.

I woke up in a bewildered state of mind, with thoughts of Marie filling my brain. I pulled myself up off the floor and sat down at the kitchen table. I looked down again at the log book and continued flipping pages, one after the other, reading intently and trying to absorb as much information as I could. Then I came across a small section with a list of numbered items. It was titled simply "Instructions." There was a list of things that were marked in red and underlined. It read:

1. Return time is determined by the exact time of arrival and point of entry. Point of entry refers to exactly when you cross over and if you cross over alone or with another person.

2. The total duration of time the hole can be open for is 24 hours. This cannot be changed in any way. If you enter alone, you must return alone and within the 24-hour time limit. If you enter with another person, you must return with that person and within the 24-hour time limit. Failure to do so on any count will result in the permanent imprisonment in that selected time.

3. Anyone left behind in another timeline will continue aging at a normal rate until death. This is true only if the specific timeline was not altered to a point where the person no longer exists for any reason.

4. In case of a power failure, the system is designed to supply power until the time traveler's return. The system is designed to disengage only when the return of the time traveler has been confirmed. Several backup power supplies are available, and the machine will choose the one which best suits the need at that particular time.

5. You cannot take with you any future-related items. All clothes worn on trips back in time must be appropriate to the style and manner of the decade. You must not make any attempts to try and attract attention to yourself. Observe and keep a low profile. Avoid any interaction with the timeline's occupants.

6. You cannot change the past. Any alterations to a past life will result in a change in the timeline and can be disastrous. Example: You cannot go back in time and give yourself the number to a winning lottery ticket. This will result in a paradox that will alter your own timeline.

The instructions continued for eighteen more pages, and I took the time to read through each one. Afterward, I closed the book and decided to do whatever it took to set things straight. I relocated myself to the living room and set up a chair in front of the archway so I could monitor it for signs of my future self. I had no way of knowing when he would show up again, or how to prepare for what he might say or do. Or did I?

I continued reading the log book, page after page, for many hours a day, for several days, until reaching the end again, back to "January 18, 2036." As I read that date, the archway began to switch on, and soon I was looking at my future self again (I'll refer to him as Doug Sr.).

He began to speak: "I know you have many questions, and we will get to the answers together, I promise." Then Doug Sr. continued, "Where is Marie?"

"I have no idea," I said with some sadness in my voice. "I haven't seen Marie in twenty-eight years."

"You must find her and bring her here."

"What do you mean, find her; isn't she, well, you know, dead?"

"The Marie of your time is still alive," he said, as if I should have known that all along. "Did you not study the book?"

"I read everything cover to cover," I replied.

"Marie must step through the time machine with you on a specific date in order to correct the past."

"I wouldn't even know where to begin to find her," I said. "Do you know where she is?"

"She lives with her two sons in Little Falls; you must convince her to make this trip with you. She will need some proof to back up your story of a time machine, so you have to bring her here, and I will help you to convince her."

"What if she doesn't? I mean, what if she just refuses to even talk to me or just slams the door in my—"

I was cut off midsentence with a loud bark from Doug Sr.: "You must not fail to bring her here!" he yelled.

"How do I contact you?" I asked. "How do I turn this thing on and off?"

"I already know exactly when you will be here, and I know that you do convince Marie to come with you. I know that you will step through the time machine on a certain date and at a certain time. I know this because I already did it."

"If I already did it, then why are we even having this conversation?"

"I remember my younger self as being a little more intelligent," he said condescendingly. "You are going to have to trust me; you have no choice. Did you ever ask yourself why you and Marie never stayed together?"

"Yes, I asked myself that question many times."

"After this is over and we reset the timeline, you will be with her."

"Be with her how, like married and kids and all that?"

"Something like that, yes."

For the first time in a very long time, a smile broke through my face.

"I will tell you this one thing, and then you must be off to find Marie and bring her here."

"I am listening," I said, moving closer to my future self.

"After we correct the past, you will have no memory whatsoever of any of this." After a brief moment, he continued, "The two of you were meant to be together; you were never supposed to break up. She was never supposed to marry another man, and you were never meant to marry another woman.

"The two of you wondered about each other all these years," he said with a crack in his voice. "This is the only thing we can't fix."

"What thing?" I asked.

"You and Marie can't regain the lost years, but you still have a future together. It is not too late."

"I haven't seen her in twenty-eight years; what, if anything, do we still have in common?"

"Don't be so quick to dismiss the possibility that your hearts still hold feelings, and these feelings will lead to other things."

What would she feel for me after all these years? I walked over to look at my reflection in the bedroom mirror. I gave myself a once-over, top to bottom. I was older now, and I'd gained some weight, and I was losing my hair.

"What could she possibly see in me after all this time?"

Doug Sr. sighed. "I cannot tell you everything," he said, "or it will interfere with your own thoughts and actions."

"I wouldn't know what to say to her in order for her to believe me. I mean, I created this thing, and now I'm not sure if I would even believe myself."

"There is some proof in the files you have; this will help convince her to at the very least take a trip and visit you here."

"But what if—" I was cut short.

"Just take along some of the documents that you will find and leave the rest up to her curiosity." Then Doug Sr. pointed his finger directly at my face and said, "You were never supposed to build this machine."

With that, he walked away slowly, still muttering something under his breath, and the viewer once again closed down.

The entire conversation left me standing there like a deer in the headlights. My head was spinning, not just from talking to myself but at the thought of seeing Marie again. Suddenly, all the past feelings came rushing back to me, and I felt like I was a kid again. My emotions were all over the place, and I found it hard to concentrate on any one thing. Then, as if crashing into a brick wall, I was reminded what Doug Sr. said about Marie dying in a car crash. My heart stopped beating for a second. I found it hard to catch my breath and think clearly. I sat down for a moment on the edge of my bed and threw my body backward. As I lay there, staring at the ceiling, I started to formulate a plan. I knew that I had to convince Marie to join me on this journey, and I knew that her life depended on it and, it seemed, my life as well.

Chapter 7

I had been left with the task of tracking down Marie; at least I knew what town she was living in. Finding out her exact address should not be too difficult. I had made the decision to move on this quickly and not waste any time. I began searching for Robert's contact information from Shultz Realty; I knew I had his business card filed away somewhere. I would call him and ask him to look up Marie's address. I knew that he could do that through tax records, and as a Realtor, he would have access to that information. I searched throughout the house, looking for his business card, and after a time, I realized that I would be able to find it with the sale documents, and the sale documents were still in the large envelope, and that envelope was ... where?

A trip to the basement apartment was needed to retrieve the document envelope. I remembered that I had filed that away months ago and had not even bothered to look inside. Reaching the lower-level apartment, I switched on the overhead light and walked over to the small file room, which used to be a bedroom. All of my important papers, folders, pictures, and drawings were stored here. I had installed a Halon fire suppression system to protect this room and the entire lower level from the possibility of a fire.

Halon is a compound in which the hydrogen atoms of a hydrocarbon have been replaced by bromine and the other halogen atoms. This system is designed to remove all the oxygen from the air, thus suffocating a fire. This is used in place of a typical fire sprinkler, which uses water to put out the fire; water would damage not only the documents but also the complex controls and computer system that was now powering the viewer. I realized that I should start referring to the viewer as a time machine, but the thought was still difficult to grasp.

A quick search yielded the envelope I was looking for, and after removing it from the file cabinet, I closed the file drawer and made a quick inspection of the controls and reviewed the monitors to make sure there had not been any glitches. A quick diagnostic of the programming told me what I needed to know: Everything was still operating perfectly. I grabbed the envelope, turned off the light, and returned to the main level. The kitchen was the brightest room in the house, and I used it quite often for reading and drawing. I sat down at the table in the chair closest to the window facing the rear yard, which was now finely manicured with a lush lawn and flower beds.

I was able to keep the cherry tree after pruning all the dead branches and treating an insect infestation which could have killed it. It would have been a shame to lose the tree, because it was quite old and was planted by my own grandfather some eighty years ago. I sat in the chair, pulled myself close to the table, and opened the envelope.

I pulled out all the documents and started to make small piles in order of importance. I found all of the documents from the sale of the home, and after reviewing them, I placed them into their appropriate pile. I noticed there was a small folder which contained some old pictures of the home back during construction; one of the pictures was labeled "734 North 7th Street, New Construction 1906," and there were other pictures of the home throughout the years, one from 1928 and another from 1950. There were other pictures, showing how the street itself looked back when all that was visible were open fields and what looked like a stable offering pony rides. There were even some pictures of children riding on the back of a pony, being led by a handler of sorts.

I put the pictures off to the side and continued looking through the envelope. Then I noticed a small card stapled to the corner of another folder, which read "Robert J. Morrison, Realtor." I removed the card from the folder, put it off to the side, and finished sifting through the papers. *At least I found what I was looking for,* I thought to myself. I picked up the business card and was about to call Robert when something struck me as odd. One of the pictures I was looking at earlier contained an image of a group of people, standing around two children riding on a pony. The picture was dated August 5, 1929, and it caught my attention as I focused on two of the people standing next to the pony.

I blinked several times and tried to make my eyes see clearer as I stared at the photo. At first, I thought my mind was playing tricks on me, and then I thought I may have needed new glasses, but the longer I looked at the image, the more reality set in. There was no way this could be; this was impossible. I sprang up and began looking for my high-powered magnifying glass. Again, I started tearing boxes and files apart, looking in drawers, until I found it on the back porch. For a second, I wondered why I would have left it on the back porch, and then I remembered: I had used it to start a fire in the grill. I didn't have any matches that day and wanted a barbecued steak in the worst way. After retrieving the magnifying glass, I scrutinized the photograph further. It took me several more minutes to convince myself that the two people I was looking at in the picture were Marie and me.

I checked the date on the photo again; yep, 1929. That's what it said. There was no longer any doubt as to the identities. I could not wrap my mind around this time machine concept; why were Marie and I in a picture from 1929? Why would we even want to travel back so far in time, anyway? What would be the reason? I continued looking at the picture intently, and now I was again scrutinizing every single pixel for clues, but nothing additional came into view. Now with my head spinning out of control, I fought the urge to scream, and instead of crumpling into a ball on the floor again, I shook it off quickly, picked up the business card, and called Robert.

My call to Robert's office was answered quickly by a cheerful receptionist. "Good morning, Shultz Realty; this is Maggie, how may I assist you this fine day?"

"Hello, my name is Doug Lupo, and I wanted to talk to Robert Morrison, please."

"Please hold, and I will connect you," Maggie said, as the sound of happy elevator music began playing on the line.

There was the sound of a click, and then Robert began speaking: "Hey, Mr. Lupo. How's it going, sir?"

"It's going quite well, Robert, thanks for asking."

"So what can I do for you, sir?" he said with hopeful anticipation.

"Robert, I need a favor and was thinking you may be able to help me."

"Sure, Mr. Lupo, what do you need?"

"I'm looking to track down a dear old friend of mine; her name is Marie Martin, and I'm told she is living in Little Falls. I was wondering if you can—"

"Look up her address?" he said, cutting me off midsentence.

"Yes, exactly; can you do that for me?"

"Sure thing, Mr. Lupo. I will need a few minutes; can I put you on hold, sir?"

"Yes, that's fine. I will hold."

After about five minutes, Robert returned to the line and said, "Sorry to keep you waiting, Mr. Lupo. I have that information you requested."

Robert began to rattle off Marie's address: "She is listed here at 136 Douglas Avenue, Little Falls." And then he asked me, "Did you need anything else, Mr. Lupo?"

"No, Robert, I will not need anything else," I said while thinking to myself, *Unless you have an easier way out of this.*

"Okay then, nice talking to you, sir. Have a great day," Robert said, and then he disconnected the line.

I wrote the address down on a piece of paper, placed it into my shirt pocket, and made ready to hit the road.

I sat at my personal computer and quickly mapped out directions to Marie's house. According to the directions, it should take me about an hour to get there. I took the folder with the pictures of the house and the picture of Marie and me from 1929. I grabbed my car keys and flew out the door.

The ride from Newark to Little Falls took about an hour, and before I knew it, I was pulling up in front of a cute little Cape Cod on Douglas Avenue. I don't know how long I sat there in my car before getting up the nerve to go and ring her doorbell. After a few deep breaths and a "Let's do this," said aloud, I climbed out of my car and walked up the driveway to the front of her home. I noticed two vehicles parked in the driveway and assumed that someone would be home. I climbed the three steps to the landing and reached down to ring the bell. As I reached for the doorbell, my hand began to shake slightly, and I could feel the beginnings of sweat forming on my forehead. I took another breath, pushed the button, and immediately heard the pleasant sound of chimes on the other side of the door.

After about fifteen seconds, I heard a woman's voice saying, "Who's got that?" and then after a few more seconds, she spoke again. "I guess I do," the woman said, and then she asked, "Who is it?"

"Um, Marie, it's me, Doug Lupo," I said with a squeak in my voice, sounding like a teenager on his first date.

"Doug who?" came back sharply.

"Doug Lupo," I said again, this time with a deeper, louder tone.

There was silence for about fifteen seconds, and then the woman spoke again: "Shit, what are you doing here?"

"I have to talk to you about something extremely important."

There was no response, so I continued, "It's a matter of life and death" (which was quite an understatement).

Again, there was no response, so I rang the bell again, hoping to agitate her just enough to open the door.

"Just ... wait a minute," she said, and the sound of clanging pots and pans immediately followed. Every minute or so, I could hear her say, "Shit," and then sounds of doors closing sharply and other noises I could not identify. "Why didn't you — I mean, you should have ... Never mind, just wait!" she said through the still-closed door.

After several more minutes, I heard the sound of the door

unlocking and then slowly opening; there she was. Granted, the last time I saw Marie, she was twenty-eight years younger (and so was I, for that matter). Now we were much older and had gone on to have separate lives, yet there she was, with her brown hair and dreamy brown eyes, looking directly at mine. She had on a pair of black pants with an oversized white blouse, which gathered in ruffles at her wrists, and the front buttoned down the length, with the first two unfastened.

My God, I thought to myself, *she is still beautiful,* and my heart began to pound hard in my chest.

"Doug," she said in a softer, more calm voice. "What are you doing here?"

"I'm so sorry for just dropping out of the clear blue like this, but I have to talk to you. I wouldn't dream of bothering you with this problem, but I don't have a choice in the matter."

Marie stood there for another few more seconds and then asked, "You want to come in?"

"Yes, I do," I replied, and she stepped aside to let me pass.

"Please don't mind the mess; we are getting ready to move and are in the middle of packing."

"I'm really sorry to bother you, Marie, but we need to talk."

"Well, come into the kitchen and have a seat. I can put on some tea if you like," she said.

Just then, my mind was transported back to the 1980s, back to my old one-room apartment, where Marie once made me tea, and then my attention came back to the here-and-now. I took a seat and looked around while Marie made herself busy, getting the tea together. *This is like déjà vu all over again*, I thought to myself.

Her home was decorated very nicely, with warm earth tones that gave off a youthful edge. There was plenty of natural light washing over the crispness of the walls and giving you the overall feeling of a stress-free environment. It was welcoming and warm and calming to the senses, and it made me feel quite at home.

"Okay, so," she said as she turned and sat down in a chair directly opposite mine. "To what do I owe this visit?"

"I have to tell you a story," I began, "and you will not believe what I have to say; in fact, you may want to throw me out into the street before I'm even done."

"I won't throw you out," she said with a smile. "That's what I have sons for," and then she just left it out there for me to absorb.

"You have sons?" I asked. "How many?"

"I have two sons; they are in their twenties." Then she stood up and said, "Hey, you guys, come out here for a minute." Two young men walked out into the kitchen and stood next to Marie. "This is Brian," she said, and then looked in the other direction and added, "And this is Michael."

I stood, extended my hand, and shook hands with Marie's sons, who appeared polite but also seemed to be sizing me up. Michael especially gave me the once-over, from head to toe, and then pushed his lips together, as if trying to decide whether to trust his mother alone with this stranger. Brian, on the other hand, looked unconcerned.

"Thanks, guys," she said, and they left the kitchen.

The kettle was whistling on the stove, and Marie sprang into action as she prepared two mugs of tea. Seeing Marie again awakened a part of my heart that had been dormant for nearly thirty years. That same old warm and fuzzy feeling for her came rushing back, like a wave crashing onto a beach.

Marie sat down, handed me a mug of tea, and said, "Careful, it's hot."

"I'll be careful," I said in return, but without a thought, I sipped the hot tea, burning my tongue.

"I warned you that it was hot," she said with a chuckle. "You look really good, Doug."

"Thank you, I was just thinking the same thing."

"You were thinking you looked good?" she said, smiling again.

"No, I was thinking *you* looked good, not me."

"I know, I was just teasing you, trying to break the ice."

"Thank you. I am a little nervous about being here. Tell me, is there a Mr. Martin?"

"Yes, there is a Mr. Martin," she said and paused a moment and then added, "but we are divorced now."

"Oh, sorry," I said.

"Don't be sorry; it's fine, trust me." Marie took a sip from her mug and then asked, "So is there a Mrs. Lupo?"

I replied, "Yes, there is a Mrs. Lupo, but we are divorced as well."

"I am sorry," Marie said. "I don't like divorce. So why have you come to see me? Tell me your story."

"How well do you remember 1984?"

"I remember it well, why?"

"You remember my coil project that I was working on constantly?"

"Yes, I remember that quite well," she said sharply.

"Do you remember what I was hoping to accomplish with my device, trying to see if images could be captured of people from years past?"

"I remember that I never thought it would ever work, but I kept that to myself."

"Well, as it turns out, it didn't go according to my original plan."

"You don't say."

"Something else happened, something hard to explain, but I need you try to have an open mind."

"My mind is wide open, ready."

"I finished my work on the coil project only a short time ago."

"Really?" Marie exclaimed. "Only a short time ago?"

"I moved back into the old Newark house; actually, I not only moved in, I purchased it."

"Oh, good for you," Marie said, shifting in her seat.

"What I have to tell you next is the unbelievable part."

"What are you going to say, you invented a time machine or something?" she said sardonically.

"Yes, that's exactly what I'm going to tell you."

Marie's facial expression changed from interest to one of concern. "Doug, you know I have always been a little gullible, right?"

"This is not — I mean, I'm not ... look at this." I handed Marie the picture of us from 1929.

"What's this?"

"Take a long hard look at it," I said.

"It's old; it's dated 1929, so ..."

"Look closer," I said a little more forcefully.

"What am I loo—" She stopped and stared at the two people in the picture next to the pony. "This is obviously a fake," she snapped. "You think I would believe a story like, what, we went back in time to 1929 and had our picture taken?"

I said nothing and let the reality of the situation work its way into Marie's mind.

"Doug, there is no such thing as a time machine ... Right?"

"You don't know the half of it. I started out wanting to see images, just images, and I would have been happy and satisfied with that accomplishment."

"But you just said that you had finished your work. I assumed that you just plugged it in and saw that it wasn't working and then unplugged it, the end!"

"But that's what I'm trying to tell you; it didn't work the way I designed it. Something else happened, and the only way for me to explain it to you is to actually show you."

"Okay, then show me," she said.

"I can't show you here."

"So where can you show me, outside?"

"I have to take you back to the Newark house in order to show you."

There was a long period of silence, and then she said, "So let me see if I got this straight: You built a time machine, and you turned it on, and somehow, for some reason, we end up back in 1929. Then we run over to the pony rides and have our picture taken and then end up where?"

"That part I'm not sure of."

"You're serious, aren't you?"

"Yes, I'm serious. Do I look like I'm kidding? Marie, do you remember when we were kids and you used to say you could tell when I was lying just by looking into my eyes?"

"Vaguely," she muttered.

"Well, look into my eyes; what do you see?"

Marie leaned over her kitchen table and began to look into my eyes, as if only to humor me. Then quite unexpectedly, she said, "You're telling the truth!"

She sat in her chair and shifted herself toward the window above the kitchen sink.

"I just can't wrap my mind around what you are saying."

"Would you at least give me a chance to prove to you that what I'm saying is true?"

"That's just it; what are you trying to prove to me, that you made a time machine?" She paused. "And then there is something else; if we went back in time to 1929 and had our picture taken, with a pony, I might add, then why don't I have any memory of it?"

"That's the part that's hard to explain; you see, in a real sense of time, we have not done it yet."

"If we haven't done it yet, then how do we have a picture from 1929 that says we did?"

"I can't say for sure, but the fact is that there is a picture from 1929 with us in it. For reasons I can't yet understand, it somehow survived through time and ended up in my possession. I hope to be able to solve this puzzle, along with other things."

"What other things? You mean there's more?"

I hesitated for a second. "Yes, quite a bit more, and I need you to help me get to the bottom of what has happened. I can't do this without you," I said with desperation in my voice.

"I'm not saying I fully believe everything you're telling me, but I do find myself intrigued." Turning back in my direction, Marie looked directly at me and said, "If I'm going to be a part of this and help you solve some great mystery, I want to know everything you know. Deal?"

"Deal!"

For the next two and a half hours, I told Marie everything that

I knew, and I didn't leave out a single detail. She added a bunch of "hmmms" and "huhs" along the way, but after I was done, she just sat there with a blank expression on her face for several minutes.

Then, as if an alarm went off in her head, she said, "So we were meant to be together, huh?" She paused. "I'm not totally turned off by that idea, you know?" Then she said, "But this thing with me dying in a car accident, that part scares me. What if we go back in time and find that we can't fix that part? And another thing: If I died in a car accident, how is it that we are having this conversation?" Marie stood and walked over to the kitchen counter and stared out the rear window. "What if something else goes wrong?" she said. "What if you end up dying in the process?" She paused again and then continued, "If we were meant to be together, do we still have Brian and Michael? What happens to them? Do they just vanish into thin air or something?"

"I don't know," I said with a depressed look. "I just don't know."

"I have to think about this; seriously, you didn't expect me to just get up and go with you right now, did you?"

"Actually, I didn't know if I would even keep your attention long enough for you to believe my story."

"I'm still not 100 percent on that, just so you know." She walked over to me, put her hand in mine, and said, "You never used to lie to me before, and I don't have any reason to think you are lying to me now. Well, actually, I do have a reason to think you're lying, but I find myself wanting to believe you and wanting to take this trip with you, but I need some time to think. I need a plan."

I smiled at Marie and recalled how she would always say she needed a plan.

I said to her, "I don't know what it is about the two of us or the circumstances that brought us back together, but one thing is clear."

"What one thing?" Marie asked.

"It appears that you still drive me crazy."

"Okay, big boy, I think it's time for you to leave," she said, chuckling again.

"I think I should as well," I said, walking toward the front door. "Promise me that you will give this some serious consideration."

"Oh, I'll be thinking about it, that's for sure!"

"If you decide to join me on this, come to the Newark house in two days."

"Why two days? Why not tomorrow, or a week from now? Why two days?"

"No reason whatsoever, I just want you to be sure before jumping into this with me."

Marie let out a sigh and extended her hand, and I in turn took it, brought it to my lips, and kissed it lightly.

"I hope to see you again," I said.

Marie said with a smile, "You never know what time will bring, Mr. Lupo."

On that note, I left Marie and returned home.

Chapter 8

My mind was all a blur as I made my way back home. Seeing Marie again brought something inside of me back to life, something I thought was dead or dormant, but now I was feeling like a kid again. This giddy excitement, unfelt and unremembered for so long, was continuing to build inside, turning out my heart for the world to see. Thoughts of her from the past came flooding back into memory: Her sweetness and beauty, which I once held in my arms and in my soul, made the day's sunlight seem pale in comparison. It wasn't long before I was pulling up in front of my house. I sat there for a few minutes with my eyes closed and smiled as the image of her face appeared in my mind's eye. It wasn't the face of the young woman I knew but the image from an hour ago. She still retained her beauty even now, many years later, and the sweetness of her aroma, which only she could pull off, filled my senses.

As I sat there behind the wheel of my car, daydreaming, I was startled by the sound of someone knocking on the passenger side window. A neighbor of mine motioned for me to roll down the window.

"Hey, Doug."

"Hey, Carmine, what's up?"

Carmine and his wife, Olivia, lived next door, and they were considered the neighborhood watch team, or the neighborhood busybodies, whichever way you cared to look at it.

"Olivia and I have been hearing some strange noises coming from your house."

"Sorry, Carmine. I have been working on a renovation project. If I made too much n—" I was interrupted sharply.

"I'm not talking about when you are there at the house," he said. "This was today, when you were out. You still live alone, right?"

I rolled my eyes and asked, "What kind of noises did you hear?"

"Well, I can't describe everything, but there was a loud humming and vibrations that we could feel under our own feet."

"Really? What time did you feel the vibrations?"

"Oh, that was just a few minutes ago, but we heard a man shouting earlier. It sounded like someone was arguing with themselves."

"I better get in th—"

I was interrupted again as Carmine continued, "The worst part was a few hours ago. I think it was just after you left; there were loud thuds, like someone was throwing cement bags to the floor." "Excuse me, Carmine, but let me go and see what's going on." With that, I left Carmine at the curb and rushed into the house.

Carmine stood and watched me enter the front door. I quickly ran inside and noticed several boxes lying in front of the archway. I ran back to the window facing the street and saw Carmine still standing there. I opened the window and told him that some boxes I had stacked in the kitchen fell over, and I had forgotten to turn off the television which had its volume up to high.

A smile came to his face, and I realized that he bought my story. I thanked him for keeping a close eye on everything while I was out, and with a wave of his hand, he turned and headed back home. I shut the window and ran back over to the archway to have a closer look at the boxes. I knew instantly that Doug Sr. had personally delivered them. They looked a little beat up, and the cardboard was stained and yellowed, as if they had been left out in the open for years.

Before I could pick up one of the boxes, the archway began to hum, and soon Doug Sr. was standing in the archway, looking at me.

"They are boxes of clothes," he said. "You will need them for you trip." He seemed to know what I was going to ask before asking it. "They are for you and for Marie when she arrives."

"I spoke to her today and explained everything; I'm not sure if she believed me or even if she will show up."

"She doesn't believe you, but she is very curious nonetheless; she will be here tomorrow morning at eight o'clock sharp."

"How do you know that?" I asked.

He just let out a sigh and cleared his throat. "I suggest you get a good night's sleep; you are going to need it." As soon as he said that, he vanished from sight.

I spent the next two hours opening the boxes and removing the clothes. I made a pile for Marie and one for myself. There were several pairs of light-colored pants and matching shirts for me, and for Marie, there were two dresses, one black and one red. There were also two pairs of woman's pants with matching tops, as well. Although the boxes were beat up, the clothes appeared to be new and never worn. There were several pairs of woman's shoes and two pairs of shoes for myself. I sat back on the floor, looked over the pile of woman's clothes, and pulled one of the silky blouses to my nose and breathed in. To my amazement, I caught the faint scent of Marie's perfume. I wondered how that could be, when the clothing appeared to be new and until today, I had not even been in close proximity to her.

Everything around me seemed to be shrouded in mystery, and knowing what I knew about Marie and the time travel situation, I started to think about her future car accident. What if we decided not to step into the time machine? What if we just turned the thing off and dismantled it? What if I stopped myself and realized that there was an older version of me running around in the future somewhere? What about him? What would happen to him if we did not go through with this? There was also that picture of Marie and me from 1929. What would happen to us if we did not go back, and why would we go back to 1929 in the first place?

I decided that I should take my own advice and get some sleep. Marie and I had a big day ahead of us in the morning, but before turning in for the night, I wanted to take a closer look at the tape recorder and small metal strip. I pulled out the recorder, placed it on the kitchen table, and took out the metal strip. The recorder, upon closer examination, did not look like it would contain some hidden secret or concealed compartment. I flipped it onto its front, leaving its back exposed. Nothing appeared out of the ordinary; that is, until I opened the battery compartment. There, where the batteries should be, I found another small metal strip connected across the first set of terminals. I picked up the other strip and moved it into position on the second set of terminals. It fit perfectly, as it clicked into the available slot. I don't know what I may have expected to happen, but as it turned out, nothing did happen. It just sat there. Then I remembered the AC power cord, reached over to the wall, and plugged it into the nearest outlet.

Again, nothing happened, and I was about to put it off to the side when I accidentally pushed the Rewind button on the tape deck. The room around me began turning darker and darker, while my immediate personal space was illuminated with a bluish light. I felt somewhat light-headed for a few seconds, and then that feeling passed and was replaced by a sharp pain behind my eyes; after a few more seconds, that also passed. Now I was able to focus on the wall clock over the kitchen stove and noticed that the second hand was not moving. I checked my watch and observed that it was functioning properly. I could see out the kitchen window; Carmine and Olivia were having their evening cup of coffee, but they were not moving at all.

Then I realized that this little machine had insulated me from the passage of time. I removed the plug from the wall and waited to see what would happen next; the device began to power down. It took several minutes before everything returned to normal. The device seemed to hold a charge for a few minutes, and I had only plugged it in for a minute or so. I wondered, if I left it plugged in all night, would it hold a longer charge? I also wondered if it would be portable and could make the trip through the time machine. It would make a good tool should the need arise to stop time. As soon as I saw myself, my older self, I would get some answers. I decided to call it a night and get some sleep. According to Doug Sr., Marie would be here at 8 a.m. sharp. I better try and look my best for the morning.

Feeling a little mischievous, I took a piece of paper, wrote Marie a welcome note, and placed it on the front door, where I knew she would see it in the morning. The note said "It's 8:00 a.m. sharp; I knew you would be here. Please come inside, the door is open." After I placed the note on the door, I washed up and made myself comfortable in my bed. I reached for a box under the bed that contained some old pictures, from when Marie and I used to date. There were so many pictures I had lost over the years, but for some reason, these pictures survived to this day. I shuffled through the small pile and came across several pictures of us at a restaurant. Marie was wearing a red dress and heels, and I was wearing a tan suit and tie.

I looked at the pictures and took notice of the expressions on our faces. We were so very happy to be together. I sunk down deeper into my bed, still holding the pictures and thinking to myself that we were so young. I could almost smell the scent of her perfume as I lay there, reminiscing about our younger years. Minutes passed, and I felt my eyes become heavy. I caught myself several times drifting off to sleep but then waking up again, still staring at the pictures. After several more minutes, I reached over to the nightstand and turned off the light.

Morning came in a flash, and as soon as my eyes were open, I jumped out of bed, took a hot shower, and made some eggs and bacon for breakfast. I decided to wait until Marie came over so that we could eat together. I put on a pot of coffee and waited for her to arrive. At exactly eight o'clock, Marie rang the doorbell. I was already at the door but waited a few seconds before opening it (I didn't want her to think I was overly anxious or anything).

"I saw your note," Marie said, as she followed up with a "good morning."

I caught my first glimpse at Marie's face, and for just a moment, I saw the younger version of her looking back at me; then as quickly as it came, she was gone, and the present-day Marie was in her place.

"See, I found it," she said as she adjusted herself.

"Please come in," I said with a huge smile.

Marie stepped through my door, as she did many times before, but in another time. The two of us had not been in this same place for nearly thirty years.

"I made a little something for breakfast," I said. "Are you hungry?"

"I could eat something," she said as we made our way to the kitchen. "Still looks the same, except the furniture is different."

We passed my bedroom, and she commented, "I remember that spot in particular," pointing to where my bed used to be some years ago. "I used to come through the kitchen door and take my clothes off and slide under the covers with you." She let out a sigh and gave the room another warm glance.

We walked into the kitchen, and again she said that everything looked so familiar, "like time just stood still or something."

"Please have a seat, and I will heat this up quickly."

Marie took a seat nearest the porch door and looked out the window facing the back yard. "Oh, my gosh, I like what you did back there; look at all the flowers, and the big cherry tree is still there." She continued, "What happened to the old wooden shed, the one your grandfather built?"

"I had to knock it down; it was infested with mice."

"Mice?" she said, lifting her feet slightly off the floor.

"Not in here, only outside."

"Oh, good," she said, shifting her attention back toward me. "So, I'm thinking all the way over here that this whole time machine business is nothing but an elaborate plan of yours to get me to come over."

"You really think that?"

"I don't know; to tell you the truth, I don't know what to think." She paused a moment and mentioned the note on the front door again. "How did you know I was going to be here today, and how did you know it would be at 8 a.m.?"

"Well, let's eat first, and then I want to introduce you to someone."

"Oh, who might that be?" she asked, adjusting her seat closer to the table.

"Let's eat, and then I have to go over the general plan with you."

"It's good to have a plan," she said with a smile, shifting to a comfortable position in her chair.

I served the eggs and bacon, and poured the coffee for the both of us. Then I sat down and we ate our breakfast.

"This is so weird, to be here again, with you, after all these years."

"I know, it is weird, right?"

"Doug?"

"What?"

"Why am I really here?"

"You are here because of everything I told you yesterday."

"So you are sticking to the story of a time machine?"

"It's not a story, it's true, and after we finish our breakfast, I will prove it to you."

"Just so you know, I'm not expecting anything, just curious about you, and I did want to see the old house again."

"Well, in a few minutes, your perception of me and our situation will change drastically."

"Drastically? I don't like that word," she said with a chuckle.

After breakfast, Marie and I cleaned up what little dishes there were and sipped down another cup of coffee before heading into my bedroom. I turned Marie around to face the archway looking directly into the kitchen and told her to stand there and not to move.

"Just stand here and don't move?" she repeated.

"Yes, just stand there, and I will be right next to you."

We stood there for several minutes, staring at the archway, until Marie said, "So what's supposed to happen?"

"Just wait," I said, and we again turned our attention on the opening.

Just then, the familiar hum of the coils began to vibrate the floor. Marie began to blink several times and stared in amazement as she witnessed the image of the kitchen begin to fade into a collage of colors.

"What am I looking at?" she asked me while squeezing my arm slightly.

"Just wait," was all I said in return.

The blur of colors had rearranged themselves into shapes, and now the shapes were becoming familiar to her. "The room is changing," she said aloud. Then a figure of a person began moving toward the opposite side of the archway. "There's someone in the house with us," she added.

The blurry figure began to sharpen, and in seconds, it became clear to Marie what was happening. She stared at the figure on the other side of the archway and squeezed my arm tightly, pulling me closer to her.

"Oh, my gosh," she said as she looked at me and then again at the elderly man in the archway. "That's you," she continued. "You're an old man!"

Just then, Doug Sr. spoke directly to Marie: "It's good to see you again, Marie."

She looked at me and then at the older Doug.

"I still don't understand what's happening," she said in a somewhat-fearful voice.

"I can't explain to you every single detail," the older Doug said, "but what I can say is that I did create this time machine and I did use it." Then he paused a moment and corrected himself: "We used it together, and we were very successful at it, I might add. That is, until the day when you didn't come back, and we could not return to our time as planned."

"Was this the day of the accident?" Marie asked.

"Yes, it was, and as my younger self has told you, I have been trapped here on this timeline for many years, missing you and blaming myself for your death.

"I should have been more careful and added more protective measures and fail-safes, but in my haste to change the past, I ended up losing you." He continued, with his head down, "We discovered early on that any changes to the past, no matter how small or insignificant they may appear, could not be cosmically tolerated. In a nutshell, my dear Marie, we caused a paradox. We meddled in things we had no knowledge of, and it took your life and imprisoned me in a place that was filled with the torture of guilt.

"There has not been a day since then that I have not relived the accident. I was the one who pulled you from the car, and I was the one who held you in my arms as you took your last breath. The ambulance came, and they were able to revive you, but you slipped into a coma and were in the hospital for a long time before passing away." He looked up at Marie with tears in his eyes. "I was there when you died the second time as well."

Marie stepped closer to the archway and said, "But I didn't die, I'm right here."

Both Doug Sr. and I said in unison, "It hasn't happened yet!"

"But you just said it happened already, and you were there when I died —twice, I might add," she said, even more confused.

Doug Sr. spoke again: "I have a plan, and if it works, we will be able to reset the original timeline and avoid the accident. You, my dear, will go on to live a wonderful life."

Marie said, "What if I don't go into your machine? What then?"

"Then time will catch up to you, and when the day of the accident comes, you will just disappear into thin air."

Marie looked horrified and said, "Then I have no choice: I have to go, no matter what."

"No matter what," Doug Sr. repeated.

I put my arm around Marie's shoulder, pulled her closer to me, and then gave her a hug. "I will be with you and I will protect you from harm, I promise."

"Oh, Doug," she said. "You weren't able to protect me before; what makes you think you can this time?"

"Because now I know when and where things are going to happen, and I will take corrective measures to avoid them."

"I wish I could believe you," she said, now with tears in her eyes. "Not at all what I expected today," she added.

"If you two are ready, we must get started," Doug Sr. said.

After a few minutes of collecting ourselves and wiping away our tears, we set to the task of preparing for our first trip through the time machine. Doug Sr. took us through the entire process; there were step-by-step instructions that had to be followed and not deviated from in any way. He explained everything, including how we were to dress. After several hours of preparation, we were ready for our first trip.

"Remember what I told you: You must be back in twenty-four hours, and you must return together at the same time. I will not be there in the past and will not be able to guide you further, so you will be on your own." Then he said, "Just make sure you are back in twenty-four hours."

Then he pushed something through the archway, and it dropped to the floor. "Here, this is your remote access control," he explained. "It will allow you to open the portal from the other side and open the portal on your side as well. It's very much like to one you have already, but it has been modified over the years." He continued, "The digital readout at the top represents where you are going, or I should say *when* you are going, so don't confuse the dates. The bottom readout represents when you are to return and will begin a twenty-four-hour countdown from the time you arrive. Do not let this remote out of your sight; you will need it to return." Finally, he added, "It will take you several weeks and many trips into the machine before you can actually repair the past. The first two or three trips are very hard on the body and will take some getting used to. You will feel very tired when you first arrive, almost like passing out from exhaustion, but you will get used to it and build up a resistance to it quickly. Today, you leave at exactly 1 p.m., and you will return at exactly 1 p.m. tomorrow. Do either of you have any questions?"

Marie asked, "Will I be able to see the younger me when I go back in time?"

"Yes, you will, and you will be able to see other family members who have passed on as well. They will not know who you are unless you tell them, and if you tell them, you will effectively change the past. I warned you about that, so don't do it," Doug Sr. said in a harsh tone. "You will be tempted to tell your former selves to avoid things or take a different path, but you must not." He added, "You will only observe and not take part; is that clear?"

Both Marie and I nodded our heads in agreement and began changing into our clothes for the trip.

At 12:30, Doug Sr. said his good-byes and wished us both success on our trip back to the past. "I have to go now, but remember what I told you. Your remote is set for Saturday, June 4, 1983. Both of you are out of the house at this time, so you will be able to arrive undetected, and you will be able to return undetected as well. Oh, I almost forgot: Here is a master key to the door. It will work in all of the time periods."

The key dropped to the floor, and Marie bent down to retrieve it. Then the viewer shut down, and the kitchen returned to normal.

We only had fifteen minutes to get ready and restart the machine with the new time setting.

I took Marie by the shoulders to face me.

"I'm scared," she said.

"I'm scared as well, but we can do this; we did it already, according to old Doug, so we should be safe."

"Eighties," Marie said.

"Eighties what?" I asked.

"Hair spray; never mind," she said. "It's a girl thing."

"Well, let's do it then. I'm ready!"

Marie took my hand and motioned for me to push the button on the remote. "A kiss for luck," she said.

I put my lips to hers, and we kissed and pulled away very slowly.

We gave each other a familiar look, and Marie said, "Now that is something I remember quite well."

Chapter 9

We both took a deep breath. I pushed the button on the remote, and the machine sprang to life. We watched as the room took on another configuration, and then there was a clicking sound. The remote's digital readout was flashing "Ready." I grabbed Marie's hand, and we took another breath and stepped through the archway. We were immediately bombarded with sounds and voices from the past (or they may have been from the future). The voices passed us as if on a very fast train, with them trailing off into the distance. There were bright lights and sharp pains in our heads. I could feel pressure on my body, as if we were under water, but I was still able to breathe. Our legs gave way from underneath, and the floor became unstable. After another sharp, more intense pain in my head, I lost consciousness.

The next thing I knew, we were lying on the floor, just on the other side of the archway, trying to open our eyes and focus. My mouth was dry, and my eyes burned. My skin felt hot to the touch. We lay there for several minutes, waiting for the sounds of the new time to catch up with us. I tried to speak, but my words were garbled. After a few more minutes, the connections from our voice to our hearing cleared up.

Marie asked, "Are we there yet?"

I started to laugh but only came up with a three-pack-a-day kind of cough. I tried again to answer, and this time it was much clearer.

"I'm glad you haven't lost your sense of humor," I joked.

Marie and I sat up slowly on the floor and strained to focus our eyes.

"This is incredible," she said in an excited tone, while looking around.

"Can you stand up?" I asked.

"I think so," she said, and we leaned on each other and stood up.

At first, our legs seemed wobbly, but after a few minutes, they regained their strength.

"So that was time travel," Marie said. "Not too bad." She instantly began checking out everything in the kitchen and then moved into the bathroom. "I'll be in here for a few," she said and closed the door behind her.

I looked around and recognized everything; all the old fixtures and finishes seemed brand-new. On top of the old kitchen table, I saw newspapers and mail from 1983. I looked out the window to the back yard and saw the old wooden tool shed, standing where it used to be. Everything was as it was back in 1983.

Just then, Marie emerged from the bathroom and said, "You know, you have pink soap in there."

"So what?" I said.

"Guys don't have pink soap in their bathrooms," she said with a sinister expression.

I said, "Pink, blue, green, white, what's the difference?"

"We will talk about it later," she said, drying her hands on a kitchen towel.

"Hey look at this," I said. "I found an envelope on the kitchen table and it was addressed to us."

"What do you mean, us?" she said.

"Just what I said: 'To Marie and Doug, open immediately and read together."

I tore open the envelope and removed a set of keys and a note. The note read "You will need a vehicle to get around in while you are here. Take these keys to the 1969 Valiant parked across the street. It is registered to Marie, and the tank is full. Also, here is some money to hold you over for the day. The currency is all pre-1983.

"For your first day, just go out for a drive and make sure you do not interact with your younger selves. Be back at the house 1 hour before departure to prep for the return. Have some fun!"

Marie took the keys and said, "I used to own a Valiant; I wonder if it's the same car?"

We walked through the house and noticed all the old furniture, including my old bed, where Marie and I got to know each other very well.

"Remember that?" I asked, pointing to the bed.

"Funny, I remember it like it was yesterday, and actually, today really *is* yesterday."

"I guess you're right about that." Marie walked over to the bed and sat down. Then she lay down on one of the pillows and said, "This is so weird," motioning for me to join her.

I walked over and sat down as well.

"I remember this smell," she said, holding a pillow to her face. "Even the smell of this house, I remember it."

Marie climbed out of bed and started to pick up everything she could get her hands on to examine it. "This is absolutely incredible," she said.

I was also picking up items and looking at them. I even found a box of old photos that went missing sometime in the late eighties.

Marie said, "Let's go check out the car. I want to see if it's the same one or not."

"Wait a second before you run outside," I said. "We have to be very careful who we encounter."

"You're right," Marie said, peeking through the living room curtains toward the street. "I can see my car," she said as she put her finger to the window.

"Let's make sure the coast is clear before jumping into your car; we don't want to attract any attention."

Marie and I gathered what we came with, took the envelope and note with us, and left the house. As we descended the front steps to the sidewalk, our hearts began to race.

"I feel like we are on the lam or something," Marie joked.

We both looked up and down the street for signs of anyone we might recognize, but all seemed quiet.

"I think we are in the clear," Marie said, reaching for my hand. "Let's go before I lose my nerve."

We crossed the street, looking as inconspicuous as we could.

"Oh, my gosh!" Marie exclaimed as she bent down to open the door. "Doug, this *is* my old car." She sat inside the driver's seat and reached over to unlock my door.

"Are you sure this is the actual old car you had back in the day?"

"I really think so," she said, gripping the steering wheel and running her hands around its circumference. "Sure feels the same."

"I don't think I was ever in this car with you before" I said with a juvenile grin.

"It was forever breaking down and sat in front of my house most of the time." Then she said, "But this sure looks like the real thing." She adjusted the mirrors and moved the seat into a comfortable position. "Ah, that's better," she said, putting the key into the ignition and giving it a turn. The car roared to life, and Marie commented that it never sounded so good. "Well, where shall we go first?"

"Let's head toward Nutley and drive up Franklin Avenue; we can see the old high school and where I used to get my hair cut at the Park Barbers."

"I like that idea; we can stop by Avondale and maybe go for a walk," Marie said, giving me a wink and a smile.

"It sounds good to me."

Marie put the car into drive, and we headed toward Branch Brook Park.

"Let's drive through the park," I suggested, motioning with my hand the direction.

Marie made a right-hand turn at the end of the street.

"This is absolutely incredible," was all Marie could say while looking at all the old stores that we used to visit years ago. "Hey, look at that," she said, pointing to a sign that read "Jug Milk." "Remember that little store?" she asked.

"I remember like it was yesterday," I said. "Funny how my memory of this time is so vivid. I could almost walk this neighborhood blindfolded."

"I know what you mean," Marie replied. "Hey, I want to see something, okay? It's just a little out of our way."

She drove past the park and up two blocks to where she once lived in a second-floor apartment. She made a left-hand turn and inched up the block slowly until she came to the house, where she actually pulled into the driveway.

"What are you doing?" I asked her.

"I want to take a quick look at the old place," she said with excitement in her voice. "I can see that I'm not home right now," she added with a little giggle.

Marie stopped the car in the driveway, and we both got out. She instinctively made her way to the rear of the home, where a staircase led to the second-floor apartment. She practically sprinted up the steps; upon reaching her old apartment door, she cupped her eyes and pushed her face to the glass window in the door.

"Oh, my gosh," she said in utter amazement. "See how small it really was?" She motioned for me to take a look.

I leaned in and looked at her old apartment, everything in one room. I recognized her bed, where she once lay very sick and hungry, and I came over to take care of her. The vision of that night again burned into my brain; it felt like it happened last night.

I asked, "Remember that night when you called me because you were very sick?"

"I do remember that," she said and touched me on my hand. "You took care of me and made me something to eat and gave me medicine." Then she said, "You were such a nice guy to do that. You know, all my memories of you are good."

"Thank you," I replied.

Marie peeked into her apartment window once again and took one last look around. She sighed, "I just can't get over how small it really was," and then turned around to face me. I noticed her eyes were watery, and it looked like a tear would fall at any second.

"We loved so close together," she said.

"You mean 'lived so close together,' don't you?" I asked her.

"Yes, lived; what did I say?"

"You said 'loved.'"

Marie touched my cheek and said, "Slip of the tongue." She smiled.

"Are you ready to leave?" I asked.

"I guess so. I wonder if this whole trip will make me cry everywhere we go."

I put my arm around her shoulder and said, "Come on, let's go, lots of people and places to see. I wouldn't mind stopping by the old King Street house to see it again."

"And I wouldn't mind stopping by my old house in Nutley as well." Marie's face lit up again as we walked back to the car and climbed inside.

In no time, we were back on the road, heading toward the park. Marie made a right-hand turn and began driving through the park. We both looked around at everything; I mentioned that it hadn't changed a bit, and then we realized we were looking at it in 1983. We both let out a laugh.

We continued on through the park until we came to Washington Avenue; we made a left turn and headed toward King Street, where I used to live from 1969 to 1980, all the while passing the stores and places we remembered.

"Oh, look: Butts N Bows, remember that?"

"Hmmm," Marie replied, nodding her head. "Oh and look: Guys and Dolls," she said, pointing to her right.

"I remember that place," I said.

We continued driving and passed the old McDonald's on the left, where the sign read "Over 10 million served." Then we passed the Brunswick Bowling Alley and continued on to King Street. We made a left at the bottom of the hill and headed up toward my old house. As we drove up to the red brick Cape Cod on the right-hand side of the road, I noticed my old 69 Chevy parked in the driveway.

"Oh, my," I said. "I'm home now."

Marie took notice of the car in the driveway and said, "The young Doug is inside the house." Then she added, "I want to park for a while and see if he comes out."

This is so weird, I thought to myself.

Marie pulled the car over to the curb directly across the street so that we both had a clear view of the house.

She turned the car off, and we just sat quietly and looked over at the house without saying a word. Thirty-five minutes passed, and we noticed some movement at the side door. Our eyes practically bugged out of our heads as we watched young Doug, dressed in sweatpants and a tee shirt, climb into the 69 Chevy and drive up the hill.

"Let's follow him and see where he is going," Marie said, starting the car and throwing it into drive. "I wonder if you are on your way to see me," she said in a girlish tone.

She stepped on the gas hard at first, and the car's tires screeched as the rubber gripped the road.

"Easy," I said, and I reminded her that we were to remain in the shadows.

"I know, I know," she said, driving up King Street.

"Look, there you are," she said, pointing to her left at Zinicola's Bakery. "Oh, my gosh," she said. "Look at you, so young and full of muscles." She sighed.

The young Doug was inside the bakery, picking up two long loaves of Italian bread. I knew this, because I did it hundreds of times as a kid.

"I bet you anything he comes out of there with two loaves of Italian bread."

"How do you know what he is going to buy?" Marie asked, looking at me puzzled.

"That's all I ever used to buy there," I replied. "Always the same thing, every time."

Just then, young Doug emerged from the bakery with, yes, two loaves of Italian bread.

"Look, you're pulling the top off of one of the loves." Marie pointed. "Now you're eating it," she said, laughing.

"I always did that," I said, "every time. The bread was always hot, and it smelled so good."

"Let's pick some up tonight before we head back to the house," Marie joked. "Oh, there he goes. Back down the hill to your old house."

"Let's keep moving; there are so many places to see."

"I agree," she said and then paused a moment. "Where shall we go next?"

"How about we drive over to your old home in Nutley? We might catch a glimpse of the young Marie."

"Why not?" she said and started heading in that direction.

We made a right onto Union Avenue and drove a block or two.

"Look, there's the White Oak Pharmacy."

"Yes, and there's Jerry's," I said, pointing over to our left.

We continued down to Park Avenue, made a left turn, and continued to Walnut Street, but before making the left onto Walnut, we both noticed Washington Grade School and barked out the name in unison. We made the left on Walnut and headed down a few blocks toward Marie's old home.

"There it is! There it is!" Marie yelled. "Oh, my gosh. Look at it," she said, still very excited.

"I don't see any cars in the driveway, you think anyone is home?"

"Mom is probably home, but I can't be sure," she said sadly.

"Let's park here for a while," I said. "Perhaps we might see her, or we might even see the young Marie stop by."

Marie pulled over to the curb and turned off the car. "You know what I would love to do right now?"

"No, what?"

"I would love to take a walk around the neighborhood." She paused. "Want to take a walk with me?"

"Sure, but first I would move the car; you don't want the younger Marie driving it away by mistake."

"Good point," she said, driving around the corner, out of sight.

Marie parked as close to Washington Avenue as she could. We got out of the car and started walking back toward her old home.

"What a beautiful day," she said, flipping her long brown hair out of her eyes. "This is so incredibly amazing," she said again and again. Then she said, "Stop!"

"Stop what?" I asked.

"Look!" She pointed to her house and said, "That's Jimmy." She paused. "My little brother Jimmy; look how cute he is, er, was." Marie sighed. "I wish I could see my mom. If this was Halloween, I could put on a mask and ring the bell, and then she would answer the door, and I would be able to see her."

We stood there at the corner for another few minutes and then decided to take a walk through Kingsland Park.

The weather was absolutely gorgeous, with clear blue skies, a temperature of 78 degrees, and a light wind blowing in from the north.

Marie said, "Come on this way," and she stepped off the curb and started walking across the street. "I remember a short-cut to the park."

"I'll follow your lead," I replied and then matched her pace and stride.

The walk to the park took us nearly fifteen minutes, and when we arrived, we were amazed at just how wonderful everything appeared. Marie breathed in deeply and then exhaled. "Oh, remember the smell of this park?" She paused and then answered her own question: "Yes, I do."

"Hey, look over there," I said and pointed to a tree on the island nearest to the water. "Do you remember that spot?"

"I think so, is that where we made out one day?" she asked.

"You really do have a good memory," I replied. "They call that the United Nations Garden."

"Oh, look over there; you see the bridge and the little waterfall?"

"Yes, I see it."

We walked around the park for at least an hour and a half, and then we started to get a little tired and decided to head back to her car.

Marie said, "Let me sit for a minute and rub my feet; they are hurting me."

We sat under a tree on a park bench, and she removed one of her shoes.

"Here, swing your foot over here," I said.

Marie smiled, shifted herself to face me, and lifted her leg up, resting it on my lap.

"Be careful what you wish for, big boy."

I took her foot into my hands and massaged it thoroughly.

Marie sat back and let out a sigh. "This is really nice."

"I'm glad you liking it," I replied. "How's about that other foot?"

Marie instantly swung the other leg over my lap.

I removed her other shoe and methodically began to rub her foot.

"You always did have magic hands, you know that?"

"Thank you," I said. "How do your feet feel now?"

"They feel much better, thank you."

"What time is it?" I asked.

"I don't know," she replied. "Don't you have a watch?"

"Oh, yes, I do. It's just about 4:30. Want to head back now?"

"I guess so," she said and then paused. "Where are we going now?"

"I thought we would get a bite to eat or something."

"What do you mean, 'or something'? What is 'something?'" she asked, giggling.

"I'm just asking if you want to get something to eat, that's all."

Marie sat up straight and put her shoes back on. Then she put her hand on my shoulder and said, "I know, I was just teasing you a little." She stood up and said, "I have an idea," and then looked right at me. Together, as if on cue, we said, "Scotto's."

While walking back to her car, we passed her house once again and overheard someone talking inside. We stopped to listen for a moment.

"That's my mom talking to someone," Marie said. "I can't tell who." She moved a little closer to the window and lifted her head to hear. "She's talking to my Aunt Kitty on the phone. Oh, my gosh." Marie broke down, kneeled on the ground, and wept. "Haven't seen my Aunt Kitty …" She cleared her throat. "… or my mom in so long. I just want to hear her voice again." She wiped her tears away with her hand and stood up. "I want to see her, Doug," she continued. "We stepped through nearly thirty years and drove about six miles. I want to see her."

"Hey, no problem, let's get the car and park in a good spot, where we can see the entire house. We will have a stakeout for your Mom. Speaking of steak, um, let's pick up something to eat and bring it back with us. What do you say?"

"I say that's a good idea, and we're coming right back here to hang out and spy on my mom, right?"

"Right."

"You still want to go to Scotto's? We can grab a couple of sandwiches and something to drink to go."

"Sounds good; let's go quickly so we can get back right away."

We drove the two-plus miles to the pizzeria and parked in a spot right out in front.

"Look at that," she said. "Amazing, and look at the pet shop and liquor store."

"It is really unbelievable, I know."

"You mind if I stay here in the car?"

"I don't mind. Tell me what you want, and I'll go in and get it for you."

"I want a nice salad with croutons and grilled chicken on top."

"And a Pepsi Max," I joked.

"Maybe just a seltzer water." She paused a moment and added, "And one slice of pizza."

"Is that all you want?"

"That's all," she said.

I walked into the pizzeria, placed my order with a waitress, and sat down at one of the booths.

I didn't want to take a chance of being recognized by one of the guys behind the counter. Jerry, the owner, came out from the back and started making a pizza. After placing it in the oven, he wiped his hands on his apron and leaned on the counter, looking out the front window. Then he turned his attention toward the rear of the restaurant and took notice of me sitting in the booth. He only looked in my direction for a moment and then turned again to the parking lot. This time, he looked harder out the window, directly at Marie's car, and began to scratch his head.

The order was ready, and I got up to pay. I handed the money to the young guy behind the counter, and he made change instantly; seconds after that, I was out the door with my food. I wasn't going to give Jerry a chance to put two and two together. I turned quickly just before getting into Marie's car and looked toward the storefront, only to see Jerry standing there, still staring in our direction.

"Do you see Jerry over there, staring at us?" Marie asked.

"Yes, he was looking at me in the restaurant," I replied. "I thought he might have recognized me."

"Did he say anything to you?"

"No, I paid and got out of there quickly."

"Well, we should get moving."

"I agree, let's head back over to Walnut."

Marie put the car into drive, and we left the parking lot rather quickly. "Is this how it's going to be, with us being all paranoid about who is going to recognize us?"

"I would assume that they might think they recognize us, but at second glance, they would have to rethink it."

"What do you mean?"

"How can we possibly be the Marie and Doug from 1983, looking the way we do? Besides, the younger Marie and Doug are still running around here every day. They would have to put if off as being coincidental older look-alikes.

"I guess so." Marie thought for a moment. "Then if that happens, and someone thinks they know us, we will have to say we are someone else, right?"

"Exactly, but I think it would be easier just to avoid uncomfortable situations; keep our distance or maybe use a disguise of some sort."

Marie looked at me and said, "You put on a mustache and beard with sunglasses, and I can get a wig with a big hat and dark glasses." She paused. "I think that might work."

"I think we could get away with it, yes."

Marie pulled up across from her house on Walnut Street and backed the car up just a bit to have the best view, yet still remain inconspicuous.

"There, we will be able to see everything from here," she said, putting the car into park and turning off the ignition.

"Let's have our dinner, okay?"

"Yes, let's," Marie said, staring at her old house. "I really hope I see my mom."

"Maybe we can call her from my cell phone and …"

"Um, cell phone?" Marie said, while giving me a half-smile.

I started to laugh and said, "That would be funny if it could work. I didn't bring it with me, anyway. There are no cell phone towers yet, at least, I don't think so." I was just talking out loud; I had forgotten *when* I was.

Marie and I finished our salads and drank our seltzer water and just sat back in the seat and focused our attention on the house. We cranked the windows down to allow some fresh air into the car. The last of the sun's rays had just dipped below the visible tree line. Lights were beginning to become noticeable in the houses along the block.

A cool breeze began to stir the newly formed leaves on the trees, creating a soft, almost hypnotic sound that filled me with a sense of peace and relaxation.

Marie sighed, "I forgot just how much I missed my old home and neighborhood," and then she added, "So many memories, things I haven't thought about in decades."

"Like what, for instance?" I asked.

"Just memories of growing up in that house." She took a breath and added, "Memories of Mom and Dad." She wiped a tear away. "Dad." She paused. "I miss him, too."

Marie wiped away another tear and cleared her throat. "So many memories," she said, looking toward the living room window and taking notice of shadowy silhouettes on the curtains. "She's in there right now; all I have to do is walk over there and ring the bell."

"You could do that, but how would you explain yourself?"

"I don't know."

"Hey, you know what?"

"What?"

"I have an idea."

"Oh, what is it?"

"Your doorbell comment got me thinking. I could go over there and ring the bell and hide."

"Do you have any idea how childish and immature that sounds?"

"Well, I —"

"I like it," she said, shifting herself to a more comfortable position. "Go now, please?"

I got out of the car, closed the door quietly, and casually walked over to the front door. I rang the bell and quickly darted around the side of the house and waited. I looked over across the street and noticed Marie, with her face looking out the window.

Just then, I heard a woman's voice say, "Wait a minute, be right there," then the sound of the front door opening. "Hello?" Pause. "Hello, who's there?"

Marie's mom had come to the door and was now standing just outside the entrance. She took a few steps down to the walkway, crossed her arms, and looked from side to side. "Anyone?" she said, taking a few more steps toward the sidewalk and looking first up the street and then down.

Just then, there was the high-pitched sound of another voice: "Mom, who is it?"

"I don't know, Jimmy, there's no one here."

Marie's brother came outside and met up with her mom at the sidewalk. I could see from my vantage point that Marie was now scrunched down, with just the tops of her eyes visible. She was watching them.

"Just someone playing a joke," Marie's mom said to Jimmy. "Let's go back inside, it's a little chilly."

At that point, they both returned inside the house and closed the door. I waited another minute or two before giving up my hiding place to return to the car. Just as I started to move, I heard a sound above my head of someone opening a window.

I scrunched down and remained motionless. I knew from the mumbles going back and forth that Marie's mom and her brother were looking out the window, trying to catch the juvenile delinquents who rang their bell and ran away. Then I remembered that I was that delinquent and sank deeper into my position.

After a few more minutes, they closed the window, and the muffled sound of their voices trailed off. I thought about running across the street and jumping into the car, but at the last second, I decided to just walk nonchalantly and not attract any unnecessary attention. When I reached the car, I noticed the windows were now closed; I opened the passenger door and got in. Marie was sitting motionless, staring straight ahead at the windshield. She didn't say anything for at least ten minutes. I could see that she had been crying; her face was wet.

Then she turned to me and simply said, "Thank you for that."

"It was my pleasure," I said quietly.

She sat for a few more minutes and then shared a thought with me: "You know, the last time I saw my mom, she passed away in bed with all of us around her. My siblings were there to comfort her in her last moments." She paused. "It is just incredible to be able to see her alive and talking and walking again." Just then, she wiped the remaining tears from her eyes and said, "I could really get used to this time travel stuff."

"I have to admit, it does have its advantages," I said, nodding my head in agreement.

Marie shifted herself again and made ready to drive away. "So where are we off to now?" she asked, shifting into drive.

"I thought we might call it a night and head back to Newark."

"Oh yes, I wanted to talk to you about that," Marie said with smile.

"What's to talk about?"

"I'll get right to the question."

"Okay."

"Where are you sleeping tonight?"

This was the first time I had given that any thought. "I guess I'll take the sofa, and you can have my bed. Is that what you are asking me?"

"Yep." She paused. "That's what I'm asking you."

"Are you okay with that answer?"

"I would have suggested the same thing," she said, now turning onto Franklin Avenue. "This situation we are in has got to be the strangest, what, date? What would you call it?"

"I have no idea what to call it," I said, folding my hands on my lap. "But I can say one thing without the slightest bit of doubt."

"Oh, what's that?"

"Even after nearly thirty years of absence, we still know how to have a good time."

"I think it's the chemicals."

"What?"

"Chemicals, it's chemicals inside our bodies that react a certain way when we are together."

"So you are saying we have good chemistry together?"

"I always thought so," she said.

"I always thought so as well," I replied in full agreement.

Marie continued down Franklin Avenue and then turned onto South Franklin and then onto Franklin Street, followed by a quick left on North Seventh Street. After a few blocks, we pulled over directly in front of my old house.

We both looked up and down the street to make sure it was safe to go inside. After confirming with each other, we quickly got out of the car and practically sprinted down the side of the house to the rear entrance. We wanted to get out of sight as quickly as possible. After climbing the stairs and opening the door into the kitchen, we entered and turned on the light. We both breathed a sigh of relief to be at the house; now we would be able to relax until our return trip to 2014.

"I want to freshen up a bit," Marie said, making her way to the bathroom. "Sorry I have to go; I've been holding it for hours."

"Hey, no problem, go right ahead."

Marie closed the door behind her as she entered the bathroom, and I immediately heard the sound of water running and then a flush.

I decided to poke around a bit and explore my old photo albums. *I kept a pretty clean house back in the day*, I thought to myself. I picked up one of the photo albums from the floor next to my bed and switched on the lamp on top of the nightstand. I sat down on the bed and started flipping through the pages. Instantly, my mind began to race as I looked at images of people I hadn't seen in over thirty years. All these pictures had been lost to time, but I remembered having them. Page after page and picture after picture, the memories came flooding back. I was in nostalgic heaven.

"Ah, I feel so much better now" Marie said, still air-drying her hands. "What are you looking at?" she asked, walking over to the bed and sitting down next to me.

"Just some old pictures I used to have."

"You and your pictures," she said and slid over closer for a better look. "I remember most of these people. Look how clear and vibrant the images are; they look brand-new." Catching herself before I could comment, she said, "They are brand-new." She paused. "This is so weird."

I turned to the last page of the album, and out fell a photo of Marie, taken here in the house in 1982.

Holding the picture in her hand, she asked, "How did you get this picture of me?"

"I took that picture one day when you came over with your friend

Margret. While you came into the door, I snapped it and have had this picture ever since."

"I look like an alien or something."

"No, you don't. I like this picture of you."

"Hmmm," was her reply.

She handed the picture back to me, stood up, and walked into the living room, where she turned on the television. Seconds later, I heard the theme song of a popular TV show I used to watch. *Dallas* was just getting started. I went into the living room, and Marie was already comfortable on the sofa.

I stood there for a minute, looking at her, and commented on how strange it was to be here with her, in my old room from 1983, on the actual sofa we had gotten to know fairly well back then. I wasn't sure if it was the room or the year or what, but looking at her sitting there on my sofa made me all warm and fuzzy inside.

"What are you thinking about?" she asked.

"I was just remembering the last time I saw you sitting on that sofa."

"I was just thinking about the same thing," she said, motioning for me to sit down next to her.

"It has been the most unbelievably fascinating day." She paused. "Who else in this entire world could say they have experienced such a day?"

"I don't think you will find any takers."

"That's for sure," Marie replied. "I see you still haven't forgotten how to show a girl a good time."

"It's been so long since I've been out with a woman. I feel like a kid again in so many ways."

"I know what you mean."

We turned our attention to the television, looking for a way to break the tension.

"Did you ever watch *Dallas*?" I asked.

"No, not really; the only thing I remember is that JR was shot, and that's about it."

Just then, the telephone rang, and we almost jumped out of our skins.

"It's only the phone," I said and instinctively went over to it and answered, "Hello?"

Marie's eyes bugged out of her head, and she made a cutting motion with her hand, trying to get me to hang up.

"Hello, Doug?"

"Yes, this is Doug; who's this?"

"It's me, Marie."

I felt the blood rush to my head as I shot a glance to Marie on the sofa.

"Who is it?" she asked, moving her mouth in silence.

I pointed to her and moved my mouth: "It's *you*."

"So what are you doing home? I thought you were away this weekend."

"I just had to pick up some clothes before I headed out," I replied, thinking fast.

"Are you still going down the shore?" young Marie asked.

"Is that what I told you?"

"Yes."

"Then that's what I'm doing."

"Your voice sounds different; are you catching a cold or something?"

Or something, I thought to myself.

Marie stood up, walked over to me, and pushed an ear close to the phone. We struggled for a second to get the phone in the best position so we could both hear.

"Are you alone?"

"Um …"

"So you have company?"

"Ah, not really company, just, ah, actually, I was just thinking about you!"

"Oh, is that so?" the younger Marie replied.

"Why did you call me if you knew I wouldn't be home?" I asked, thinking fast again.

"I just wanted to leave you a message on that crazy phone message machine of yours to have you call me when you got back." She paused. "Since I have you on the phone, can you call me when you get back? I want to do something."

"Sure, but do me a favor."

"What?"

"Call right back after we hang up and leave your message."

"What for? I already told you."

"I just don't want to forget to call you; besides, I like hearing your voice."

"You like hearing my voice?" the younger Marie said with a doubtful tone. "Are you sure you are alone over there?"

"It's just you and me, I swear!"

Marie pulled back from the phone and started to laugh under her breath. I shrugged my shoulders and motioned that I didn't know what else to say.

"Okay, I'll call right back and leave a message. See you when you get back."

"Okay, see you when I get back," I said and hung up the phone.

A few seconds later, the phone rang again, and this time, I let the machine pick it up.

Marie sat back down and said, "I wouldn't answer that thing anymore."

"I don't plan to," I replied.

The young Marie left her message, and I sat down again next to Marie.

"This day keeps getting stranger and stranger," she continued. "We will have to be cognizant of our surroundings and be more careful."

"I know," I said. "Force of habit to answer the phone; sorry, that wasn't very smart."

"Not to change the subject, but what time tomorrow do we go back?"

"As close to one as we can; I'd say 12:55 should be acceptable."

"What day will it be?"

"The same day and the same time we left."

"You mean …"

"Yes, it's like we were never here."

"It's hard to imagine that we lived an entire day in 1983, and we still have the entire day ahead of us in 2014." She thought for a second. "So if we went on a time trip that lasted ten years, we could still return at the exact time we left?"

"Yes, that's correct, but —"

"But what?"

"We would have aged ten years before our return, and family and friends in 2014 would still be the same age as when we left."

"So long trips are not a good idea?"

"Not a good idea," I repeated.

"The show is over," Marie said, pointing to the television. "I wonder what's on now."

I turned around in my seat and began looking for the remote.

"What are you looking for?"

"The remo— Never mind. I'll get up and change the channel."

"Thank you, I did it the last time," she said with a grin.

I turned the knob until we found a good old-fashioned black-and-white movie on Channel 13.

"Oh, leave this on," Marie said.

"I've seen this one, a long time ago," I said; without thinking, I spoiled the ending: "She dies after first going blind."

"Don't tell me everything." She paused. "I want to see it for myself."

With that, we finally settled in for the night, with Marie leaning to one side of the sofa and me on the other. It wasn't long before we both fell asleep, in our seemingly uncomfortable positions.

Several hours passed before I woke up and nudged Marie awake.

"Um, what's the matter?"

"Time for bed," I said.

"Okay," Marie replied.

We started walking into the bedroom when the last of the sleepies left her brain.

"Hold on, big boy," she said, putting her hand against my chest and stopping me in my tracks. "What are you doing?"

"What do you mean?"

"We said we were not going to sleep together, right?"

"Right."

"Then where are you going?"

"You will need something to sleep in; I think I may have an oversized t-shirt and a pair of sweatpants that may work for you."

"Oh, I thought —"

"No, I'll get something for you and for myself to sleep in, and then I will take the sofa like we planned."

"Oh, I just wanted to be sure." Marie sighed, either from relief or disappointment, I couldn't tell for sure, but after we changed, we retreated to our designated sleeping areas.

Marie made herself comfortable in my old bed, and I propped up a pillow and added a blanket to the sofa, making myself comfortable as well. It was extremely quiet in the house, so much so that any sound at all seemed to be amplified in some way. I lay there on my back, with my arms across my chest, staring at the ceiling and watching the occasional reflection of a car's lights wash over the walls. Every few minutes, I could hear Marie inhale and then exhale deeply, followed by a sigh and a slight humphing sound.

"Are you okay in there?" I asked.

"Yes, but I can't sleep now," she continued. "I was just thinking that I never slept in your bed alone before."

"I know."

"Don't know if I like it," she said, standing at the doorway to the living room and looking at me on the sofa.

"Would you rather have the sofa?" I asked.

"I think I'd rather … we should …"

"What?"

"Are you going to make me say it?" she asked, now standing directly in front of me.

Looking up at her in the dimly lighted room opened a floodgate of memories, and all the affection I once felt for her came rushing back.

"Is it hot in here?" I asked.

"Yes, it is," she replied.

I got off the sofa, scooped her up into my arms, and carried her into my bedroom. I held her close as I kissed her, still holding her in my arms. Marie threw her arms around my neck and pulled me close with a hug that almost cut off my circulation.

"Oh, my gosh," she said as we both got into bed. "I never thought I'd ever be with you like this again."

"I can't tell you how much I missed you over the years," I said while holding her face in my hand.

"I missed you too," she said as we slipped down into the blankets and made love for the first time in nearly thirty years.

The morning came quickly, and I was the first to wake up. I wondered if there was any food in the house to make a quick breakfast. I looked in the refrigerator and found a dozen of eggs and some bacon. I even found some bread to make toast. The only problem was I couldn't find a toaster, Now that I think about it I never owned a toaster, so I used a frying pan. I cooked the eggs and bacon and toasted the bread. Just as I was finishing up the breakfast, Marie came into the kitchen.

"Smells wonderful," she said, walking over to the table. "What did we do last night?"

"You know what we did, you were there!"

"I mean, did we do the right thing?"

I moved up against her and gently lifted her face upward to look into her eyes. "I have no doubt in my mind that what we did last night was the right thing."

She hugged me tightly and smiled, still in one of my old t-shirts as she sat down for breakfast. "What time is it?"

"9:30," I replied and began serving the eggs and bacon.

"We still have nearly three and a half hours before we head back to 2014, right?"

"That's right; why do you ask?"

"I wanted to make a phone call."

Breakfast with Marie was very pleasurable; we talked about old times and how everything was now so fresh in our minds. Being back in 1983 had ignited a flame of memories inside the both of us. Our conversation carried on while we washed the dishes. I washed and she dried and then put everything back in its proper place. Marie finished drying the last plate and put the dish towel down on the counter.

"There, all done," she said, turning on her heel and facing me.

"I'm curious, who did you wish to call?"

"First, I want a kiss, and then I'll tell you," Marie said, holding her arms open.

I stepped in close, put my arms around her, and drew her to me. She threw her arms around my neck, and our lips met.

"Hmmm," Marie said. "I always loved the way you kissed me."

I pulled back slightly, looked into her eyes, and asked, "What about now?"

"I still love the way you kiss me."

"I still love kissing you," I replied, and after another huge hug, we separated.

"I should get dressed."

"Wait just a minute," I said. "You haven't told me who you wanted to call."

"Let me get dressed first and I will tell you."

We took turns in the bathroom washing up and changing back into our time traveling clothes. Afterward, Marie tapped me on the shoulder while I was looking out the kitchen window into the back yard.

"What are you thinking about?" she asked.

"I was just thinking about us, actually."

"Oh?" she said, rubbing my back. "What about us?"

"I'm a little scared about the future."

"Scared? Why?"

"I don't want to lose you again, and this car accident thing has me very worried. I don't know all the facts the lead to that terrible day. I don't like not knowing how and why it happened. I'm scared that I might have had something to do with it or I might have not done something to prevent it."

"Whatever it was or however it happened, I know you will figure out a way to stop it," she said, putting her hand on my cheek.

"I hope so," I said, changing the subject quickly. "Who do you want to call?"

"I want to call my mom and actually have a conversation with her." She took a step backward and added, "I called here last night, and you were able to speak to me, so I figure I could call my mom and have a conversation without difficulty."

"I think you may be able to, but you would have to be very careful not to say anything that gives you away. You will have to stick to everything in 1983, do you know what I mean?"

"I know exactly what you mean, and I will be very careful."

With one hour to go before our jump back, Marie picked up the phone and dialed her old number. After a few seconds, the operator came on and said that the number was disconnected. She tried again, and the operator repeated the message.

"Why isn't this working?" she asked, talking to the phone.

"Are you dialing the right number?" I asked.

"I think so."

"Wait, let me check something," I said and walked over to the nightstand next to the bed. "I used to have a, oh, here it is," I said.

"What is that?"

"My old phone book," I said, lifting a small black book off the table. "Your number should be in here."

"Clever," she said, now looking over my shoulder.

I flipped the pages to the back of the book, where I found Marie's old phone number, right next to a scribbled heart and arrow drawing. She moved back over to the phone, and I read her phone number out to her.

She dialed again, and this time someone answered. "Hello?"

"Hello, Mom?"

"What happened, did you forget something?"

"Forget something?" Marie repeated.

"You just left here," her mother said. "How did you get to a phone so quickly?"

"I'm over a friend's house, using their phone," Marie said.

"Okay, so what's the matter?"

"Nothing's the matter; I just wanted to talk to you."

"You talked to me all morning; I would think that you're tired of me by now."

"Oh, Mom, it's so nice to hear your voice." Marie paused and then added, "On the phone."

Marie continued her conversation with her mother for another twenty minutes. I tried not to eavesdrop on them but kept one ear open for anything that may raise a flag or two. She was very careful not to say anything suspicious or out of the ordinary.

After a while, she simply ended her call.

"Good-bye, Mom, I love you," she said and then hung up.

Pretending not to have heard a thing, I asked if she enjoyed speaking to her mother. With tears in her eyes and a smile from ear to ear, she cupped her hand in my shirt and pulled me into her.

"I can't tell you just how much it meant to me to hear her voice again," she said while burying her face in my neck. "Thank you," she said and then returned to the bathroom to splash a little water on her face.

"We have fifteen minutes to get ready," I said. "I'm about to push the remote."

"Wait a second, I'm almost ready," she called, drying her face with a towel. "Let's do this," she said and took her place next to me. "Go ahead push it."

I took her hand and pushed the button on the remote. The machine began to vibrate, and the image of the doorway changed. We waited until the remote's digital readout spelled out "Ready," took a deep breath, and walked across the threshold together. The return trip was quite pleasant, and we did not feel any pain in our heads or hear the sounds of voices or see any bright lights, like when we went into the past. We were met by a cool jet of air as we stepped forward, and the floor under our feet glowed until it became almost transparent. The walls melted away until we found ourselves floating in a weightless environment. Still holding fast to Marie's hand, I tried pulling her closer to me but could not fight against the effects of the portal. The return trip forward seemed to take quite a bit longer than the trip back. I wasn't sure just how long we were in the machine, but during the process, we remained totally conscious and fully aware of our surroundings and each other.

We noticed the pitch of the machine began to change and the vibration began to slow down. Our bodies began to feel heavy as the effects of gravity made it presence known. The floor and walls began to materialize, and it was then that I heard Marie's voice. It seemed to be coming from everywhere.

"This is so freaking amazing!" she yelled, followed by laughter.

The next thing I knew, we were standing upright on the floor, just in front of the archway. The last of the vibration ended, and the room was now in full view. Marie and I did not move for several seconds, trying to get our bearings. I looked down and noticed we were still holding hands; our fingers were devoid of blood from squeezing so hard. It took a few more seconds to pull them apart and take a step into 2014.

Chapter 10

I checked the read out on the remote to confirm that we arrived at the correct time the readout flashed July 8, 2014, 1:00 p.m., we have arrived at the exact same time as when we left.

"I have never had a better time in all my life," Marie said, shaking off the pins and needles in her hand. "So what happens now?"

"I guess we wait for our orders from Doug Sr.," I joked.

At that exact moment, the archway began to hum to life, and we knew why. We turned slightly, faced the machine head-on, and waited for it to complete its cycle. As soon as the image was clear, we heard the sound of Doug Sr.'s voice.

"I suspect that the two of you enjoyed your first day in 1983?"

We both nodded our heads in agreement.

"From this point forward, it will become more difficult," he said solemnly. "You have seen the picture of yourselves from 1929, yes?"

We nodded again.

"This cannot take place" he said, holding up a copy of his own. "This," he said, raising his voice, "this is the reason Marie dies in the car crash."

Marie and I stood there with our mouths open and remained speechless.

"Let me explain this to you in detail," Doug Sr. continued. "I am not totally sure how it happened that the two of you ended up in 1929. Either the remote malfunctioned or the settings were accidentally changed; either way, this jump set up a series of events that ended in Marie's death."

"How could something we did in 1929 affect Marie in 2022?" I asked intently.

"Doug, this is directed at you." Doug Sr. pointed at me with a shaky finger. "We created a paradox," he said, raising his voice again. "Somehow, you ended up in 1929 instead of 1979, as was originally intended." He continued, "The two of you stepped into 1929 on Monday, August 5, at twelve o'clock; miraculously and without incident, you were undetected by a house usually full of people." He paused a moment. "Our grandfather was busy in the back yard, constructing a tool shed with the help of some of his sons; our uncles were helping him. Our grandmother just happened to be at the market, and the house was empty at this time." He took a breath and continued, "As soon as the two of you realized what was happening, you ran out the door and down the dirt road."

"Dirt road?" I asked.

"Yes, at this particular time, the roads around the home were not paved."

Doug Sr. paused, held up an old newspaper clipping, and began to read aloud: "Tot saved from fatal injury." He turned the article toward us, and we recognized the picture of the child.

"That's the boy on the pony!" Marie yelled.

I stepped forward just enough to get a closer look at the picture. The hairs on the back of my neck were standing up. "What happened?" I asked.

Doug Sr. took a step closer to the archway as well. "The two of you panicked when you arrived in 1929; instead of just returning as soon as you realized your mistake, you ran out of the house." He took another deep breath. "You found yourselves wandering around the neighborhood, looking for something to keep you busy until you could find a way back into the house to return. You ended up at the pony ride just two blocks from the house."

"There was a child walking alone near one of the horses. Suddenly, the horse was startled and began to kick. The horse would have killed the child had Marie not pulled him out of harm's way." He paused.

"Are you saying that Marie was not supposed to save the child and let the horse kill him?"

Doug Sr.'s face began to turn red, and his breathing became shallow. "I need a minute," he said and sat down in a chair, facing us. "The parents of the child were very appreciative and treated the two of you to a fine dinner that evening; they also had a picture taken with the woman who saved their little boy."

"So what was the harm of saving him?" Marie asked.

"By itself, the act was heroic, but when applied to the timeline, the result ended in your death. This child grew up and had three sons; the youngest of the three grew up and had two sons of his own." He continued, "The youngest of the two grew up and had a daughter, and it was this daughter who hit you in a head-on collision on December 26, 2022." He paused. "Do you understand what I'm telling you?" Doug Sr. asked. "That child should have died in a horse accident; you were never supposed to be there to save him."

Marie dropped her head and realized that what he was saying made perfect sense. "It would be hard to just allow a child be killed right in front of me, when I had the ability to save his life," she said, lifting her head again.

"So what must we do to correct this from happening?" I asked.

"You will again travel to 1929, three minutes before the other Marie and Doug arrive." Doug Sr. stood and approached the archway again. "You will have only minutes to convince your other selves to return." Then he said, "The shock of coming face-to-face with another you will be overwhelming to the unsuspecting pair."

"What can we possibly say in a few minutes to make them return without delay?" I asked.

"The other Marie and Doug have knowledge of the car accident as you do; use that to convince them to go back."

"Can't we just push them back through the archway and be done with it?" Marie asked.

"No!" bellowed Doug Sr. "You must not come in direct contact with them; if you do, then you will all die."

Marie said, "Oh, and I thought this was going to be difficult."

"You will need a week to recover from the effects of the time jump and we still have more to do," Doug Sr. said. "We will meet back here next Saturday at 11:30 a.m. and prep for the jump to 1929." He continued, "If we are successful, we can avoid the car accident, and Marie's life will be spared."

"What happens to us after we turn back the other Marie and Doug?" I asked.

"You must wait until the portal recharges."

"How long does that take?" Marie asked.

"The portal will be fully functional for the next time jump in twenty-three and three-quarter hours." Then he added, "The remote will inform you when it is ready."

"Where do we go while we wait for the machine to recharge?" I asked. "We can't just stay in the house with everyone there."

"You will have to leave the house and return the next day," he said. "There is a window of one minute and forty-five seconds in which you have to enter the home, start up the machine, and make the return trip," he added. "There will be no one in the area at this time to interfere." Then he said, "This will be the only time in which you can return undetected. If you fail to return, you will have to remain in 1929, and if that happens, I will no longer exist, here in 2036."

"We will not fail," I said, turning to Marie.

"We must not fail," she replied. "I like living too much."

Doug Sr. removed his remote control from his pocket and walked over to his side of the archway.

"We will talk again before the next time jump," he said; he raised his remote, pointed it to the archway, pushed a button, and his image slowly faded away.

"One minute and forty-five seconds? What is this, a James Bond movie?" Marie said, throwing her hands up in the air. "What am I to do in the meantime? Just go about my life as if none of this is happening?" She turned to me and asked, "What are you going to do now?"

"I'm going to recalibrate all the sensors and run a program diagnostic, for starters. Then a hot shower and maybe some dinner; care to join me later?"

"How can you just go back to doing what you do?" she asked. "Aren't you even a little bit scared?"

I walked over to her, took her hand, and kissed it. "I'm so scared that I'm about ready to jump out of my own skin, but my focus on saving your life overpowers that fear."

"Good answer," Marie said, smiling. "I think I will join you for dinner, but first I want to go home and check on the boys."

Marie picked up her small pile of clothes that she arrived in yesterday and went to the bathroom to change. "I'll be right back. I'm going to freshen up and change out of these clothes."

"Okay, I'll be in the downstairs apartment, running tests on the equipment. Come down when you are done. I want to show you the brains to this machine."

"I'll meet you there," she said and disappeared into the bathroom.

I grabbed a hand full of almonds from the bowl in the kitchen, shoved them into my mouth, and headed down stairs to the control center.

I pulled my chair close to the computer work table and sat down. I entered my password on the terminal and opened to the main diagnostic program. I entered a code to begin a level one diagnostic. This is a very low-risk diagnostic tool; however, it can detect any discrepancies in the overall program sequence and make corrections. I entered "Yes" to start the process and moved to the other terminal. I typed in my password and opened to a review program that records every detail of past jumps. With this tool, I can analyze the entire process as it happened and look for anything out of the ordinary, such as power spikes or losses. I can even scan for the smallest details such as our heart rhythm, blood pressure, body temperature, and the level of perspiration during the time jumps. One of the best details is that the system records every sound, including what we say, and the upper level scan tool details what we think by scanning our brain wave patterns and converting them into speech.

I ran the review program and watched the line graph's peaks and valleys, paying close attention to the highlighted danger areas indicated in red at the top and bottom of the screen. *Hmmm*, I thought, *everything well within normal levels.*

Just then, Marie called to me from the foot of the stairs: "Hey, where are you?"

"Back here," I said and waved my arm for her to see.

"Oh, I see you," she said and walked to the rear, where I was seated at the terminal. "Wow, what a setup," she said, looking at all the blinking and beeping screens. "Can you get HBO on this?" she joked.

"Yes, and Cinemax as well," I replied with a smirk. "I have to set up terminal #3 to test all the sensors and then run the calibration program, just need a few more minutes to set up."

"Take your time, I just wanted to tell you I was leaving anyway," she said, looking at something that interested her on terminal #2. "What's this Marie level 4 thingy?" she asked, pointing to the screen.

"That is the volume set point for audio playback."

"You mean you're recording what we say?"

"Everything we say and think," I replied.

"No freaking way, what we think?" She paused. "Amazing, just amazing." Then she said, "Well, let me go home, and I'll be back later, around seven. Is that a good time to come back?"

I hit the Enter command and started the scan on the sensors. "There," I said, "that will run for five to six hours; let me walk you out to your car."

Marie climbed into her car, and I shut the door after her. She rolled down her window and said, "I almost forgot to tell you."

"Tell me what?" I asked.

"Come closer." She motioned with her hand. I bent down next to her, and she gave me a kiss so light and sweet that it made me light-headed.

Even after what we had just experienced jumping through time, her kiss made me feel exhilarated. I smiled at her and said, "See you later, my dear."

Marie smiled in return and put her car into drive, and off she went. Just as she was leaving, I yelled out loud to drive safe. I stood there on the sidewalk and watched her drive away until her car was no longer visible.

I returned to the command center and double-checked each of the terminals to make sure the programs were running, and then I walked back upstairs. I sank back into my cushy sofa in the living room and in seconds fell fast asleep. When I awoke from my nap, I felt refreshed and energized and began to run scenarios in my brain. What can we possibly say to ourselves to make them turn around and return without hesitation? I thought about it for hours, but nothing made any sense. Then I asked myself a different question: What would *I* need to hear in order for me to turn around without question?

Around six o'clock, I once again checked the monitors at each of the terminals. Terminals #2 and #3 had completed their programs, but terminal #1 was still running. Up to this point, the monitor indicated over eight hundred possible solutions to various program configurations. It would take a few more hours to read through each one and make the subtle changes that would fine-tune the overall performance and speed of the programming.

I would come back to this later on tonight, after Marie and I had our dinner. I noticed one of the small indicator lights on the power panel was lit. The system was completely powered up. I returned back upstairs, jumped into the shower, and then changed my clothes to get ready for Marie to return.

At seven, I ran around the house and cleaned up a bit, expecting Marie to arrive any time now. Having a few minutes, I decided to open the log book and look up when the next time jump would be. According to Doug Sr.'s notes, the next jump was scheduled for next Saturday. So that meant I had a week to get to know Marie again, without having to worry about any kind of schedule. I continued to read the notes in the log book; most of the entries were calculations and prep mods, but as

I continued to read, something about the magnetic flux levels struck me as strange. According to these readouts, the energy level for the jump back was set for only one person. Marie and I were scheduled to return together, so why were the settings so low?

Just then, I heard a car door shut, and I put the log book down. I walked over to the living room window and saw Marie walking up to the house. She climbed the front steps and was about to ring the bell, but I was ready for her and opened the door just as she was pushing the button.

"Wow, automatic doors, I like that," she said. I held the door open and she came inside. "Hey there," she said.

"Hey, good to see you. Give me a second, and I will be right with you."

"Take your time, I'm in no hurry," Marie said, taking a seat on the living room sofa.

I ran into my bedroom and retrieved my wallet and car keys, checked to make sure my cell phone was fully charged. "How hungry are you?" I asked Marie.

"Starving, actually," she said, giving her stomach a slight rub.

"I know a really good Italian restaurant not too far from here called Angelo's; are you in the mood for Italian?"

"I'm in the mood for a certain Italian," she said with a slight giggle.

I winked at her, smiled, and said, "Let's go."

Dinner was absolutely fabulous, everything from the service to the food to the company I was keeping with Marie. It felt just like old times again with her; we talked about everything and filled each other in on the missing years. I had set aside the time so I could relax and enjoy our night out together, and for the most part, I forgot about the discrepancy I discovered about the next jump. After dinner, Marie and I decided to continue our date at the Park Pub in Nutley. We had not visited the place in nearly three decades and weren't sure that it still existed, but we were feeling a little adventurous and decided to just go for it. To tell you the truth, I think the last time I was at the pub was with Marie over thirty years ago.

We climbed into my car and took the scenic road toward the old pub, making some detours along the way as we passed by where I used to live in Nutley and then another quick pass by Marie's old house as well.

"Wow, they remodeled the entire exterior," she remarked. "It looks totally different from how I remember it."

After sitting in the car for a few minutes, staring at the house, we pulled away and headed for the Park Pub.

Aside from some minor exterior renovations, the interior looked pretty much the same. As we stepped into the pub, we were instantly transported back in time to the days when we used to meet there for a drink. We took a booth in the rear of the pub so that we could have a little privacy. I wanted us to have a nice evening together and didn't want to trouble her with the details of the next jump until I had time to investigate it further.

"This place hasn't changed a bit," Marie said, looking around and running her hand along the back of the booth. "Even without your time machine, I feel like I'm twenty years old again."

"I feel the same way," I replied with a wink.

A very cheerful waitress came over to our booth. "What can I get you guys?" she asked.

"I think we will have a pitcher of your finest beer and two glasses, please."

"What kind of beer would you like?" she asked, showing us a menu to choose from.

"Coors Lite looks good," I said, and Marie nodded in approval.

"I think the last time we were here we had pitchers of beer as well," she said, smiling at me.

The pub's mood lighting reflected off of her face, complimenting her features further.

The beer arrived, and the waitress put two glasses down in between us. "Care for anything to munch on?" she asked.

"No, this is good for now," I said. "Thank you."

The waitress disappeared, and I poured the beer.

"Cheers," Marie said, raising her glass.

"Cheers," I repeated. "What do we drink to?"

"Let's drink to us," she said, smiling.

"To us," I said in return.

After our third pitcher of beer, we were feeling no pain. Marie, I must say, could hold her own when she drank; in fact, she was in better shape than I was. After we polished off the last of the beer, we decided to take a walk through Nicolas Park, directly across the street from the pub. I was feeling fairly stable until we stepped outside and the fresh air started to fill my lungs. My head began to feel the effects of the alcohol, but it wasn't unpleasant.

"Let's sit on the swings," Marie said, half-sprinting to have the first pick.

"Wait for me," I said in a somewhat slurred voice, almost falling into chains that held the swing. I took the swing next to her, and we began to swing like two little kids.

After a few minutes, we slowed to a stop, and I swung my swing sideways into her and locked my legs around her.

"Whatcha doin', Mr. Lupo?" Marie asked.

"Whatever do you mean?" I said, laughing.

"What is it about you that has me feeling like a kid again?"

I pulled her close to me, touched my nose to hers, and gave it a little Eskimo treatment. I could see her eyes glisten with moisture, and her tongue wet her lips. I felt my head swimming with delight at the thought of kissing her sweet lips. The moment came, and we kissed; my body partially melted right off the swing. Her hair was so soft, and her perfume was intoxicating. I had a vision in my head of the opening to *Love American Style,* that sixties TV show with all the fireworks.

"Oh, my gosh," Marie said, pulling away slightly. "What are you doing to me?"

"Maybe I'm trying to get you to fall in love with me," I said, kissing the tip of her nose.

"I think it's working," she said, kissing me hard on the mouth.

We made out like two teenagers on our first date, and the world stepped aside to give us this moment together. After a while, I stood up and began to push her on her swing, and each time she came back to me, I kissed her on her neck and then sent her on her way again. After this, we strolled through the park and walked off some more effects of the beer.

"You have become a very romantic person, Doug," she said, looking down at our hands now clasped together as we walked.

"What do you mean I have *become* romantic?" with the emphasis on "become." "Wasn't I romantic years ago when we used to date?"

"Um, you were always romantic," she replied. "You always knew just how to make me feel good." She gave my hand a squeeze.

I looked at her and asked what she wanted to do next.

"I have no other plans," she said, leaving the floor open to me.

"Stay with me tonight," I said.

Our walk through the park came to a sudden end as we changed our course and headed to my car. The ride home was pleasant, and Marie rested her head on my shoulder the entire way.

I thought for a moment, *What if I had not invented the time machine? Would I have had a reason to look Marie up?*

If I hadn't invented it in the first place, would we have stayed together and eventually have gotten married? Who could tell about such things? I was sure about two things: Each day I spent with her made me want to spend more time with her, and I feared losing her to whatever happened in the past (and future).

With all of these thoughts going on in my head, I knew that I had to remain focused on what we needed to do. This had to be priority number one: She must not die in some stupid accident, and we must not fail to stop it from taking place. I said "we," but I was thinking there was something I was missing in this equation. What was it?

As soon as we arrived at the house, Marie excused herself and went into the bathroom. I plopped down on the sofa and thought about today's events; so much had happened in the last few days. Now, I was sitting in the house where Marie and I first got to know each other. Just last night, we were watching television and rediscovering ourselves in 1983, right here in this exact room. Now, just a day later, I was sitting here in 2014, in the same room, waiting for her to join me on my sofa. With all that was going on and all the complicated issues we had waiting for us, we still found the time to give to one another. I closed my eyes, put my head back for a second, and started to imagine life without the time machine. I considered the possibility of another life with Marie.

I had drifted off to sleep when Marie came into the living room, turned off the television, sat down beside me, and ran her fingers through my hair.

"I'm sorry," I said, "I guess I drifted off for a bit."

"No problem, sweetie; are you going to sleep out here tonight?"

"What, out here? No," I said, still a little groggy. "I want us to be together tonight, all night."

"Then come into the bedroom. I'll be waiting for you," she said in her sexy bedroom voice.

I sat up for a moment, shook the sleep away, and then used the bathroom to freshen up. I walked into my bedroom and saw Marie lying on top of the covers, dressed in a red and black teddy.

Oh, my gosh, this woman still made me feel like a teenager; every part of my body was wide awake. I removed my clothes and joined her on the bed. We embraced, and for a long time, we just cuddled, whispering to each other how much we missed this feeling of being so close on so many levels. I looked into her eyes and lost myself in that place where the world outside played no part. We kissed and stared into each other's eyes, running our fingers lightly over each other's face.

"I never forgot this face," I said to her. I memorized every minute detail and burned her image into my mind. There it stayed all these years, keeping me sane through all the tough times.

We held onto each other as though the end of the world was right around the corner. I felt a desperate need to lose myself inside of her. Nothing else mattered now; it was only Marie and Doug, in the here-and-now, that made any sense.

We drifted off to sleep several times during the night, waking up after an hour or so each time. It wasn't until the very early part of the morning that I started to think about that discrepancy of the energy levels on our return trip from 1929. I knew that if we entered together, we must return together, so why was the reading so low? This question grew louder in my head, begging for a reasonable explanation. I turned to my side and faced Marie, who was now sleeping quite soundly. I watched as she took in a breath and then exhaled. She had a slight smile, no doubt dreaming of our time together today. Just then, I had a memory from some thirty years ago, of me doing the same thing: watching her sleep. I smiled and found a more comfortable position on my pillow, still facing her.

My thoughts about the time machine settled, and I found myself become very relaxed as my body found a comfortable niche next to Marie. The wind outside was starting to blow hard against the rickety windows. I could hear every little creak they made as they rattled. I was beginning to drift off to sleep, and the last thing I saw before closing my eyes was Marie's peaceful face, asleep on my pillow.

Chapter 11

The morning came quickly, and the sound of a thunderstorm woke us up. The rain outside was beating against the windows, and we both found the sound relaxing. Marie found a place against my chest, nestled her head into a comfortable position, and draped her arm across my stomach.

She sighed, "Hmmm."

I kissed the top of her head and could still smell the sweet fragrance of her hair. We lay there, breathing sighs of delight.

"Are you hungry?" I asked after a while. "I can make us a nice breakfast."

"I could eat something for sure, and some coffee," she said, stretching.

"Why don't you take a shower? I'll get things started. I'll take one after you and then we can sit down to eat."

"Hmmm, sounds good," she said and threw one leg over the bed; she didn't move for a minute or so, and then the second leg joined the first, and off she went into the bathroom.

I put the coffee on and whipped up a quick batch of pancakes and omelets. Marie stepped out of the bathroom and went into the bedroom to get dressed. I jumped into the shower and was ready in no time.

We sat and had our breakfast, and when we were done, we cleaned up the table and washed the dishes.

"I won't be able to see you again until next Saturday," Marie said with a pouty frown.

"Oh, not till Saturday, huh?"

"I have a lot going on this week at home with the boys."

"I understand completely; besides, I have quite a bit going on here, getting ready for this next jump."

"I thought that was already set up by, um, Doug Sr.," she said with a bit of laughter.

"It is already set up, but I want to make sure that everything goes according to the plan."

"Any reason why it shouldn't go the way he said it would?" She paused. "The first jump went very well, in my opinion."

"Yes, it did go very well, but you can't blame me for wanting to be careful; besides, we still need to figure out what to say to ourselves to get them, I mean us, to turn around and go back."

"That's right," she said. "What the heck can we possibly say to them that will work?"

"I don't know; what would we have to hear in order for us to turn around?"

Marie and I spent the rest of the morning snuggling on my sofa, watching television until the time came for her to leave.

"I just wanted you to know something, Mr. Lupo," she said.

"Uh oh," I replied.

"I never thought, even for a moment, that I would be together with you like this again." Then she continued, "You have re-energized me and made me feel wanted and loved." She put her arms around my neck. "I haven't felt like this in so long, maybe as long as thirty years."

"I know exactly what you're saying. I feel it as well."

"You have stirred up things in my heart that I thought were dead." She put her head against my neck and hugged me.

I hugged her in return, and we both looked up at the same time and said, "I love you." The emotional rush was way too much for either one of us to ignore, as we both broke down and sobbed.

"All these years without you; I missed you so much," I said.

Marie hugged me even tighter, burying her head in my chest. When she did pull away, she noticed that she had left a stain on my shirt from her makeup and tears. "I can't wear makeup with you for a while, not if I'm going to cry like this," she said.

I kissed her forehead and then her nose and then her lips. "You're beautiful," I said.

Marie went back into the bathroom to fix her makeup and dry her eyes. Afterward, she picked up her things and kissed me good-bye. "Let's talk about what we need to say to ourselves this week," she said, tapping me on the arm. "I will be here early on Saturday so we can go over whatever we need to before the jump."

"Please be here as early as you can," I said. "I want to be ready for anything."

"I'll be here around nine o'clock; is that a good time?" she asked.

"That's fine," I said, kissing her hand.

We stood there for a minute, neither one wanting to make the first move toward the door. I pulled her close to me, wrapped my arms around her, and kissed her.

"Time to go," I said.

"I'm going," she said and walked out the door.

I watched her get into her car and drive away. My heart was still racing from the overwhelming feelings I had rediscovered with her. I walked from room to room, playing the night over again in my brain. I was lost in thoughts of us and for the longest time forgot about the log book.

Shit! I thought. *The log book.* Everything I was feeling came to an abrupt halt, as I stood there eyeing the huge binder, wishing that what I read yesterday was just a part of my imagination. I hesitated to open it up again, but I knew I had to. I took a deep breath and pulled the binder over to me on the kitchen table. I swallowed hard and opened to the page that described the jump to 1929. At first, I thought I had made a huge error in my reading the first time, but as I continued to read, I noticed that my concerns were justified. For some unknown reason, only one person was making the trip to 1929 to turn Marie and Doug around.

I moved into the bedroom, still holding onto the binder and

reading every entry. Just as I was about to flip a page, the archway began to vibrate. I knew what was happening and just took up a position in front of it, waiting for Doug Sr. to appear. *I have some questions for him,* I thought, *and he better not try to bullshit his way out of an acceptable answer.*

The archway finished its process, and Doug Sr. was standing in front of me on his side of time.

"I know, I know," he said, holding up his hand.

"You know what?" I asked.

"I know you have questions about the jump to 1929," he said, lowering his hand.

"Why didn't you tell me that only one of us was going to be making the jump? You said yourself that the both of us would go."

"The two of you did make the jump the first time, and as you are aware, that caused a disturbance in the timeline."

"You call Marie's death a disturbance?" I barked.

"It is what it is," he replied.

"So who is returning to 1929 to stop Marie and Doug from changing the timeline?"

"You are," he said harshly.

"Where is Marie in this?" I asked. "Why isn't she returning with me?"

"She will return with you, but," he paused and then added, "she will not survive the jump."

"Why won't she survive the jump? It seems that we have a little experience with this now."

"You have much more experience than you realize," he said solemnly.

"I'm not following you," I said.

"You have tried this forty-two times already, and each time has ended with the same result."

"What result is that?" I demanded.

"You were not able to convince the first Doug and Marie to return, thus she will save the child and then die in the car accident."

"We made forty-two attempts at trying to repair the altered timeline?"

"That is correct," Doug Sr. said, walking around in a small circle with his hands behind his back.

"How is it I have no recollection of any of these jumps?"

"Returning to the wrong timeline erases the short-term memory of the jump," he said, stating a fact.

"Because I do not remember the jumps, I must not be in the correct timeline, is this correct?"

"Correct," he said again, stating the obvious.

"So I am not supposed to be here in this house, talking to myself and trying to repair a broken timeline?"

"Remember when I said you were never supposed to build the time machine in the first place?" he asked, looking right at me.

"I remember, but here I am, talking to an older version of myself."

"Ask yourself this," he said. "What do you do for a living?"

"What do you mean?"

"Who do you work for? Where is your job? How can you afford to pay for your projects?"

I stood for a moment, searching my brain. "I'm a — I work for—"

"You don't know, do you?" he sighed. "I have had this discussion with you many times, and it is always the same response."

"So if I don't belong here, where do I belong? What timeline is the correct one?" I asked Doug Sr.

"Neither you nor I are in the correct timeline," he said, pushing his fist into his hand. "There are at least forty-two others such as yourself and Marie who are also in a similar situation."

"So Marie has survived other jumps back to 1929?" I asked intently.

"Yes, she has."

"So why must she die on this trip? What makes this particular timeline different?"

"I believe Marie is the key that will reset the original timeline."

"How can you be sure about your facts? You said yourself that we have done this forty-two times. So forty-two times, you were wrong. You may be wrong this time as well."

"Early on with my experiments, I thought that we were the key to resetting the original timeline." He paused. "I thought that if we were taken out of the picture, then the machine would not be built, and Marie would not have to die in a car accident."

"So did *I* die in one of these attempts to fix the timeline?"

Doug Sr. just stood with his back to me; he did not answer at first, and then, after a few minutes of muttering something under his breath, he said, "Yes, in timelines six, seven, eight, and nine."

"I died four times, and you are still an old man; how is that possible?" I asked, slamming my fist into the doorway.

"You died in an alternate timeline; it does not affect us in ours," he said, as if repeating a broken record. "I have had this same conversation with you many times, and you always ask the same questions."

I stood there for a minute and tried to reason out the problem. Why would Marie's death repair a timeline that was not correct to begin with? I turned to face Doug Sr.

"Tell me why."

He picked up a book from his kitchen table, walked over to the archway as close as he could get, and opened it for me to see. "You see all the time entries for each of the jumps?"

"Yes, I do," I replied.

"Look at the far right column for each jump."

"I'm looking at them."

"Do you see the boxes with check marks in them, next to your name and Marie's?"

I scanned the boxes and noticed that Marie's box was checked in some cases. I also noticed that my box contained check marks in some cases. I looked down the page to jumps six, seven, and eight; only my box had a check mark in it.

I looked at Doug Sr. and asked, "Does this mean what I think it means?"

He pulled the book out of view and said, "Yes, it does."

"So on these jumps to 1929, either Marie or I die as a result to repair the timeline?"

Doug Sr. said, "You are starting to get it."

I turned away and began walking in circles, kind of like my older twin.

"I think I understand what is going on," I said aloud. "Each time we make a jump back, we are only repairing some small part of the original severed timeline."

"You do have it," he said. "Impressive that you were able to deduce the answer in such a short time; this is promising." Doug Sr. actually smiled. "Continue," he said, rubbing his hands together.

"I can't be sure, but it looks like we are nearing the end of the repair and that Marie will die to complete that repair." I looked at Doug Sr. for confirmation.

"Not quite the end, but next to the end," he answered. "One more jump after this one will finish the repair, according to my calculations."

"So one more trip after this one, you say." My mind stopped short before buying into his figures 100 percent. "I'm still not sold on the idea that Marie will have to die."

"You always say the same thing, and we always end up doing it my way," Doug Sr. roared. "I don't remember being so hard-headed," he continued. "Wait, yes, I do."

The tension in the room seemed to ease a bit; we looked at each other, and smiles broke out on both our faces.

"We want the same thing," I said, still looking at Doug Sr.

"Yes, we do, and I feel that we should keep that in mind as we move forward on this."

"I agree and will try to work with your plan."

"Good, very good" Doug Sr. exclaimed.

After Doug Sr. disappeared, I went to work on my own plan for the next jump. Yes, I knew I told him I would work with his plan, but I had some ideas of my own. Marie and I could cross over together and return together. I had no intention of letting her die; I believed I had the solution that would get the first Marie and Doug back safely to the original timeline, but I would have to act fast and in stealth mode. My older counterpart could not know what I was about to do. For this to work, I would have to get Marie's full cooperation.

I spent the entire rest of the day recalculating the control settings for the jump on Saturday. There was no room for error with any part of this plan. Doug Sr. felt that his younger counterpart would follow his direction on this, and I needed him to believe that was true so he would not interfere. I would put my own plan into operation. I worked into the night with the reconfiguring of the power settings; I was increasing it to the maximum level, giving me a little extra backup if needed. The second part to this plan was going to be even more difficult. Marie and I would need to work in synchronized fashion in order to pull this off. Tomorrow, I would ask her to come over so I could lay out the plan in detail to her. I finished up the reprogramming around 4 a.m. and needed to get some sleep. I left the control system in slow power-up mode, in order to gradually increase the storage capacity so that there was no chance of a short-circuit when it was needed the most. After another check of all the settings, I turned in for the night.

When I woke up around eleven, my head was a little groggy. I needed a hot shower and a full breakfast in order to get my brain working properly. Afterwards, I gave Marie a call, and her son Michael answered the phone.

After the customary greeting, he called out, "Mom, it's for you." He covered the phone slightly, but I could still make out what he was saying: "It's that guy from the other day."

"Hey, how are you?" she asked.

"I'm fine, can you talk?"

"Sure I can talk, I'm talking right now," she laughed. "What's up?"

"There have been some new developments, and I need to see you."

"Okay, so you want to come over or do you want me to come to the house?"

"I need you to come to the house; there is something we need to practice, and I can't just tell you about it. I need to show you."

"You sound different," she said. "Is everything all right?"

"Let's just say that it will be, but I need your help."

"Well, you got it." She paused for a moment and asked, "When do you want me?"

"Can you come over today around four?"

"I will be there," Marie said with some degree of excitement in her voice.

"Great. I will see you then," I said and hung up the phone.

I pulled out the tape recorder, plugged it into the wall, and began to charge it up. I remembered the cocoon effect the unit provided, shielding the user from the passage of time. I needed to reset the parameters on the device to protect both Marie and me on our next jump.

After about an hour, I was able to unplug the unit and switch it on for a trial run. I pushed the Rewind button, as I did the last time I used the device. This time, I knew what to expect and waited for the protective shield to complete its sequence. I compared my watch to the clock on the wall; I was fully protected from time.

I started measuring the amount of time the device would continue to work at full strength and also made some observations as to the extent of my ability to manipulate objects around me. I walked across the room and tried to pick up a notebook that was lying on the kitchen counter. The force field would not allow me to grip it into my hands. When I tried again, I managed to only push it off the counter, and there it stayed, frozen in midair. I checked the time on my watch; the charge of the device was now passing the three-minute mark. My theory of a longer charge was correct.

I moved away from the counter and walked into the bedroom. I observed that there was no change in the protective shield. I continued to walk into the living room and looked out the window to the street. The neighbor's children were riding their bicycles but motionless, and the tree leaves were still and unmoving. I checked my watch again; four minutes and counting. I walked back into the kitchen and noticed the notebook was closer to the floor than before, and I realized that the charge was starting to fade.

I stood there and watched as the speed at which the notebook fell increased until it hit the floor. I checked my watch and noticed that a full five minutes had passed before time resumed to its proper speed. If I was correct, I should be able to provide enough charge on the device for two and a half minutes for two people. That should give me enough time to put my plan into action. As soon as the device completely powered down, I plugged it back into the wall. The next test would require a jump through the time machine. I want to make sure I was able to take the device with me on the jump to 1929.

My observations with the tape recorder were encouraging in respect to being able to move the notebook off the counter. Now I wanted to see if Marie and I were able to use the device together. I would show it to her when she arrived later; in the meantime, I needed to get myself ready. I jumped into the shower, changed into something comfortable, and waited for Marie to arrive. While sitting at the kitchen table, I began looking through some of my old diaries; I wanted to find a date that would be interesting to both of us. I opened up a diary from 1980 and just happened to notice the date: July 1, 1980. At first, I did not remember the significance of the date, and I began to read the words I wrote a long time ago. This was the day that I first met Marie Stefanelli.

Many thoughts raced through my mind as I sat there reading my description of Marie at the pizzeria where we both worked, and the exchange of glances and a brief conversation, where she joked that I was cute but a little too young for her. As I continued reading, I was reminded again of Marie's beauty and her ability to melt a guy's heart just by looking him (that guy being me, of course). I put the diary down, stared out the window, and began to daydream, like a teenager thinking about a cute girl in school. When my brain returned to normal mode, I thought that this would be a good date to test out the device with Marie. I thought we could go incognito to the pizzeria and sit in a booth to watch the two young lovebirds at their first meeting.

As soon as Marie arrives, I thought, *I'll spring it on her and see what she thinks.*

It was nearly four o'clock, and I knew that Marie would be arriving any minute, so I double-checked the recorder to make sure it was still charging. I wanted to make sure the time machine controls were set for the test jump. I walked over to the living room and picked up the heavy binder that logged every detail of every jump and every test I had made (or would make). I paged through the book until I came across a notation for July 1, 1980. I began to read the technical details of the jump and then noticed some remarks written in red ink along the left margin. The note indicated that arrival time was exactly 9:01 a.m.; there was no indication of occupancy. A separate note just below it stated that the departure time of 8:59 a.m. the following day was successful. With this information, I picked up the remote and punched in the arrival date, Tuesday, July 1, 1980, and then the time: 9 a.m.

Just as I finished programming the remote, I heard the doorbell ringing, followed by a series of small knocks. I walked to the front door, opened it, and was greeted by Marie's smiling face.

"Hey, come on in," I said to her.

"Thanks, I think I'm on *time*," she said, making air quotes with her hands and stepping inside as I closed the door behind her.

"What's this?" I asked, pointing to the paper bag under her arm.

"Bagels; I brought bagels," she said, walking into the kitchen and placing the bag on the table. "What's the matter, you don't like bagels?"

"I love bagels, especially with cream cheese and jelly."

"Hum, I like them toasted with butter," she said, giving her stomach a small circular rub. "So what's all the mystery?"

"I think I discovered a way out of this mess."

"Oh, what did you come up with?" she asked.

"Here, take a look at this," I said while passing the small tape recorder over to her.

"What is it?" she asked.

"This is our chance to repair the timeline."

"A tape recorder?" she said, giving me a confused look.

"Well, it's not just a tape recorder, it's a —" I paused and then said, "Here, let me show you."

I walked over to where Marie was standing in the kitchen, put my arm around her waist, and pulled her close to me.

"What, are we going to record something?"

"Not exactly," I said. "Don't move unless we move together."

"What is this thing going to do, give me a shock?" she asked.

"No, it will not shock you, but just don't make any sudden movements; just follow my lead."

Marie stood motionless, took in a deep breath, and held it. "Ready," she said, pushing out the word while still holding in her breath.

I reached over and pushed the Rewind button. The room around us began to grow dark, and at the same time, we noticed that a small space around us was becoming brighter.

"You see that?" Marie asked.

"Yes I do," I said. "Wait, it gets better."

We waited while the device finished enveloping us in its protective cocoon of light, shielding us from the passage of ordinary time.

"You smell that?" Marie asked.

I gave the air a sniff and concluded that a faint burst of ozone was released during the startup; strange that I hadn't noticed that before. We stood there practically motionless until I was sure the device had finished doing its thing.

"So this is some kind of nightlight?" Marie remarked.

"No, not a nightlight," I replied. "Something much more than that." I pointed out the kitchen window and told her to look outside.

"It's dark out there, but the sun is out, and there are no clouds in the sky," she said.

I nudged her away from the window and led her to the living room, where I could give her a better example of what was happening. Meanwhile, I kept my eye on the time; so far, forty-five seconds had passed, and the power level was holding. We walked over to the window facing the street, and I asked her to look outside and tell me what she saw. She moved the curtain out of the way and glanced outside.

"It's still dark," she said. "Wait, what the —" Marie paused a moment and gasped. "Are you fucking kidding me? Nothing is moving out there! Nothing." She looked at me and then again out the window and then back at me again. "Are you trying to say that this little tape recorder can stop time?"

"That's exactly what I saying, but wait," I said. "I need to try something." One minute and thirty-five seconds had passed, and the device still appeared to be working at full capacity. "There, over by the sofa." I pointed at the lamp, sitting on top of the end table. "I want to see if we can knock it off the table without breaking the protective shielding."

"Why would you want to knock the lamp over?" Marie asked.

"Just trust me on this, okay?" I replied.

We walked over to the lamp and both reached for it, careful not to touch it. As soon as we were within six inches of the lamp, it moved backward, sliding across the table as if on ice. We backed up and then lunged forward, and again, the lamp moved, this time slamming into the wall behind it. It just stayed there, as if glued in place. We backed up again and watched in amazement as the lamp began to fall, ever so slowly at first. I checked the time and noticed that a full two minutes had passed. At two minutes and twenty seconds, the lamp landed on the floor, and then we noticed the light in the room begin to change back to its proper intensity. At two minutes thirty seconds, we heard the lamp make a crashing sound, as its base separated from the rest of it and tiny little pieces of ceramic sprayed across the floor. At two minutes thirty-five seconds, it was all over.

"Why did we break your lamp?" Marie asked, looking as if we had just lost the family pet.

"I needed to test my theory on object manipulation while inside the protective shield."

"So now you have a large time machine and a portable one to take on vacation or something," she joked.

"Not quite," I said, "but it is a powerful tool we are going to use to set things straight."

As soon as the demonstration was over, I released my hold on Marie and took the device back into the kitchen, where I plugged it back into the wall. Marie followed and commented that she could have used that device back in high school; she would have been able to walk right up to the teacher's desk and copy all the answers for a test. Of course, she was only kidding, but she may have used it for that reason if she wanted to, and no one would ever know.

"I guess now is a good time to discuss your big plan to save the day," Marie said as she sat at the kitchen table.

I took the chair next to hers, looked her in the eye, and told her that I had thought of a way to reset the original timeline.

"How do you know for sure what the original time is?" she asked.

"I don't know," I said. "I'm not really sure about anything anymore, but I do know that I have to try something. I can't just sit here and hope for the best."

"I guess you're right about that. So what's the plan?"

"You remember what Doug Sr. said about the original Marie and Doug screwing up the timeline by saving the little boy from the horse accident?"

"Yes, of course."

"You also are aware that we must prevent them from doing that anyway we can. Remember what Doug Sr. said about how many times this was attempted and the outcome always ended in failure?"

"What do you mean? There were other times?"

"Oh, that's right, you were not part of that conversation. He told me that this was attempted forty-two times already by other versions of us."

"You're not saying that there are forty-two other Maries and Dougs running around out there, are you?"

"See that's the part that troubles me."

"What part?"

"The part about there being multiple Maries and Dougs, running around in different timelines. You know what happens to all of us if this works, don't you?"

"No, what will happen?"

"We all will just vanish into thin air, and the only survivors will be the originals. Who knows if we are even alive in another timeline?"

"That's a scary thought," Marie said, closing her eyes and pushing her lips together. "I guess there is no way of telling what the real Marie and Doug are doing right now."

"Well, Doug Sr. said that the original you and I walked through the time machine into 1929 and changed everything. We are going to meet them face-to-face, and I'm guessing no matter what we say to them, they will not be convinced to return.

"Let's face it: A few minutes is not enough time to explain something so complicated. What we must do is not give them a chance to realize what's happening. As soon as they step through the machine, we can push them right back to where they came from. As far as they will know, the jump will not be successful. I'm guessing Doug will just do a quick head scratch and run to the controls to see where the problem occurred. I figure he will see that the intended date was somehow changed by some type of accident."

"Yes, but what about the original timeline?" Marie asked.

"That's just it, I don't know what will happen, and if what Doug Sr. said is true and the original timeline is reset, there may not even be a time machine at all."

"So what's next?" Marie asked.

"We have another test to make on the device. I have to make sure it can be transported through the time machine. I also have to make sure it will work in the past as it does in our time."

"So when do we make this test on it?"

"We will be ready in a few hours; in the meantime, we need to see what we can wear as a disguise."

"What disguise?"

"Oh, I forgot to tell you: We are going back to 1980 for the test."

"Wow, 1980? You're kidding!" Marie exclaimed. "Where are we going?"

"I was going to surprise you, but I guess it's better if you know. We are going to Scotto's Pizzeria on July first.

"Why does July first seem familiar to me?" Marie asked.

"It's the first time we ever met," I said. "I thought it would be interesting to see the young Marie and Doug interact. What do you think?"

"I say, let's do it. I always wanted to remember how that all went down with us meeting and what we said to each other."

"Great, now let's go through the clothes we have and see what we can wear so as not to attract any attention from anyone."

Chapter 12

There wasn't much to work with, with the pile of clothing given to us by Doug Sr., and in the end, we just decided that hats and sunglasses would be the best way to go. With only a couple hours to prepare, we took my car to the Wal-Mart and picked up hats and sunglasses for the both of us. Marie chose the largest, darkest sunglasses I had ever seen and tried them on for size.

"What do you think?" she asked, turning to me and modeling the huge glasses, which covered nearly her entire face, from the bridge of her nose up.

"Oh, it's definitely you," I said. "Now all you need is a big floppy hat that will cover your head, and you are all set."

I found a western-style hat and a pair of aviator sunglasses that completely hid my eyes. Afterward, we grabbed a quick bite to eat at Wendy's and then were on our way back to the house.

When we arrived, we noticed a little commotion a few houses down, where a gathering of people were milling around, talking amongst themselves. I walked over with Marie and asked a neighbor what was going on.

Ralph Petri was a retired fireman; he and his wife had settled in the neighborhood a few months ago. "There appears to have been a murder upstairs," he said, pointing to the second floor of the two-family home.

"Where are the police?" I asked.

"As far as I know, they were called over an hour ago, but you know how that goes," Ralph said, throwing his hands into the air.

"Does anyone know what happened?" I asked.

"All I know is that a young man was found stabbed to death."

"Who was it?"

"That I don't know," he said. "Oh wait, Greg may know; he seems to know everything that goes on around here." Ralph reached over and tugged on the back of someone's shirt.

Greg Finch was a slender, tall man with bright green eyes and very long fingers that reminded me of the French fries Marie and I had at Wendy's.

"Hey, Ralph," Greg said as he turned around.

"Any idea who was killed?" Ralph asked.

"Some young real estate agent; a local kid, I think," Greg said as he rubbed his chin with his hand, as if more information would make its way to the surface. "That's all I know." He turned around to face the house again.

I turned to Marie, pulled her aside, and whispered in her ear that I hoped it wasn't Robert, the kid who sold me the house.

"Oh, my gosh," Marie said. "If that's true, then the police will be questioning you at some point."

"Yeah, if they ever get here," I said in a sarcastic tone.

I took Marie's arm and led her away slowly back to the house.

"You know, if the police looked into our bags right now and found our disguises, they might think we had something to do with that," Marie said with a crack in her voice.

"Let's get ourselves together and prepare for this test jump. The device should be ready shortly."

Marie and I both squeezed ourselves into my small bathroom, washed up a bit, and tried on our disguises. We were a sight to see, and we even started to laugh at one another. I checked my pockets for anything that might not be wise to carry with me on the jump back to 1980. I emptied my wallet and removed the credit cards but kept my license, just in case. I opened a drawer to my bedroom dresser, pulled out some cash dated 1980 and older, and stuffed it into my wallet. The dated cash was given to me by Doug Senior along with the clothing items. Marie did the same, and we patted down each other, looking for anything we may have overlooked.

When we were sure that all the precautions were taken, I picked up the remote control and the tape recorder; we walked over to the archway and made ready to push the Engage button.

"Wait, you forgot something," Marie said, holding her hand over the remote.

"What did I forget?" I asked.

"How are we getting to Scotto's when we arrive in 1980?"

I smiled at her and said one word: "Taxi."

"Taxi," she repeated. "That works for me."

With that, we held hands and turned to each other; Marie kissed me smack on the lips. "For luck," she said.

"For luck," I said in return. I was just about to push the button when there was a loud rap at the front door.

"Newark Police" was all that we heard; I started to move toward the door, but Marie pulled me back.

"Let's do this thing," she said and gave me a smile.

I checked the time on my watch and made a mental note: 9 a.m. I found the Engage button on the remote and pressed it. Instantly, the machine began to hum to life, and the image of the room in front of us began to change. Another loud rap on the front door, and again we heard an officer say, "Newark Police." We ignored it and focused our attention on what was in front of us. The humming sound became louder, and the objects in the room were becoming clearer and were now definable. Another loud rap at the door, and this time, we heard the sound of the door being kicked in. The crash of the door hitting the wall was the last thing we heard as the remote flashed "Ready," and we stepped into the archway and disappeared.

For some reason, we both ended up on the floor just in front of the archway. As soon as our heads were clear, we were able to stand up and regain our balance quickly.

"That wasn't too bad this time," Marie said.

I agreed with her and immediately began to scope out the kitchen.

Looking around, I noticed that the kitchen was empty. There was no table or chairs, and as we looked around, we noticed that the rest of the house was empty as well.

"Oh, shit," Marie said. "What happened?"

"I don't know," I replied. "Wait, I do know," I said. "1980, yeah, that's right, both my grandmother and grandfather had just passed away, and the house was cleaned out to make ready for a renter. My father bought this house from all his brothers and sisters, and I ended up being his first tenant."

"So right now the house is empty?" Marie asked.

"That's right; we should not have any trouble coming or going."

"So what do we do first?"

"Let's call for a taxi," I said and with that, I turned for the phone on the wall but found nothing. "Oh, shit, that's right, I had the phone installed after I moved in."

"So now what?"

"If I remember correctly, there's a pay phone down the street at the supermarket; we can call from there. Come on, let's take a walk."

We slipped out of the house quietly and were very careful to look in all directions before venturing forward. We made it to the sidewalk without anyone taking notice of us. We began to walk toward the supermarket. We passed the house on the left where just minutes before, a young man had been murdered, but that would not happen for a very long time (as a matter as fact, the kid wasn't even born yet).

We continued walking past the remainder of the homes until we came to a vacant lot, which was owned by the church around the corner. At that point, we crossed the street and continued up one more block to the supermarket. Just as I remembered, I found the pay phone and reached into my pocket for some change for the call. I came up with nothing and had to go inside the store to break a dollar. Afterwards, I stepped back outside, picked up the phone book attached to the bottom of the pay phone, and looked up the nearest cab company. Checker Taxi was just a few blocks away, and I gave them a call.

After hanging up the phone, I told Marie that the taxi would be here in ten minutes, so we just waited for it to arrive. When the cab arrived, we got inside. I told the driver where we were going, and off we went. During the ride, both Marie and I just stared out our windows, looking at all buildings that have since been knocked down or renovated. The cabby took all local roads and avoided the park. As we continued, we passed the Channel Lumber store on Franklin Avenue, and then we continued farther down and passed Nutley High School and then the Franklin movie theater and Peerless, the stationery store where I bought my first diary.

It wasn't long before we arrived at Scotto's Pizzeria. I paid the driver and gave him a little something extra. Marie and I arrived a little too early; the restaurant wasn't open yet, so we decided to just go for a walk to pass the time. Having an hour or so to kill, we walked past the flower shop where I used to buy roses to leave on Marie's windshield. We continued walking and went past the old Stop and Shop, where I worked in my high school days. Everything looked so new and so old, at the same time.

Our walk took us to the Bradlees store, which was one of the strip mall's anchors, and we decided to go inside and have a look around. "I remember when all the Bradlees stores went out of business so many years ago, and here it is again, all brand-new," Marie said while looking in every direction at the same time.

We visited every department in the store, and Marie commented over and over that "you can't get these anymore."

She asked if it would be okay to purchase some underwear from the store, because she always liked the brand. I told her I didn't think it was wise, due to the unforeseen problems it might cause if someone from the future were to get their hands on them.

"Are you kidding?" she asked. "How could my underwear cause a problem?"

With that, she turned and held up a pair for me to see. "Nice," I commented, and a smile developed on one side of my face.

"You're blushing," she said and returned the garment to the rack. "I guess we have more important things to think about right now."

After spending almost an hour in Bradlees, we left the store and headed back toward Scotto's. It was nearly eleven o'clock; the doors were open, and the lights were all on. I commented to Marie that the younger versions of us would be arriving soon, and it would be a good idea to go inside and find a seat where we could see everything.

"I can almost remember this day somewhere in the back of my mind," Marie said, as if searching for a spark in the middle of a dark room.

We walked into Scotto's and were instantly met by the aroma of fresh pizza cooking in the oven. We both just stood there for a moment, letting the mixture of smells penetrate our senses. We gave each other a quick glance just to make sure our disguises were effective. Then without any further delay, we walked over to one of the booths that were positioned right smack dab in the middle of the restaurant. At this position, we would be able to see everyone. Marie agreed, and we took our seats.

We were only seated for a minute or so when a voice rang out from behind the counter, saying that someone would be right with us. The voice spoke in broken English, and we knew without a doubt that it was Jerry, the owner of the establishment, who was too short to see over the counter. All you could make out from our vantage point was the top of his balding head.

"I just had a crazy thought," Marie said, touching my hand across the table.

"What's that?" I asked.

"What if the younger me waits on us; then what?"

"Then nothing; just play it cool and pretend that you have absolutely no interest in anything except eating your meal."

"What if I recognize myself?" Marie asked, becoming a little nervous.

"Just keep cool and keep your eyes on me; leave your hat pulled down as far as it can go."

Another minute passed, and we noticed some movement at the front of the restaurant. There were some cars pulling up directly in front, and we noticed some people moving toward the entrance. Marie and I tried hard not to appear to be nosey, but we couldn't help ourselves.

Just then, I took notice of the young girl who just walked into the restaurant in her waitress uniform. She had long brown hair and walked with a spring in her step; her smile seemed to light up the room as she went along. The young girl passed directly in front of our booth, and when she did, she left behind the scent of her perfume. Marie pulled her hat down very low, partially covering her face.

Marie muttered under her breath, "Oh, my gosh, that's me."

The young Marie disappeared into the back of the restaurant for a few minutes and then returned and went directly over to Jerry, behind the counter.

They spoke quietly for a few seconds, and then young Marie walked over to our booth.

"Hi, I'm Marie, I'll be serving you today," she said with a smile, while handing us two menus. After retrieving a pen from one of her pockets and an order pad, complete with a sheet of carbon paper, she was ready to take our order.

"Can you give us a minute or two?" the older Marie asked.

"Sure," she said, and then, in a slow motion voice, she added, "Just wave me down when you folks are ready."

The younger Marie then turned on her heel and walked back to the counter.

"This is freaking me out," Marie said as she sank deeper into her seat, trying to make herself somehow less visible.

"Just pick up your menu and pretend to read," I said. "It should give you some cover while allowing yourself to observe what is going on."

"I don't know if I can do this, I'm too nervous," she said, sitting up straight.

There was a little commotion behind the counter as we heard Jerry complaining about some pizza dough that had gone bad in the refrigerator. Then the next thing we noticed was melon-sized balls of raw dough being tossed into a trash can, one after the other, just to the other side of the counter.

I caught young Marie's attention and signaled her to come over to our booth.

"What are you doing? I'm not ready yet," Marie said, a little agitated.

"I thought we could use some coffee to help wake up our brains."

"Have you decided what you want?" young Marie asked, standing in front of our booth with pen and pad in hand.

"We'll just have two coffees for now," I said, smiling directly at young Marie. "We're not ready to eat just yet.

"That's fine; two coffees, coming right up," she said and was off in a flash.

"You looked right at her," Marie said, giving my hand a little pinch.

"It would be rude to speak to her and not look at her, don't you think?"

"Yes, but she might recognize you or your voice or something," Marie said as she turned slightly to observe the younger Marie prepare the coffees.

"You're forgetting one important thing," I said.

"Oh, what's that?" Marie asked.

"You have to remember that the younger Marie … shhh, here she comes," I said.

"Here you go two coffees; milk and sugar on the table," the young Marie said. "Just let me know when you would like something to eat or if you want more coffee. I'll be right over there."

"So what were you going to say about what I forgot?" Marie asked.

"I was going to say that the young Marie hasn't met me yet, so there would be no reason to think she might recognize me, and as far as you are concerned, I doubt she would stand there and reason out that she was taking to an older version of herself, just out of the blue."

Marie sat for a moment and thought about what I said; she slowly started to straighten up and seemed to regain her confidence. "You know, you are 100 percent correct," she said, now smiling. "I forgot what year this was and what happens today."

Marie sipped her coffee and commented that it still tasted too strong. "This is why I switched to tea, I think," she said as she took another sip.

Just then, we both noticed two young men coming into the restaurant. One was taller than the other, and they were both dressed in a typical uniform with a white button-down shirt and white pants. They walked over to the counter, where Jerry was busy loading new dough from the kitchen. We could hear them talking to Jerry for a moment but could not make out exactly what they were saying, something about one of them being the new guy. Then all three of them walked into the kitchen, leaving the counter unoccupied, except for the younger Marie.

The expression on Marie's face was frozen in place. She sat in amazement as she recognized the shorter man and let out a sigh. "You were so fucking cute," she said, tapping my hand on the table.

The younger Marie sat down at one of the booths, filling the salt and pepper shakers and the sugar dispensers as well. She moved from one booth to the other, arranging them in a predetermined fashion so that everything looked uniform. The taller young man emerged from the rear of the restaurant, took his place behind the counter, and immediately went right to work.

Marie and I recognized him as Lou Gencarelli, who was my old high school friend. Lou had arranged for me to get the job at the restaurant by speaking to Jerry on my behalf. I was going to start out by washing dishes; from there, it was entirely up to me just how far I was willing to go. I had always wanted to know how to make pizza and other Italian dishes, so this was a good opportunity for me. Sounds of slapping came from the counter area as Lou pounded the balls of soft raw dough into flat disks and then, using his fists, stretched the dough into perfectly round disks. He then placed it down on the wooden paddle before adding the tomato sauce and mozzarella cheese.

Both Marie and I watched him prepare at least three pizzas in a total of five minutes. They were all in the pizza oven, and now the restaurant was engulfed with a pleasant aroma. The younger Marie was still busy making her way from booth to booth, continuing to fill the condiments. A group of elderly people walked into the restaurant and stood at the door.

The younger Marie took notice right away, walked over to them, and asked if they needed a booth. They spoke for a minute and then followed her to a booth near the front of the restaurant. They didn't want to walk all the way to the back. After they were seated, the younger Marie handed them each a menu and told them that she would return shortly to take their orders.

Meanwhile, my younger self was still in the back of the restaurant with Jerry. From what I remember, he was showing me around and explaining what my duties would be. The younger Marie was busy now other customers, and the place were starting to fill up. We noticed a second waitress enter the restaurant, and Marie recognized her as well.

The young Marie passed by our booth several times, and each time, she said that she would be ready as soon as we were.

"This is all so incredible," Marie said. "I feel like I should be getting up and waiting on tables."

We continued to watch as more customers poured into the restaurant and were seated immediately by young Marie or the second waitress. Lou was very busy at the counter, and then he was joined by another worker, and the two of them continued making pizzas and working the register. The young Marie saw that every customer was taken care of and then finished up with the last two booths that needed condiment filling. Just as she sat down and began the ritual, Jerry re-entered the main restaurant with the young Doug in tow. They walked right past the younger Marie and went directly behind the counter, where we could see all the heads moving from one side to the other. Jerry's head was barely visible, but you could still make it out. I could see the top of my head following behind Jerry wherever he went. Jerry and the younger Doug were behind the counter for quite some time before they both emerged to head back toward the kitchen area.

The younger Marie was busy filling a sugar dispenser when Jerry stopped for a moment and introduced the younger Doug to her. "Dis-a Marie, she's waitris, okay?" he said, pointing to young Marie sitting in the booth.

The younger Doug barely had the time to say hello before he was taken back to the kitchen to start washing dishes. Marie and I sat in our booth with our eyes glued to what was happening. The younger Marie slid to the edge of the booth and watched the younger Doug and Jerry walk to the kitchen. When she turned around again, we noticed the expression on her face.

"Looks like she likes him," Marie said.

"I think so," I replied. "I thought we had more time to talk when we first met."

"I thought so too, but I guess that was it. Not quite what I expected," Marie said, a little disappointed.

The younger Marie stood up, walked over to our booth, and asked if we decided what we were going to have.

"I would like a slice of pizza and a Pepsi Max," Marie said.

"A Pepsi what?" the younger Marie asked.

"Oh sorry, I mean just a Pepsi, please," Marie said, clearing her throat.

"We have Coke, is that okay?"

"Yes, that's fine," Marie said.

"And for you, sir?" Young Marie now turned her attention to me.

"I'll have the same thing she's having."

"Thank you," the young Marie said and turned slightly to keep watching us as she walked toward the counter.

She filled the cups with soda and peeked out the side of the machine once or twice, looking at Marie and me, seated in the booth. I noticed a puzzled look on her face as she headed back to our table with the drinks. She placed the cups down, retrieved two straws from her apron pocket, and placed one on each side of a cup.

"I'll be right back with your pizza," she said and disappeared again.

"I've been meaning to have a slice of Scotto's pizza for years now but never had the time to stop by," Marie said, rubbing her hands together.

"I haven't had a Scotto's slice in over thirty years myself."

"Nice treat, huh?"

"You can say that again."

While we waited for our slices, we noticed young Doug poking his head out from the kitchen, was trying to get someone's attention at the counter. After several unsuccessful tries, he walked out to the front, passing by young Marie, and then went behind the counter. We could not hear what he was saying, but Lou followed him back into the kitchen. If I remember correctly, I needed rubber gloves for washing the dishes.

After a few minutes, young Marie brought our meal to the table and said, "If you guys need anything else, please let me know," and off she went.

"I think I'm very polite and professional, and I smell nice," Marie said with a huge grin.

"You left out something," I said.

"Oh, what's that?" Marie asked.

"You left out that you were beautiful, as well."

"Hmm," Marie sighed. "What do you mean, *was*?" She laughed.

We ate our meal and decided to hang out another hour, just to observe the youngsters, and then we would head back to the house for some additional tests on the device. I had to make sure it would work after traveling through the time machine and being subjected to the intense magnetic field. Marie finished her slice and sat back in her seat, now completely relaxed.

"I wish there was more to see what happens to our first meeting," Marie said, sounding a little disappointed again.

"I know how you feel; I wanted to see a little more myself."

We finished our sodas, and I waved at young Marie to come over to our booth.

As soon as she arrived, I asked her for the check.

"Why didn't you just ask her from across the room, you know, make the 'give me a check' signal with your hand?" Marie asked.

I responded with an "I don't know" gesture by shrugging my shoulders.

"You know what I think?" Marie asked.

"No, what do you think?"

"I think you just wanted to look at the young Marie up close."

"I think you're right," I said. "It may have something to do with her eyes."

"That's right; you always liked my eyes, didn't you?" Marie asked.

"I still do," I replied, and we both smiled at each other.

The hour past quickly; Marie and I decided to use the restrooms before heading back to the house. The restrooms were located in the back of the restaurant, and they provided a good look into the kitchen area. About this time each day, the staff gathered for lunch in the kitchen around a table near the rear exit. Marie was the first to use the restroom, and she walked very slowly past the kitchen. She looked inside to see if everyone was gathering around the table, including young Marie and Doug. Marie tried hard to make out what they were all saying as they ate and laughed. Marie did notice that the young Marie and Doug were engaged in conversation and were laughing together. After using the restroom, Marie reported to me what she witnessed in the kitchen. After another minute or two, it was my turn to use the restroom, and I followed Marie's lead and walked very slowly toward the kitchen.

I caught young Marie saying to young Doug that it was a shame that he wasn't older, and then young Doug replied, "How old do I have to be, anyway?"

I remember that conversation somewhat, but my recollection of it was slightly different. I always thought that Marie had said that in front of one of her friends, and not at the lunch table, and not on the first day. Still, it was such a great sight. Anyone could see that these two young souls were really digging each other.

When I returned to Marie in the booth, I told her about what I heard.

"I'm surprised that I did that in front of the guys," Marie said, giving her head a scratch. "I remember that happening a little different."

"You know I was just thinking the same thing. I remember it happening different, as well."

We both brushed if off as something due to our long-term memory not being as good as it should be and decided is wasn't important.

Marie and I stood up and looked around the old place one more time, breathing in the aroma as if to store it in our olfactory files. Before leaving our booth, I left young Marie a twenty-dollar bill as a tip. Marie gave me a wink and a nod of approval. We walked to the front, paid our tab, and used the pay phone to call a cab. While we waited outside the restaurant, we peered inside every few minutes just to be nosey. The cab pulled up directly in front of the pet shop, and Marie and I climbed inside. I gave the cabby the address, and off we went.

On the way back to Newark, Marie and I were very quiet. We were both processing the day's events into our memories, to be pulled out and reused at a later time. The ride back to the house was quick; before we knew it, we were back in the kitchen, getting ready for another test with the device. Everything in my plan depended on the device working as well as it did before the jump to 1980; everything came down to this test. If this did not work, my plan of saving Marie's life and restoring the timeline would be destroyed.

I set the device on the window sill and plugged it into the wall outlet. I wanted to make sure it was fully charged before attempting the test. Marie and I sat on the floor of the living room and just talked for a few hours about old times and how being together after so many years was strange and wonderful at the same time. After at least three hours had passed, I decided that it was time to test the device.

Marie and I walked into the kitchen, and I unplugged the unit from the wall and handed it to Marie. We stood close to one another, one arm around each other's back, pulling at each other until we were like one person before I made ready to push the Rewind button. We held our breath and gave each other our customary good luck kiss, and then I pushed the button. Instantly, the space around us began to turn brighter, as the room grew darker. We knew right then and there that the device was working. It took a good fifteen to twenty seconds for the unit to power up and reach its designed functional state.

I monitored the time closely on my watch; thirty seconds passed, and we were now fully cocooned in the protective time shield. I nudged Marie forward and asked her to walk over to the heavy, old-fashioned refrigerator. I want us to use our shield as a sort of battering ram to try and move the refrigerator. If we could accomplish this, moving the original Marie and Doug should be a breeze. We positioned ourselves about six feet in front of the unit and lunged forward at the thing. As soon as the tip of the shield made contact with the refrigerator, it lifted it off its front legs and tipped backwards, almost crashing into the window behind it. We stopped and moved backward, and the refrigerator fell forward again with a crash, as it returned to the floor.

Overwhelmed by the successful test of the device, we turned to one another and hugged tightly, almost dropping the device on the floor. We released, and I quickly checked the time on my watch; fifty-eight seconds had passed, and the unit appeared to still be fully charged. We walked over to the living room and peered out the window into the street, noticing the traffic light on the corner. It was eerie to see that the light was in the process of changing from one color to another, from yellow to red, not quite yellow and not quite red, somewhere in between.

We moved back into the kitchen and waited for the unit to discharge. According to my watch, two minutes thirty-five seconds passed before its power supply depleted, and time resumed to its normal setting.

Marie breathed a sigh of relief. "I'm so happy that neither one of us has to die."

I turned to her, gave a nod of approval, and pushed my lips together in deep thought.

"What's the matter?" Marie asked.

"I was just thinking about what will happen after we are successful resetting the timeline."

"Isn't that what we want?" Marie asked in earnest. "Isn't that the plan?"

"That's what we want, for sure; you and me, in our timeline. There is still something troubling me about this, something I can't put my finger on it."

I left Marie standing in the kitchen, now confused about my doubt and concern of the unknown intricacies of time displacement. I walked slowly from room to room, my hands clenched together behind my back. I needed time to think, as a thought was emerging from deep inside my brain and working itself to the surface, trying to make itself known. The harder I thought, the more my head hurt, but still, I felt something was there, something important, something we needed to know.

Marie took a seat on the living room floor, which was still carpeted, and lay down on her back, with her hands behind her neck, supporting her head in a way where she could still watch me walk around in circles. It wasn't long before she drifted off into a light sleep. I decided to lay down next to her and take a power nap. I needed to clear my mind and focus on what was giving me so much doubt. I snuggled up close to Marie and put my arm around her; she turned on her side, and I drifted off into a restless sleep.

The night passed quickly, and the faint glint of sunlight was peeking through the cracks in the window shades, hitting our eyes and waking us up.

Marie was the first to sit up. "Oh, my gosh," she said, giving out a stretch and a yawn. "I am so stiff, I can hardly move."

I followed her lead and sat up as well, encountering the same problem.

"How long have we been asleep?" Marie asked.

I checked my watch and found that about nine hours had passed. "What time is it now?"

"It's just about six o'clock," I replied.

"What are we going to do while we wait until our return jump?" she asked.

"Well, the return jump will be just before nine o'clock. So we have a few hours to prepare," I said, while plugging the tape recorder back into the wall outlet. "First, we need to freshen up and eat something. I don't know about you, but I can use some coffee."

"Mmmm, that sounds good," Marie replied, "but what are we going to do about washing up and brushing our teeth? We didn't bring anything with us, and there's nothing in the house to use."

"I know, we left in a hurry, with the police right behind us. Shit," I exclaimed, "the police; they were right behind us. When we return, they will be there in the house. How do we explain not answering the door, and furthermore, why would they break down my door just to question me?"

The few short hours instantly became shorter in my mind, as the problems mounted, one on top the other. I still hadn't figured out what was troubling me last night; was it the device or maybe what we observed with the interaction between young Marie and Doug at the pizzeria? Whatever it was, we still needed to freshen up and have a good hot meal.

There was a Travel Lodge not far from us on Washington Avenue in Bellville; we would be able to wash up and brush our teeth and have a nice breakfast.

"I always think better on a full stomach," I told Marie.

"So where are we going?" she asked while fixing her hair as best she could.

"Remember the motel on Washington Avenue, where you took me on my birthday a long time ago?"

"I do remember that," Marie replied with a glint in her eyes. "I remember wine and food and other things," she said, giving me a wink.

I winked back and felt my face become hot.

"Oh, my gosh, you're blushing." Marie reached over and touched my face with her cool hand. "We were so damn cute back then, weren't we?"

I agreed with Marie that what we had when we were young was very special; I leaned forward, kissed her several times, and hugged her so tightly that she almost lost her breath.

"Everything all right?" she said, looking directly into my eyes.

"I hope so," I replied.

We left the house in our usual stealth mode, trying extremely hard not to attract any attention to ourselves. We walked down to the supermarket, and I called a cab to take us to the motel.

"Another trip down memory lane," Marie said with a huge smile.

I turned to her, offered my hand, and she took it. We stood there at the supermarket for the next ten minutes, discussing possible stories to tell the police when we returned. Whatever we came up with and how clever we thought we could be, it would be nearly impossible to convince them that what they thought they saw with our disappearing and reappearing was all in their minds. In any case, our return jump today would prove to be unforgettable.

The cab arrived, and Marie and I jumped in. I gave the cabby an approximate location of the motel.

"Oh, I know that place very well," the cabby said, and off he went, like a man on a mission.

Marie and I sat back in our seats, trying to absorb all of the information we had collected over the last twenty hours or so.

"I don't know about you," she said, "but I feel that the odds are against us."

I looked at her and said that I felt exactly the same way. We both took in a deep breath and said nothing for the remainder of the ride to the motel.

After the cabby pulled into the parking lot, Marie and I exited the vehicle and walked into the rental office. The elderly man behind the counter was extremely overweight and had a bit of old-person smell of cigarette smoke and body odor, mixed in with a little beer; it had been quite some time since his last bath.

"Can I help you?" he asked.

"Yes, we would like a room for a couple of hours," I replied.

The man slowly stood up and waddled over to the counter, giving us a quick look up and down. "Just for a couple of hours, huh?"

"Yes, we just need to freshen up and have something to eat and then we will be leaving."

He handed me a registration card and asked me to fill it out. "How long did you say you needed the room?" he asked, looking directly at Marie, who up to now was still discreetly covering her nose.

"We just need a couple of hours that's all," Marie replied.

I finished filling out the card and handed it back to the man.

"Let's see here," he said, holding the card close to his face in order to read it. "Mr. & Mrs. Smith," he said, looking up at us. "1200 1st Street, New York." Then he looked at me and asked, "Is this correct?"

"Yes," I replied and gave Marie a sinister smile and a wink.

"Okay then," the elderly man said, "that will be $30, paid in advance," holding out his hand.

I reached into my pocket, pulled out the thirty dollars, and handed it to him.

"Okay, fine, here are your keys; there are fresh towels in the room. If you need anything, call me here at the desk." With that, he returned to his chair and slowly sat down.

Before leaving, Marie asked, "Do you have toothpaste and toothbrushes, soap, and shampoo?"

"You will find what you need on the counter in the bathroom," the man said, and he picked up his word find magazine and went to work.

We left the rental office, walked over to room #26, and opened the door. The room was clean and very well stocked, just as the man at the rental desk said.

"You mind if I use the bathroom first?" Marie asked as she closed the door behind her.

"Sure, go right ahead," I said, talking to myself and sitting on the edge of one of the beds; I turned on the television. I flipped through the channels until I settled on watching a cartoon. I needed something mindless to help clear my head and help me to think. I watched as one little character tried to outdo the other in a series of unsuccessful attempts at mutual destruction.

For whatever the reason, I found it enjoyable and settled back on the bed to continue to watch. Marie was still in the bathroom, and now I could hear the sound of the shower running. Then something in the cartoon caught my attention, something funny but still interesting. One of the little guys caught the other naked in the shower, trying to blow him to bits with a bomb. Then it occurred to me that if Marie and I were, let's say, engaged in some sort of sexual activity, it would be a good excuse to give the police as to why we hadn't answered the door. Then again, this would have to look believable as well, and that would mean we would have to be naked.

Marie emerged from the bathroom with a towel wrapped around her and her hair pulled back off her neck and tied with a black ribbon.

"It's all yours," she said and moved over to the large mirror above the dresser. "The guy was right, this place has everything." She began patting her legs dry with a second towel.

"After I take a quick shower," I said, "I want to discuss what we can do about our little police issue."

"I'll be here," she said and continued drying herself.

I walked into the bathroom and found a toothbrush and a small tube of toothpaste ready for me on the counter top. Marie had arranged everything in order of need; even my towel was laid out neatly ready for my use. She seemed to have a magical touch that turned any ordinary thing into something beautiful. I could really use her around the house to brighten up the place. I took a fast shower and brushed my teeth, dried myself off, and used some of the deodorant left out for me on the counter.

I emerged from the bathroom wrapped in a towel, and as the cool air hit my skin, I felt much better. Marie was nearly dressed already and was putting on some final touches of makeup.

"I didn't have much to work with," she said as she added a little eye shadow. "I didn't think that I was going to need any of these things."

I removed my towel and systematically redressed myself in yesterday's clothes. I took a quick sniff of my shirt's underarm area and noticed that it was not unpleasant. I finished dressing and Marie did the same; we were both ready to leave. We gave the room one final inspection to make sure we did not leave anything personal behind and closed the door behind us as we left. We walked over to the rental office, dropped off the keys, and asked the elderly man to direct us to a restaurant where we could have a hot breakfast.

"There is a place not far from here, about a mile or so, called Alison's," and he pointed in the direction we needed to go.

We thanked him and headed down Washington Avenue in the direction of Alison's.

The temperature was starting to heat up, and the humidity was climbing steadily. Marie and I walked the mile and a half to the restaurant and a waitress led us to a table near the window.

"Will this be okay?" she asked.

Marie and I looked at each other and simultaneously answered yes. We ordered coffee and the breakfast special, which was two eggs over easy, a short stack of pancakes, and two sausages. We sat quietly, staring out the window, until the waitress placed our order down in front of us and poured the coffee.

"Thank you," I said, and Marie did the same.

"Just let me know if you need anything else," she replied. "I'll be right up front," and then she was gone.

We looked around; Marie and I were the only people in the restaurant, so we could talk freely. We ate our breakfast and drank our coffee, and the waitress followed up by pouring each of us a second cup. "Will there be anything else?" she asked.

"No, thank you, just the check please," I said.

"I'll be right back with that," she said, and then she was gone.

"So what's this idea of yours to get out of trouble with the police?" Marie asked, tapping her spoon to the side of her coffee cup.

"Well, you'll have to keep an open mind on this one," I told her.

"As long as I don't have to parade around naked," she joked.

I said nothing and just looked at her blankly.

"What?" Marie asked.

"That's my idea," I said.

"What, that I put on a show for the police to take their minds off of arresting us?" She paused. "Do you know just how crazy that sounds?"

The waitress brought the check, and I asked her to wait while I gave her the money and her tip.

"Oh, thank you, sir," she said as she slipped the five-dollar bill into her pocket and disappeared from view.

"Think about it for a moment," I said. "If we were naked and having sex, the police would consider that as an explanation as to why we did not hear them knocking on the door."

"So now you're naked, too?" Marie said with a strange grin. "Isn't there something, anything else you can come up with that would not include us taking our clothes off?"

"I'm up for suggestions," I replied.

"Let me think about it," she said, crossing her arms and beginning to laugh.

"What's so funny?"

"You," she said. "One way or the other, you always seem to be able to get me to take off my clothes." She shook her head.

"Strangely enough, I can't think of anything else that would work under that condition."

"Damn, Doug, that's going to be embarrassing as hell," she said and started to laugh again, and this time, I joined her.

Before leaving the restaurant, I called a cab to take us back to the house. Marie and I waited in the air-conditioned vestibule for it to arrive. On the way back to the house, she appeared agitated and nervous.

"What's the matter?" I asked. "Are you okay?"

"No, not really," she said. "I am not looking forward to doing this peep show for the Newark police."

"It's not for the Newark police, it's for us to stay out of trouble long enough to correct the timeline. Can you imagine if we were arrested and put into jail? What chance would we have to put my plan into action?"

"I didn't think about it like that," she said quietly. "I guess we have to do whatever it takes to make it right again."

I slid over closer to her, put my arm around her shoulder, and gave her arm a little squeeze. "It's going to be all right, Marie; somehow, it will all turn out all right."

"How do you know that?" she asked.

"I don't know how I know, I just know, you know?"

She started to laugh and put her head on my shoulder. Before we knew it, we were pulling up in front of the house. We waited a minute or so before getting out of the cab, making sure it was safe to do so. I paid the cabby, and he drove down Seventh Street until he disappeared. Marie and I made our way back into the house and discussed our naked plan of action.

I checked my watch and noticed that we still had another full hour before making the jump back to 2014. Marie and I rehearsed possible scenarios as to what we might face with the police. Marie wanted to keep her clothes on and gave me several reasons why she thought that would be better. We went back and forth several times until finally agreeing that naked was the best option.

"I must say, here and now," Marie exclaimed, "this time travel stuff is for the birds." Then she continued, "I mean it has its good points, but the bad things that can happen far outweigh the good stuff."

"I agree with you, it is far too painful to travel through time. Even under the best and strictest conditions, there is always a chance to screw things up. After we correct the timeline, I'm going to destroy the time machine."

Marie looked puzzled and asked, "Didn't Doug Sr. tell you that you were never supposed to build it in the first place?"

"Yes, he did, as a matter of fact. I was just thinking that all of this, everything we are doing now, will not even be a memory to anyone. We may not even have a place in the original timeline. Who knows if we even exist at all?"

With twenty minutes to go until our return jump, Marie asked nervously, "How are we going to be able to just show up naked and have everything come out okay?" She paused. "Really, Doug, I'm having second thoughts about this."

"Marie, listen, I just had a brainstorm."

"Please tell me it doesn't involve pole dancing," she said in a shaky voice.

"As a matter of fact, we will not even be there when the cops burst in."

"Excuse me?"

I walked into the kitchen and unplugged the tape recorder from the wall. I turned around and held it up for Marie to see.

"This little device will get us out of trouble."

"I'm not following you."

"Just before we re-enter the time machine, we push the Rewind button, and by the time we emerge in 2014, we will be shielded and protected from time. What we do is walk right past them, and then we wait outside on the sidewalk for the police to come out. Then we can question them as to why they broke down my door."

"Holy brainstorm, Batman," Marie said. "Why didn't you think about this before? You had me worried for no reason."

"I'm sorry, it just came to me. I wish I would have thought of it sooner myself. Do you think I like the idea of exposing myself to strangers?"

Marie said nothing and then I heard her giggle under her breath.

"Oh, now you think it's funny?"

There wasn't much time to discuss the intricacies of the tape recorder idea, so we were just going to have to wing it. At least Marie and I had some experience using the device, so we should be able to pull this off.

"Remember to stick as close to me as possible after I turn this thing on," I said.

"You're paper, and I'm glue," Marie said with a smile. "Just glad I'm not taking my clothes off for this trip."

"I feel the same way," I replied as I looked out the window facing the back yard. "I feel like we have been gone much longer than twenty-four hours."

"I was just thinking that exact same thing," she replied.

I checked my watch and took note that there were only ten minutes to go until our jump to 2014.

CHAPTER 13

With only a few minutes to go before our jump, I checked the device to make sure it was secure. Marie and I took our positions in front of the time machine, and we pulled each other close. Just before we engaged the device, we gave each other a kiss for luck, and then I pressed the Rewind button, and we stepped through the time machine. Our return trip was instantaneous and completely uneventful. We materialized directly in front of one of the police officers, almost nose to nose. The second officer had his gun drawn.

"It's a good thing we didn't go through with the naked thing," Marie said. "He may have shot off your little Dougie."

"Very funny. Come on, let's get out of here."

Marie and I walked right past the two officers, out the front door, and down the steps to the sidewalk below. There we waited for the device to power down. As we waited, we took notice of the large crowd of people that had developed in just a few minutes. There was even a Channel 7 News truck parked on the street. Several police vehicles had parked diagonally in the roadway, blocking traffic from both ends.

"This is a big deal," I said.

"The victim must have been very well known around here," Marie commented.

We continued to wait for another minute or so for the device to completely power down. The crowd began moving, and the sounds around us started to become more audible.

"What do we say to the police when they question us?" Marie asked, gripping my arm tightly, as if trying to squeeze out a reply.

"That depends on what they ask us, I guess."

The device finished its cycle, and time returned to its proper setting. We continued to wait on the sidewalk for the police to come out of my house. As we waited, the crowd grew in size; people were asking each other what had had happened.

One of the neighbors saw Marie and me standing on the sidewalk and walked over to us. "Hey, you guys all right?" she asked. Nancy Gluck lived a few doors down; her husband served in the military and was just now on tour in Afghanistan. "We thought for sure something had happened to you as well."

"Why would you think something happened to us?" I asked.

"You don't know, do you?" Nancy looked grimly at both Marie and me.

"Know what?" Marie asked.

"The victim ..." Nancy's words came slowly. "The victim is your son."

Nancy's eyes dropped, and she cleared her throat. Marie and I were dumfounded, as we looked at each other but did not say a word. We knew we didn't have a son, at least have one together. Michael and Brian were Marie's sons, and they were, as far as we knew, safe and secure back in Little Falls.

Nancy reached over, gave us both a quick hug, and said, "I'm so sorry." She walked away, with tears in her eyes.

"What the hell is she talking about?" Marie asked, throwing her hands in the air.

"I have no idea," I replied.

"What the hell happened on this last time trip?" Marie pulled at my arm. "What did we do? What did we change?"

I could only shrug my shoulders and offer no comment. Just then, the two officers walked out the front door and saw Marie and I standing at the foot of the steps. One of the officers walked up to us.

"Are you the owners of this house?" he asked.

"I'm the owner," I replied. "My name is Doug Lupo."

"And who is this?" he asked, looking at Marie.

"She's a friend," I replied. "Her name is Marie Martin."

"Martin?" the officer repeated, now visibly confused. "I was told that the parents of the victim lived in this house and that they may have been subject to foul play."

"Is that why you broke down my front door?" I asked.

The officer gave me another confused look and said, "Just wait here."

He pulled his partner aside for a private conversation, looking back over his shoulder several times in our direction, and then they both returned.

"Mr. Lupo, is it?" the older officer asked.

"Yes, I'm Doug Lupo," I said, and I looked at both officers. They appeared totally confused.

"We are sorry about your door, but I'm afraid we may have gotten some bad information."

"What do you mean?" Marie asked, looking directly at the second officer.

"We were told that the parents of the victim may have been subjected to foul play."

"Yes, we were told that by the other officer."

"We knocked on the door several times, but there was no answer, and we were under the impression that the perp might be hiding in the home."

"The perp?" Marie asked.

"Yes, ma'am, the perpetrator, the person who might have been responsible for the homicide."

"Officer, we are obviously not harmed, but we are very confused. Can you please explain to us what is going on?"

Again, the two officers huddled for a quick conversation, and then the second officer said, "Your son Robert was found shot to death in your neighbor's home."

"Our son Robert?" Marie's voice rose with obvious concern.

"Yes, ma'am. I'm sorry, can you two please wait here while we process the crime scene?" Then he paused for a moment, leaned over to the other officer, whispered something into his ear, and then turned back to us. "Someone will be with you shortly to take a statement; in the meantime, please stay out here."

With that, the two officers returned to the house.

Marie leaned over to me and whispered, "What the hell is he talking about, our son Robert?"

"I have no idea. The young man from the real estate company, who sold me this house, his name was Robert, but he's not related to me whatsoever."

"Why do all these people think this young man is our son?" Marie turned to me. "Doug, what did we do?"

"We didn't have the time to put a family together, if that's what you mean."

I felt my legs begin to wobble, and a sensation of unsteadiness and lightheadedness filled my body. Suddenly, new memories were surfacing in my brain, and what I thought I remembered about my life was no more. The old memories were replaced by the new ones, and after a time, I knew that Robert was indeed my son. Marie was experiencing exactly the same thing, as we leaned against each other to keep from falling down.

"What is happening?" Marie's voice rang in my ears, distant and unclear.

My vision blurred, and my legs gave way. The next thing I knew, I was waking up inside an ambulance.

Marie was on the cot next to me.

"Mr. Lupo," a voice echoed in my head. "Can you hear me?" It was a woman's voice, almost childlike in nature. "Mr. Lupo," the voice repeated. "Can you hear me?"

I replied in a slurred tone, "Yes, I can hear you."

Then the first aider turned her attention to Marie and did then same with her. "Mrs. Lupo, can you hear me?"

Marie replied with a garbled "Yes," and then the young first aider asked, "Can you sit up?"

"I think so," Marie said and made the effort to position herself upright.

I did the same, and as I sat up, I noticed the commotion outside. They were bringing out a body from the crime scene home. It was covered with a sheet and placed into another ambulance.

Marie was looking at the same thing, and she broke down in tears.

"Why is this happening?" she asked. "Before we left, we didn't have a son; now we do, and he's been killed? How is that possible?"

The young first aider handed Marie a cup of water and told her to drink, which she did.

She also handed me a cup, and I followed in turn. "You both have had quite a shock, I'm so sorry," she said and turned to the rear door and gave it a few knocks.

The door opened, and a tall slender man looked in.

"I'm Detective James Murdock," he said in a low voice, taking out a badge and showing it to us.

The young first aider turned to us and said, "The detective is just going to ask you some questions." She stepped out of the ambulance and said, "Good luck."

Detective Murdock climbed into the ambulance with us and took a seat next to Marie.

"I know this is not a good time for either of you, but I have to ask you both some questions," he said. "I need to ask you now, while the information is still fresh in your heads."

"Please, Detective, first tell us what's going on," Marie said. "Everyone seems to think that our son Robert was killed."

I looked at Marie's expression, and our eyes communicated to each other of the acceptance of the fact that we had a son.

"Robert Lupo was identified by your neighbor, Margret Fletcher, who claims that she came home and found his body in her house.

"Mrs. Fletcher also told us that she has known Robert for a period of several years and that she had a relationship with him." He paused. "Are you aware of this?"

Marie and I were searching for a response, using our new memories as a guide.

"Robert told me one time that he had a girlfriend but never mentioned her name or where she lived," Marie said in a solemn tone.

"Mr. Lupo, were you aware of Robert's affair with Mrs. Fletcher?" the detective asked.

"Robert never mentioned that to me, but I remember seeing him a couple of times leaving Margret's house; until just now, I never gave it a second thought" (which was not far from the truth).

"Were you aware that Mrs. Fletcher's husband died approximately four years ago of esophageal cancer?"

"Yes, I remember that now," Marie said, then clarified her reply to say only, "Yes, I remember."

"Mrs. Fletcher, according to your neighbors, became a loner and shied away from people, only leaving the house when she absolutely needed to," the detective said, reading from his notes on a small pad he carried with him. "Furthermore," he said, "this is not confirmed, mind you, but according to Mrs. Fletcher, she and your son Robert were becoming serious in their relationship, and according to Mrs. Fletcher, they were going to become engaged."

"I had absolutely no idea that Robert was thinking about that," Marie said.

With each passing minute, as we continued to speak with the detective, new memories were entering our minds, memories of Robert as our son, Marie and I as husband and wife, and our life together.

Still, at the same time, we retained other memories of a different life separate from what we were now discovering. Reality as we knew it was bending, distorting, and rearranging itself; there were two sets of memories at the same time, but which memories were the correct ones?

"Mr. and Mrs. Lupo, are you aware of anyone who might want to cause harm to your son?" the detective asked, and both Marie and I answered simultaneously with a no.

We continued speaking with the detective for another hour, and then he finished up the interview and thanked us for our time. He gave each one of us a business card.

"If you can think of anything else, please call me," he said, and with that, he politely said good-bye and stepped out of the ambulance.

Marie and I sat motionless for a long while, waiting for our brains to catch up with all the new information.

"What happened to Brian and Michael?" Marie asked. "Am I still their mother?"

"What about my daughter, am I still her father?"

"This young man, Robert, who is supposed to be our son, I have memories of him, yet I can't feel him in my life or in my heart, as I do with Brian and Michael. How can I remember two different lives at the same time?" Marie asked, looking directly me.

"I don't know," I replied. "It seems that no matter how insignificant we think something is and how careful we think we are, something is always changed on every time jump."

The door to the ambulance swung open, and the first aider asked if we were well enough to walk. We both answered yes and climbed out.

"If you are sure you're okay, then you can go home now," she said and closed the door. "We have another call now and have to go."

She got into the front of the ambulance and drove down the street.

Marie and I, still in a state of shock, walked slowly back to the house. I closed the front door as best I could and secured it with a few screws so that it would remain locked for the evening.

"So what do I do now?" Marie asked.

"Do about what?"

"Should I call home asked Marie and see if either one of the boys answers the phone?"

"Give it a try," I said. "I'm curious to see what happens."

Marie picked up the phone and called her number; an automated message came on and said that the number was disconnected. She froze and just looked at me, shaking her head in disbelief, and then hung up the phone.

"So now what? Do I stay here or go home?" Marie asked, pacing back and forth. "I can't stay here, anyway. I don't have any clothes to change into."

She opened the closet in the bedroom to prove her point but found it completely filled with her things.

"What the hell?" Marie yelled. "Where did this come from?"

"Are they your clothes?" I asked.

Marie replied, "Yes, I recognize everything; these are all mine, I'm sure of it."

Bewildered and confused, Marie and I tried hard to make sense of everything that had taken place upon our return to 2014. I picked up the massive log book and searched for entries that might explain our situation. After a few minutes, I found an entry dated July 10, 2014, at 9 a.m. The entry read as follows: "Upon our return with the aid of the device we avoided the police and were able to get ourselves outside. Robert is now our son, the children are gone, and the timeline has been altered; unexpected meeting with Doug Sr., sensation of small earthquake, and possible paradox, according to Doug Sr."

I put the log book down and scratched my head. When did I meet with Doug Sr.? Just then, the archway began to vibrate, and both Marie and I knew what that meant. Doug Sr. was making a house call. We stood in front of the archway and waited for the time machine to complete its sequence.

Doug Sr. appeared on the other side, obviously agitated over what had happened. "What the hell were the two of you thinking?" he said in an angry voice. "You changed the past, and it has caught up with me here."

As soon as he finished his sentence, the entire house began to shake violently; it continued for several seconds.

"What is happening?" Marie asked.

Doug Sr. replied that what we were feeling was nothing to what he had experienced. "Every time you change something in the past, it affects everything going forward, and as it moves further into the future, its effects become more violent."

"I was only testing out a theory with —"

Doug Sr. interrupted and bellowed, "I told you what you need to do; who told you to go out and think on your own?" He took a breath. "This is what happens when you don't follow the plan."

"Who's plan?" I asked.

"*My* plan," he replied. "We can still salvage this, but you are not to defer from the plan in any way; do I make myself clear?"

Marie began to cry and sat down on the edge of my bed.

"I just want this thing to end, one way or the other," she sobbed.

Doug Sr. and I gave her a moment and then continued our discussion.

"I don't like your plan," I snapped. "In fact, I will not allow Marie to die or have any harm come to her on this trip to 1929. Do I make myself clear?"

Doug Sr. took a step backward and replied, "Remarkable; you are the first to take a stand with me."

I continued, "Unless you give me a better option, I am moving forward with my own plan."

"It is true that I will not be able to stop you, but I can manipulate events in such a way that you will eventually yield to my wishes."

"What do you mean, manipulate?" I asked.

Doug Sr. paused for a moment and then said, "I understand Robert died of a gunshot to the stomach."

"Yes, he was killed by a —" I stopped and looked Doug Sr. in the eye. "How do you know he was shot in the stomach? I did not mention that to you."

Doug Sr. walked out of view and did not return for several minutes.

"I'm slipping up," he said from out of view. "Getting old and forgetful."

I asked him again how he knew where Robert was shot.

Cold and unfeeling, Doug Sr. replied, "While you were away on your little excursion, I visited Robert and shot him."

Marie leaped from the bed and yelled at Doug Sr., "What the hell happened to you?" She paused, wiping a tear from her eye. "You were such a nice person when I knew you, years ago; what did you hope to accomplish by murdering someone?"

Doug Sr. dismissed Marie with a wave and then said, "You have no idea what my world has become because of this fucking machine!"

He took a breath and continued, "What I did, I had to do, in order to prevent a paradox of unprecedented proportions." Then he added, "You changed the past and altered the future, and because of what you did, time as we know it was fractured and distorted."

"What did we do that was so bad?" I asked.

"Your trip to Scotto's started a ripple in time that was amplified a thousand times before it was felt here. I must admit you surprised me by reasoning out a plan of your own. You were the first to do so, and it left me scrambling to repair the damages."

"What damages are you talking about?"

"Really, I remember myself to be much more intelligent and observant," Doug Sr. said. "What happened in the restaurant? Was it as you remembered from your memory of the past?"

Both Marie and I looked at each other and realized that we did, in fact, observe anomalies between what we saw and what we remembered.

"That's right, you remember now, don't you?" Doug Sr. bellowed. "Sometimes, the human memory can be a tricky thing, and what we think we remember is not in actuality what happened." He paused. "Because you were there, you interacted with young Marie just long enough to change the timeline. She was not supposed to notice young Doug for a few more hours; because of you two, you caused her to slow down with filling the salt and pepper shakers in the booths. Because of this, she was sitting in a booth when young Doug and Jerry passed by." He took another breath "Are you starting to understand what I'm saying?"

"I understand that we should not have interacted with anyone in anyway," I said to him. "We were not there in the past to interfere with young Marie, so the timeline was altered."

"Now you're getting it," Doug Sr. roared. "Late, but at least you understand."

"Tell me, why do we have two sets of memories?" I asked Doug Sr.

"You shielded yourselves with the protective time device; this prevented your brain waves from being totally rearranged."

Marie interjected with a question: "So what does Robert have to do with all of this?" She moved closer to Doug Sr.'s image in the archway. "And why are Brian and Michael gone?"

Doug Sr. took in another breath and then exhaled loudly, replying, "Because you changed the way young Marie and Doug met, and because of this, they married young and had a son who became involved with the wrong people and developed a taste for drugs.

"Robert's addiction escalated to the point that he became desperate for more and more drugs," he continued. "He became delusional and was going to kill you both in your sleep and take whatever money he found just to get his next fix." He paused. "If he succeeded in killing you, then the plan to reset the original timeline and to restore the original Marie and Doug would be lost forever."

Marie reached toward the elderly Doug but stopped just inches away from the magnetic field of the archway.

"I hate what you have become," she said bitterly.

Doug Sr. turned his back to Marie and lowered his head.

"It's only because you do not fully understand," was all he offered in return.

I moved closer to Marie, put my arm around her, and pulled her away from the archway.

"Please, Marie, come and sit down," I said.

"I don't want to fucking sit down, I want this nightmare to just go away," she said, pushing me away. "You did this," she said, pointing her finger at me. "You," she said again, this time with less heat. "I don't know why I —" She stopped and broke out into a sob, and then she threw her arms around my neck and hugged me tightly. "I'm sorry I said that. I don't know where that came from." Tears were streaming down her face.

Taking a deep breath, I responded only with a sigh and returned a reassuring hug. As we stood there, comforting each other in our time of need, we almost forgot about Doug Sr., who was now watching us intently from his side of the archway.

"I remember when you held me like that many years ago," he said softer and in a gentle voice.

"I lived a lifetime without you, and I have spent every waking minute of every day trying to get back to you." He paused and removed his thick glasses from his face, revealing moisture under his eyes; he was crying. "I haven't cried in over fifty years," he said, wiping them away dismissively. "I have grown hard and unfeeling, and my only wish is to end this miserable existence." He stepped closer and looked right at Marie. "I have always loved you and needed you but couldn't have you," he said. "You were taken from me many years ago, and I was left behind, with only your memory to sustain me. I don't expect you to understand my obsession to end this torment, for that is what it has become for me."

He lowered his head, and a single tear rolled off one of his wrinkled cheeks and hit the floor at his feet.

"I thought about ending my life many times over the years, and it would have been easy to do, but that would not bring you back into the world, and the world needs you, and I need you, so that was not an option." He pressed on, saying, "I have no choice but to repair what has taken place. I don't have much time left. Soon I will die, and with my death, there is no one to mourn for me. I have distanced myself from everyone I ever knew, with only one solitary thought in my head: getting you back, so I'll continue on until death comes to relieve the pain." He returned his glasses to his face. "Before I go, I want to repair the original timeline, where you, Marie, live a full and wonderful life with the man you love with all your heart and soul."

He turned to me and nodded, indicating that I was that man. "And you, Doug, will enjoy a lifetime of love and happiness with the woman you have always loved." He then nodded in Marie's direction. "We need to work together and trust each other for this to work. I can't do it alone." He stopped, thought for a moment, and repeated, "Alone."

Until then, I was quiet and gave Doug Sr. his moment to open up and say what he needed to say, getting a lifetime of pressure off his chest, but now I needed to focus on the task at hand: prepare for the trip back to 1929.

"Is there anything you want to tell me before we make the trip back to 1929?" I asked.

"There is nothing more you need to know," Doug Sr. replied. "Just prevent the original Marie and Doug from doing anything and send them back the way they came, and everything will return to normal."

I raised a hand and said, with some degree of doubt, that he previously told me that there would be one more jump after this, and that this would be next to the last.

Doug Sr. sighed and said, "That was then, and this is now; because of recent events, the second jump is no longer necessary."

I looked into Doug Sr.'s eyes, trying to see if I could detect any sign of untruth. I could not find it.

"When you get there," he said, "you will know what to do." Then he turned and took a final look at Marie and said, "I love you," and with that last word echoing off the walls, his image vanished, and then he was gone.

Chapter 14

Feeling the overwhelming pressure of having the world on our shoulders, Marie and I thought it best to get a good night's sleep before preparing for the last jump. We washed up and prepared for bed. Marie knew where to find everything she needed, thanks to her additional memories. She changed into an oversized t-shirt and crawled into bed. I changed into my sleep pants and a t-shirt and slid in beside her. Before long, we were huddled together under a single sheet on the bed, holding each other close and whispering that we loved each other and that everything was going to be all right. Feeling the effects of the day and the emotional stress on our bodies, we began to drift, and in minutes, we were asleep.

The next day, the neighborhood was busy with activity, with our neighbors milling around and talking to one another, no doubt discussing the prior evening's event. I peeked around the living room curtain and noticed two police vehicles parked in front of Margret's home. My guess was that they were still processing the crime scene. Across the street was a dark, unmarked car, which probably belonged to the detective we met last night. As I continued to look outside, Marie walked up behind me and hugged me. I turned and kissed her.

"Want some breakfast?" she asked, as she moved toward the kitchen.

"Yes, I am a bit hungry," I replied. "You know I could use some —"

"Coffee?" Marie finished, smiling.

"Yes, coffee sounds good," I replied and followed her into the kitchen.

Marie and I worked together and prepared eggs and bacon; she even toasted corn muffins, which she had baked the before.

Corn muffins? A question entered my head: *Marie made corn muffins?* I sat down visibly confused and asked Marie, "When did you make corn muffins?"

"I made them yesterday, before we left for the store, remember?" she said and began humming to herself as she finished pouring the coffee.

"Wait a second, something is not right about this," I said. "I don't remember you making corn muffins."

"It's not the first time you forgot I did something, sweetie." She bent down and gave me a kiss. "Come on and eat; we have a busy day ahead of us." She sat down at the table.

I stared at Marie, who was already enjoying her first sip of coffee. "I don't —"

"Just eat," she said. "You always feel better after you have eaten."

As I put the first morsel of food to my mouth, I heard strange voices in my head. I closed my eyes and saw a large crowd of people with police cars and ambulances.

Marie touched my hand and brought me back. "Are you okay, my love? You seem a little out of it."

"I'm fine, I guess, just a little confused. Wait," I said; I ran into the living room, threw open the curtains, and looked outside. Everything was quiet, as usual, not a soul around.

Again the voices in my head and the visions of a commotion or … something, I don't know. What was I thinking about, just a few seconds ago, something about police cars?

"Hey, your breakfast is getting cold!" Marie called. "Come on."

I turned around and headed back into the kitchen to have breakfast with my wife. Wife!

"There it is again," I said.

"There what is again?" Marie asked.

"Voices in my head," I said.

"You have been working too hard on that project of yours," she said, tapping my hand.

"I guess I just don't —"

"Come on and eat your breakfast; it's getting cold."

I managed to get through the meal but felt dizzy and confused the entire time.

"Marie?"

"Yes?"

"Tell me something."

"Sure, what do you want to know?"

"How long have we been married?"

"Really now, don't tell me you forgot our wedding," she said, with disappointment in her voice.

"Really, how long? I want to know."

"We were married in 1987, you know that," she said, now sounding concerned. "What's the matter with you?"

"I don't remember our wedding," I replied.

"What do you remember?"

"Something about Brian and Michael and police cars and drugs, and yes, someone was hurt, shot, shot and killed!"

Marie just sat there with a smirk.

"I'm not kidding, something is wrong. Brian and Michael, Brian and Michael." I repeated the names over and over and turned to look at Marie for some sort of acknowledgment.

"Who are Brian and Michael?" she asked.

I ran into the bedroom and pulled out the log book and paged through it for any information about a loss of memory of any kind. I came across an entry for July 10, 2014: "7 p.m. Came home from the store, conducted test with tape recorder, successful. Loaded new program into computer, eliminated ghost server, added new hard drive, increased power for final jump."

I stood there with my head spinning, and then the room began to spin as well; then, everything went black.

I woke to the cool sensation of a wet cloth on my head and the sound of Marie's voice guiding me back to consciousness.

"You passed out," she said, dabbing a cool towel over my face. "How do you feel?"

"I feel a little groggy; what happened?"

"Like I said, you passed out; you ran in here and opened your big book, and then you were on the floor."

I went to stand up.

"Are you sure you're okay?"

"Yes I'm fine; let me up, please."

I knew the second I stood up that I had to prepare for our time jump.

"There is so much to do for the jump," I told Marie.

"Will you relax? Everything is all set, you said so yourself."

"When did I say that?"

"Last night, just before we went to sleep, remember?"

I shook my head and replied with a confused no.

"Look," Marie said, pointing over to the bed. "All our clothes for 1929 are already laid out. The tape recorder is plugged into the kitchen outlet. All we have to do is get dressed, grab the recorder, hit the button on the remote, and go."

"How could I ever manage to do without you?"

"I was just wondering the same thing," Marie said as she kissed me on the cheek. "Now, come on, let's get ready."

I closed the log book and put it off to the side. Marie went into the bathroom to shower and get ready. I waited in the living room for her to emerge from the bathroom so I could take my shower. While sitting on the sofa, faint sounds of voices echoed in my head, nagging at my brain.

"Okay, you're next," Marie said before turning on the blow dryer in the bedroom.

I took a very long and very hot shower, letting the steam penetrate every pore on my body. When I finished and opened the bathroom door, steam wafted out and rolled across the ceiling. I grabbed a second towel and began to dry my hair as I walked in the bedroom. Marie was putting on some final touches of makeup. She was already dressed in her 1920s clothes and struck a pose for me.

"So what do you think?" she asked.

"Beautiful," was all I could say.

I dressed in my 1920s clothes and put on some hair gel, combing it back into the style of the time. I picked up the old pocket watch, set it for the correct time, and placed it securely in my vest pocket.

"I love these shoes," Marie said as she slipped her black heels on. "I'm not sure about this dress, though." She turned to show me where it came together just below her waist. "It's a little tight here, doesn't move well." She gave a tug on the fabric and then let it go. "It will have to do," she said, taking one last look in the mirror.

"I'm almost ready," I told her and sat down on the edge of the bed to tie my shoes. Afterwards, I stood up and asked her to give me a once-over to make sure I didn't forget anything.

"Did you take some money with you?" Marie asked, reaching into both front pockets of my trousers and giving me a little squeeze.

"Hey," I said, "no time for that; we have to go soon."

"Just teasing you, honey."

I grabbed a handful of dollars from the 1920s pile and placed them in my pocket. I took one last look in the mirror and pronounced myself ready. Marie and I knelt down together near the edge of our bed and said a prayer that we would be successful with our mission. Before starting the time machine, we swept through the house, making sure everything was in its proper place. We didn't want to come back to a messy home. I unplugged the tape recorder from the wall outlet and held it tightly under one arm. We positioned ourselves in front of the archway and gave each other a kiss for luck. I double-checked the date and time on the remote, Monday, August 5, 11:55 a.m., and pressed the Engage button. The archway sprang to life, and the familiar sound of a vibration filled the air. Everything had come down to this; what would be waiting for us when we returned? Would we still be together?

Who could say? When it had finished its sequence, we were ready to step into 1929.

Marie and I held hands firmly and stepped through the archway into 1929, leaving 2014 behind. The trip itself was instantaneous and quite enjoyable; we didn't end up on the floor this time; in fact, we arrived standing upright and were immediately aware of our surroundings. Getting right down to business, I checked the remote control display: "Monday August 5, 11:55 a.m." flashed across its face. I pulled out the pocket watch and marked the time.

"We have exactly five minutes to prepare for Marie and Doug," I said.

"I'm as ready as I'll ever be," she exclaimed.

"Remember the plan; stay as close to me as you can, and move when I say, not before."

I took a quick look around just to make sure we were alone. Everything appeared quiet, although I thought I noticed some movement out in the backyard. I checked the time again: 11:56 a.m.

"Only four minutes until they arrive," I said to Marie.

"What's going to happen to us after they are gone?"

"I don't know for sure; Doug Sr. seemed pretty confident with the plan the last time we spoke to him."

"What time is it now?" Marie asked.

"It's 11:56, no, 11:57 a.m., we still have three minutes. Listen, the device takes about twenty to thirty seconds to power up, so at exactly 11:59:30, we will turn it on."

"I'm getting really nervous; my palms are sweating," Marie said as she gripped my arm tightly. "Before this happens, I just want to tell you something." She pulled me around to face her. "No matter what happens, I want you to know that I have treasured each and every day I have had with you." She kissed me hard on the lips and added, "I have always loved you."

We were feeling the pressure of the clock ticking away seconds, bringing us closer to the inevitable.

"I want you to know, as well, that life is not worth living if you are not a part of it. You are life to me," I told her.

Marie squeezed my arm harder; I could feel the moisture of her sweaty palms through my shirt.

"I'm scared," she said.

"I am too, honey," I replied.

I checked the time: 11:59:00.

"We have thirty seconds before switching on the device. Remember now, move when I move; we will only have one shot at this."

"I'm with you," she said.

Another glance at the pocket watch: 11:59:20.

"Get ready," I said and pulled her close. I could feel her shaking nervously now and holding on to me as tight as she could.

11:59:30

"Here we go."

I pushed the Rewind button on the tape recorder, and it began its powering-up sequence. At 11:59:45, the archway began to hum, and the perimeter of the wooden molding began to glow a neon blue color. This was the first time we were witnessing a time traveler appearing from this side of the device. At 11:59:50, we could see the faint outline of two figures begin to appear, crumpled side by side on the floor, just in front of the opening. The recorder was nearly ready, just a few more seconds. We continued to observe as the original Marie and Doug fully materialized at our feet. It would only be seconds before the device would be fully functional, allowing us to push them back into the portal.

They began to stir and open their eyes. The original Marie was looking directly at us; her facial expression changed from confusion to outright fear. The original Doug began to move, trying to get to his feet. He opened his eyes; he, too, was looking directly at Marie and me, and his expression also changed to fear. As the two of them began to help one another up off the floor, the device began to perform its designed function and shielded us from the passage of time. The original Marie and Doug were now frozen in a posture with legs bent slightly in our direction. We noticed they were wearing exactly the same clothing, right down to the very last stitch.

"Now?" asked Marie.

"Wait a second, I replied; "just want to make sure we are ready."

"Look at them," she said, tilting her head slightly. "Look at them together." She sighed. "They are so cute."

When I was sure the device was functioning, I told Marie to get ready.

"I'm ready," she replied.

"On the count of three, just like when we tested it on the refrigerator, okay?"

"Okay," was her reply.

"One." We bent forward slowly, as if getting ready for the start of a race. "Two." We gripped each other tightly, forming one person out of two. "Three!" We lunged forward, stopping about six inches from them.

Unlike the refrigerator test, we experienced great resistance, like running face-first into a wall. An ear-piercing vibration, like a small explosion going off inside our heads, knocked us backward, and we tumbled to the floor. The concussion blinded us for a few seconds, but we regained our composure quickly and tried to stand. Shaking our heads, trying to remove the last of the horrible sound from our brains, we focused our attention on the archway. Both Marie and I tried hard to regain our sight, rubbing feverishly at our eyes.

"Do you see anything?" Marie asked.

"Not yet, you?"

"I see something, can't quite make it out."

Then at the exact same moment, while squinting in the direction of the archway, Marie and I saw what had happened.

The original Marie and Doug were gone; we were successful in our mission to prevent them from altering the timeline. Seconds passed, and our vision cleared enough to check the time on the pocket watch; it read 12:00:32.

"Thirty-two seconds," I said aloud, shaking my head in disbelief.

"What's thirty-two seconds?" Marie asked.

"That's all the time it took to complete the task and set things straight. Thirty-two seconds," I said, repeating it several times.

Marie took a deep breath and gave herself a quick brush-off.

"I don't feel any different," she said.

"Neither do I. My guess is that we are still protected by the protective time shield of the device."

Just then, we both realized that we were, in fact, still surrounded by the bluish glow of the bubble.

"So now what?" Marie asked, sounding a little impatient.

"Now we wait until the device powers down, but after that, I don't know. If we must stay here for the next twenty-four hours, we will have to leave the house like we did before but keep away from people and not interact with anyone. I don't want to make any unnecessary changes."

"How do we not interact with anyone?" Marie asked.

"Well, we will just have to do our best; remember what Doug Sr. said about how the simplest things can effect huge changes in the timeline? So we will go for a walk and try and stay busy until tomorrow, when we have to leave."

"I'd like to take a walk," Marie said, "but not in these heels; they will hurt my feet for sure."

"I know how you feel; the shoes I'm wearing are a little tight. I'm sure to get a blister or two along the way."

"You are not suggesting that we walk around for the next twenty-four hours, are you?"

"Not at all," I replied, "just stay as busy as we can, maybe take a room in a hotel somewhere to pass the time."

"Hotel room, huh?" Marie's eyes widened, and a smile washed over her face as she took my arm. "I can think of a few things to do while in our hotel room."

"I can think of a few myself," I told her and kissed her lightly.

It was at this moment we noticed that the bluish glow surrounding us began to fade. There was a shudder of vibration under our feet.

"That didn't happen before," Marie said, taking hold of my arm again.

"No, that has never happened before," I replied, pulling her closer to me.

The device continued to power down, and time, that is the time in 1929, slowly began to return to normal. We felt another shudder of vibration under our feet, this time a little more intense, and then another, followed by yet another.

"What's happening?" Marie asked; we looked all around for something that could be the cause but found nothing unusual.

It took a few more seconds for the device to completely power down, and the vibration continued, like huge invisible waves slapping against the beach. The air around us began to feel cold, and our warm breath was now visible as we exhaled. The device was now off, completely powered down, and the vibrations stopped.

The air temperature around us continued to drop dramatically.

Marie pulled herself closer, looking for warmth. "Doug," she said, "something is happening to me."

"I know, I can feel the cold as well."

"No, not the cold, something else," she said and backed away just enough for me to see what she was talking about. "I'm feeling light-headed," she said.

I looked at her, beginning with her head and working my way down until I noticed it. Her feet were gone, vanished, yet the rest of her body was still there.

"I'm floating," she said, in a faraway voice. "Doug?" she called out. "Where are you?"

"I'm right in front of you."

"I can't see you!" she cried.

I pulled her close to me and wrapped my arms around her, trying desperately to hold on. Little by little, her body began to dissolve in my arms, disappearing without a trace.

"Marie, can you hear me?" I yelled.

"I can hear you," she said, but her voice trailed off slowly.

"I don't know what's happening!" I cried. I tried with all my might to hold her body together, but it was useless; she continued to dissolve.

"Marie, my Marie, please stay with me," I bellowed. I fought to keep her fading substance with me, but to no avail. Only her face remained.

"Love you," she said in a barely audible voice.

I cupped her face in my hands; it felt icy cold, and I guided her to look at me. Her face became smaller as it dissolved away, leaving behind only her pretty brown eyes, and then they too were gone. When the last molecule of Marie vanished, I felt another shudder of vibration under my feet, and then, the sound of a woman screaming filled the room. I turned in the direction of the sound to find a young woman wearing a faded blue dress, staring at me in utter amazement and shock.

Her hair was pulled up tight into a bun behind her head, and she wore a crucifix around her neck. At first she said nothing and stood there, motionless. She then took hold of her crucifix with one hand, kissed it, and then crossed herself. I knew who she was in an instant by the old photos I had seen. This woman gave birth to four boys and five girls, who later became my father and my uncles and aunts; she was my grandmother, Marie Lupo.

Another wave of vibration swept under me, almost knocking me off balance, but it did not seem to have any effect whatsoever on my grandmother. She continued to stand there, motionless, kissing her crucifix and muttering a prayer. Another vibration, more intense than the last, rocked into me, lifting me off the floor, and there I hovered, without touching down. My grandmother's eyes were closed tightly, and she continued to pray. I felt the sensation of weightlessness and became dizzy and disorientated. I felt disconnected from the world around me as all my fears, worries, and concerns melted away, and then everything was black. I could still hear the sound of my grandmother praying, but then the sound of her voice started to drift away. Soon, I was left not only in the dark but unable to hear anything. I felt the last part of me drift off into nothingness, like the last grain of sand in an hourglass, passing into another place. My last thought was that of Marie, her face burned into my memory, and then I was no more.

Chapter 15

"Hello, anyone there?" I heard a deep, rumbling voice in the darkness. "Hello?" This time, it was a little closer and a little less intense. "Is anyone there?" the voice repeated, moving toward me.

I could not see anything, and I could not feel anything. I didn't know if I was standing or lying down or what. The voice rang out again, and this time, it was right in front of me. I tried to respond, but no words would form. I concentrated, and tried again, and then I was able to speak.

"I'm here," I said. "Who are you?"

"It's me," the voice responded, and then I felt pressure on my hand.

Excitement began to build inside of me as I realized that I had some degree of feeling in my body.

"Just give it a few minutes," the voice came, now more feminine.

I realized that it was a woman who was speaking to me. I tried to take air into my lungs and concentrated on my eyes.

"I want to see," I said. "I can't see."

"Relax, just give it a few minutes. You will be fine." The woman's voice was growing clearer.

"Marie?"

"Yes, sweetie, it's me," she answered and touched my hand again.

I didn't know how long it was until all of my senses returned. The first image I saw was that of Marie, looking down at me.

"Can you see me now?" she asked.

"Yes, I see you just fine. Where are we?"

"As far as I can tell, we are nowhere," she said, looking around as if to prove a point.

"How can we be nowhere? We have to be somewhere," I replied and gingerly lifted myself up to a standing position.

"I'm so glad you made it," Marie said. "It was very scary being here alone."

I looked around in every direction but could not make out a single landmark. I turned to Marie and asked, "How did you find me in this vastness?"

"I don't know for sure. I can't explain it," she said. "It's almost like I was being directed gently in your direction."

"I'm glad you were here for me," I said. "It must have been scary for you not to have someone there when you arrived."

"Oh, I was not alone," Marie said, answering quickly.

"What do you mean, you were not alone? Who was with you?"

Marie hesitated before answering, "Remember when Doug Sr. told us about the other Maries and Dougs, running around in different skews of time?"

"Yes, I remember; why?"

"Well, they are all here somewhere, or they *were* here, at least when I arrived," she said.

I looked around, but all I could see were clouds and bright lights. I didn't see anyone else except for Marie.

"There is no one here but you and me."

"Yes, we are the last ones," she said, moving closer to me. "One of the Dougs helped me to recover when I first arrived and stayed with me until you got here."

"How long have you been here wandering around?"

"I have no idea; for some reason, time here has no meaning. That is what they said, anyway."

"You mean to tell me you were a witness to all of the other Maries and Dougs, all running into each other at the same time?"

"It's not like that at all," Marie exclaimed, sounding annoyed that

I wasn't catching on fast enough. "You explained it to me; that is, the other Doug explained it."

"But —"

Marie interrupted, "Do you want to know, or don't you?"

"Sorry, go ahead."

"You told me that all of the Maries and all of the other Dougs had to be present before they paired off and left."

"Paired off?"

"Yes, each couple found each other, and then they walked off in that direction." She pointed. "The other Doug who stayed with me until you arrived left with another Marie."

"Where did they go?"

"I don't know, they just walked in that direction until they were gone." Marie pointed over to a very intense light somewhere off in the horizon.

I stood there for a minute and looked over to where she was indicating. I felt a pull at my heart and a sudden yearning to move toward the light.

"How do you think they knew who was who?"

"I don't know that either, they just did," Marie said with a smile. "Just like I found you, they found each other." She paused again. "Oh, and get this: Doug Sr. was here, too."

"What?"

"That's right, and he found his Marie, as well." Marie smiled again. "He said to thank you and that he knew you would do the right thing. Not for nothing, but I looked pretty good as an old lady, very elegant and refined."

"You saw yourself as an old woman?"

"Yes," she said. "Pretty weird, huh?"

"Yes, very," I said in return. "I bet you look beautiful as an old woman," I said, touching her face.

"There's only one way to find out," Marie said, facing the light that we would be walking toward and then looking at me. "Where do you think the road will take us?"

I thought for a moment, wanting my reply to sound meaningful. "To our new life, I guess," and with that, we walked, hand-in-hand, secure in the knowledge that somehow, somewhere, and at some point in time, the earth had a place for us.

Epilogue

So we all know what happened to all the Maries and Dougs who were floating around in different timelines. Each one found their way to each other and lived happily ever after; even Doug Sr. found his Marie after many years of living alone, in his miserable existence, missing his one true love. The original Marie and Doug found their place in the world and built a life together, as did all the others. So whatever became of Robert, the nice young man who in one timeline worked as a Realtor?

When the original timeline was reset, Robert's life was also changed. Robert worked as a Realtor for ten years before he met the girl of his dreams, and they married. They built a house in Budd Lake, New Jersey, where they raised three children. Robert and his wife were very happy and worked hard to provide a happy and safe environment for their family. Robert's wife, Melissa, passed away at the age ninety-three, leaving Robert alone and heartbroken. Robert missed his Melissa so much that exactly seven days later, he passed away as well. Now they were reunited in the afterlife for all eternity.

It seemed as though everyone was privileged with a happy ending, finding the answers to questions they had their entire lives. They found love and contentment, holding onto it with all of their human strength. The world had become a friendlier place for lovers in love and for the lost souls who wandered around, looking to rest their weary bones. All seemed as it should be, as it was supposed to be, without question or limitation.

Life continued on for all of our friends and their families, until they faded away into a memory, to make way for the younger generations. This was always the plan and had been so since time began. With everything in its place and everything right in the world, who would have thought that one little tape recorder left behind in 1929 would create such a stir?

The plan was for Marie and Doug to return to their time with the device when they finished their task; however, as we know, they went on to a much better place, leaving it behind for someone else to find.

The concept of using magnetic tape to record audio was imagined by Oberlin Smith in 1888, and the first recorder was invented by Valdemar Poulsen in 1898. Magnetic tape was developed in 1928 by Fritz Pfleumer. A compact version of this was not available until much later.

The first cassette player was introduced to the audio market in 1963 by Philips. It hit the European market initially and came to the United States the following year. The compact cassette became as popular as LPs were by the late 1970s.

Because no one had seen a compact tape recorder in 1929, it was questioned by my grandfather, who at first glance thought it was some type of fancy cigarette case. He imagined that the power cord was for keeping it secure, so that it could not be accidently pushed off the counter.

My grandmother thought that it might have been used as a paperweight but didn't know what all the buttons were for, except for the Eject button, which opened the tape compartment. After many years of just sitting on the counter (cigarettes were not very common at the time), the device was removed and stored away in a closet.

Years passed, and then in 1980, my grandfather died in June, and my grandmother followed him to eternity exactly seven days later. The house remained empty for nearly a year, until I moved in and breathed new life into the tired old place. I spent all of my free time cleaning, repairing, painting, and restoring the house. I made it my home and enjoyed the ever-present feeling that the spirits of my grandparents were still around, keeping a watchful eye on me. I was just eighteen years old, happy for the most part, and settled into my first real place of my own. It wasn't until I removed the last of the boxes in the bedroom closet that I came across a weathered old cassette recorder.

I was very interested in the little recorder; it looked very old, but the manufacturer's label said that it was only three years old. The plastic case was yellowed and had a patina that suggested that it was much older, and the plastic itself was brittle and dried out. One of the buttons in particular, the Rewind button, was much dirtier than the others, suggesting extensive usage.

I put the recorder aside and continued to remove the contents of the final box. There were several folders that contained medical documents that belonged to my grandmother. Most were evaluation reports about the condition of her pacemaker and other physical ailments.

There were several birthday cards that read "Happy Birthday Grandma" on its cover as well as a handful of anniversary cards. I continued paging through the documents and came across some old bank statements and a copy of the original deed from the early 1900s. On the bottom of the box was an envelope that contained more medical records, but these were different. Further investigation revealed a history of mental illness reports. I sat with my back up against a wall and read through the pages. It said that my grandmother, Marie Lupo, was placed in a psychiatric hospital for observation. There were many progress reports in the folder as well.

The first report was dated Friday, August 9, 1929. Dr. Carl Desantis wrote a brief description of Marie's claim to have seen ghosts in her kitchen; they had vanished right before her eyes. The description was followed by several medical terms and the opinion of the doctor who indicated that he believed that she indeed saw something that day and determined that is was only a hallucination brought on by a traumatic experience. There were many pages of these types of reports relating to my grandmother's "condition," as it was referred to.

I continued reading and discovered that she had three years of intense psychoanalytical sessions with the good doctor, until he released her from his care sometime in 1932. The actual date was blurred from the document, due to what appeared to be water damage. As I continued paging through the documents, I came across an old picture, dated Monday, March 24, 1930. The picture itself was yellowed and had once been torn in half and taped back together; it contained hairline cracks that ran across the face, ending in jagged edges along its perimeter. The black-and-white picture itself was still clear as crystal and showed what I recognized as a cassette tape recorder.

I looked at the picture several times and then compared it to the recorder I found in the box. There was absolutely no way this could be possible; they didn't have this kind of technology back in 1930. My curiosity was getting the better of me, and I dug deeper into the pile of papers, hoping to find additional information that might shed some light on this strange situation. After several more minutes, I came across another picture with a small note still attached to it by a rusty paper clip. The picture was that of a young woman displaying something in her hand.

The something in her hand was the tape recorder, and the woman in the picture was my grandmother. The note attached to the picture said "Mrs. Marie Lupo, March 24, 1930, and paperweight." If this was some kind of trick, it was very elaborate, but something inside of me was offering another suggestion.

I continued to read through the documents and found a letter from my grandfather to my grandmother, apparently while she was away in a hospital for some sort of testing. He wrote a very heartfelt letter, saying that he missed her and wanted her to come back home, that he was sorry he doubted her and he believed her now. I wondered what he meant by that. Then he continued to say that he would show her what he meant when she returned. "Just tell them whatever you think they want to hear, but just come home," is how he ended the letter.

What I found next really knocked me for a loop. It was an old newspaper article torn and faded to the point where it was almost unreadable. There was no date, but the headline read "Housewife claims living with ghosts." The article mentioned my grandmother and told a story about a visitation of two people one day in 1929 in her kitchen. According to my grandmother, she first witnessed two people who looked like they may have been in some kind of terrible trouble. "They looked scared" was how she put it. She went on to say that the woman ghost vanished slowly right in front of her, and the other ghost, who was a man, tried to hold onto her as she faded away.

Then soon after, the man vanished as well, but not quickly, as my grandmother told the story. "They dissolved like fine dust in the wind," she said in her description. "That's why I didn't think they were real ghosts."

My head began to spin as I read the sentence again; if she didn't think they were ghosts, then what did she think they were? If not for the tape recorder, I would have just wrote this off as some kind of mental breakdown and moved on, but the device was fascinating because of its debatable history, and each bit of information that presented itself made it more so. Then just when I thought I knew all there was to this crazy story, I found something else.

Reaching into the bottom of the box, I found a heavy leather journal. Its cover read simply "1931–1944." I opened the journal and began to read the first page; the bottom half was missing. The entry was handwritten, apparently with the use of a fountain pen. The letters were spread wide on the page but clear enough to make out what they said. "So that everybody doesn't think I'm crazy" is how it started. It continued, "Maria was right, the little box is something special, but we don't know where it comes from." Then my grandfather sketched a picture of the recorder, and I have to say that it was spot-on, with the exact dimensions and texture. I never knew that my grandfather had any artistic ability. He continued, "I plugged the thing into the wall and nothing happened," and then he added, "When I unplugged it from the wall and pushed down the Rewind button, something happened to me." The rest of what he was trying to say was cut off.

I spent the rest of the day and part of the night reading my grandfather's journal, which talked about everything freezing in place whenever he would press the Rewind button. My curiosity got the better of me; I pulled the recorder over to me and pushed the Rewind button, but nothing happened. I thought to myself that what I was doing was very silly and moved the thing over to the corner. I didn't know what to expect; maybe, at the very least, I would hear some kind of static through its speakers. Then I remembered my grandfather saying that he plugged it into the wall and then unplugged it and pushed the Rewind button. I plugged the recorder into the wall and then immediately unplugged it and pushed the Rewind button; nothing. I tossed it aside and decided to turn in for the night. My eyes were burning and dry, and they were irritated further by rubbing them to the point of making them swollen. As soon as I hit the mattress, strange imaginings filled my head with countless possibilities of what might be the real story behind the recorder. I slowly drifted off to sleep.

Friday came quickly, and I scrambled to wash up and get ready for work. Both Marie and I always looked forward to Fridays; the end of the work week and the knowledge that Saturday was right around the corner. I worked for a large pharmaceutical company in Clifton as a heavy-duty pipe cleaner; basically, I clean dirty pipes. The job leaves me a lot of time to think about what I want to do with my life. One thing I can say for sure is that I do not want to be a pipe cleaner. The day moved along quickly, and I was soon driving home, with the smell of raw vitamin E infused into my uniform. It's not a bad smell, but it does tend to be overwhelming.

While driving, I lowered the windows to help vent out the interior of the car. I felt the fresh air across my face, and it seemed to clear my mind. I got to thinking about the recorder again. I couldn't imagine why my grandfather would make up such an elaborate story. Who in their right mind would think that you can freeze something by use of a tape recorder? What an imagination, right?

I reached down and tuned the radio to an oldies station, and immediately Cousin Brucie was introducing a song and making a joke. I let my mind drift as Dion's "The Wanderer" played over the air waves. I started to sing along: "I'm the type of guy who never settles down, I'm never in one place, I roam from town to town." Then it hit me, a feeling of déjà vu, like I had lived another life in someone else's body. Then the feeling started to overwhelm me, and I realized that it wasn't my life I was sensing but my grandfather's. I was seeing events through his eyes. What I was seeing wasn't clear, but wave after wave of images flooded my thoughts.

There were images of my grandmother and the house and the recorder. I let my mind wander a little too much, and my car began to move into oncoming traffic; I was snapped back into the here-and-now by the horn of another car that came within inches of me. All I could hear as the guy in the other car passed me was "Asshole!" I swerved out of the way, steered myself back on the right side of the street, and pulled over to shake it off.

As soon as my car came to a complete stop, I realized I had a flat tire; at the same time, the strange sensation of cigar smoke filled my nostrils. I recognized the pungent odor immediately as my grandfather's cigar. The smell always made me gag when I visited my grandparents' house as a child. Gramps would sit for hours in his chair in the kitchen, looking out the rear window and complimenting himself on a job well done with some backyard project or other. The conversations were always the same, as he and my grandmother talked about all their aches and pains and how certain members of the family never came by to see them anymore.

Then they would talk about dying and where they wanted to be buried. It was all as a matter-of-fact kind of conversation they would have, along with my father and mother, who would be sitting at the table as well. My brothers and I would be in the living room, watching their black-and-white television in the hopes of seeing one of our favorite shows like *Hee-Haw* or *Laugh-In*. I would be sitting there, drawing pictures on sheets of paper that my grandmother would give me. The visual imprint of her handing me sheets of paper has never left my memory. Strange how certain things tend to stick in your memory. My brothers Ralph and Dave would sit so close to the television screen that they were almost a part of the show. My mother would constantly tell them to sit back because it was bad for their eyes. Sure enough, they ended up needing glasses very early on in their lives. Even with the three of us two rooms away from the kitchen, we could still smell the unmistakable odor of cigar smoke. We all had it on our clothes when we got home from our visits.

I sat for a few minutes, clearing my head, and then get out to change the tire. I opened the trunk of my car and found the spare tire; it looked in worse shape than the flat tire. I jacked up the car and made the exchange and climbed back into the driver's seat. I started the car, put my hands on the wheel, and noticed that they were shaking. I gripped the wheel harder to steady them and looked up to check my rearview mirror before pulling into traffic. I froze in place as my eyes caught the outline of a person sitting in the back seat.

There was no body to speak of, just the outline, which seemed to refract the surrounding light in such a way as to form the shape of a body. The smell of cigar smoke filled my nostrils, and my eyes began to water. I let out a cough and turned my head quickly for a better look. I half-expected the image to be gone, but instead, it became more dense and detailed. The image sank into the seat, as if its weight increased, and soon I was able to recognize who it was.

Gramps let out a breath filled with smoke in my general direction. I coughed and gave my eyes a rub with both hands. I was praying that the rubbing would make the image of my grandfather disappear, but it didn't.

"Doug," my grandfather said, expelling my name at the end of his puff of smoke.

"Gramps?" I asked.

"What are you doing with the tape recorder?" he asked in a scolding tone, as if I were a puppy that just peed on the floor.

"I haven't done anything yet and ..." I stopped. "How the heck am I talking to you, anyway?"

"That's not important, what is important that you stop right now with your curiosity about the tape recorder."

I felt the air in my lungs decompress as I exhaled my next sentence.

"Then why did you leave behind all this information about it?"

"I never intended to keep that information," he said, lowering his translucent head. "I meant to destroy everything when I completed my testing of the thing." He paused a moment and then asked, "Do you know what that thing is?"

"A tape recorder that can make things cold or freeze stuff," was my reply.

"What in the world gave you that idea?" he asked, again with another puff of smoke.

"I read your journal, and it specifically said that when you pushed the Rewind button, things froze in place."

Gramps laughed and said with a wide grin, "Good, that's what it's for: making things cold, but it doesn't work anymore."

"I agree that it doesn't work," I said. "I actually tried it a couple of times, but nothing happened."

"Do me a favor and just destroy it, and burn all my notes."

"Why do you want me to do that?"

"I don't want you to get into any trouble by freezing anything accidentally."

"Gramps, I just want to know one thing."

"What's that?"

"I want to know the truth of what it is and what it does."

"It's better if you do not know," he said, now visibly agitated. "You were always asking questions as a child; you never seem satisfied with a simple answer. You always wanted to know more and more."

"Gramps, I'll make you a promise."

"What?"

"If you tell me the truth, I will destroy everything according to your wishes."

"Doug," he said in a low tone, "I really don't know what the truth is."

"Just tell me what you do know about it," I replied.

"Your grandmother found the thing on the kitchen floor one day, after she said she witnessed an apparition of two people dissolving into thin air." He took another drag of his cigar and let out a huge blast of smoke. "You know by my notes and the other documents that she was in a hospital for quite some time; we all thought she was crazy." He paused. "I thought she was crazy too, and I agreed to have her committed for psychiatric observation and treatment."

"I know that already. I read your notes and the reports from the doctors. Tell me about the device; what is it?"

"I was using it as cigarette holder," he said. "I liked the way the lid would flip open when you pushed in the button." My grandfather lifted his hand, and the stub of his cigar vanished, and a new one appeared, already lit and ready to smoke. He took another drag and again blew the smoke in my direction.

"You know that smoke is killing me, right?" I said sarcastically.

"I came across the special function totally by accident when I pushed the Rewind button, and everything stopped."

"What do you mean, everything stopped?"

"I mean time stopped." He looked right at me and said again that time itself stopped.

My mind was racing, searching for a twinge of reality in what my grandfather was telling me. I picked up my head and looked at him; he was still puffing on his cigar.

"So what happens when time stops?" I asked him in a nonchalant, matter-of-fact tone.

"What do you think it means?" He paused. "It means that everything just stops; people stop moving, the clock stops ticking, the wind stops blowing, even sound itself stops"

"So what happens to you when you stop time?"

"Nothing happens to me," he replied. "I'm in some kind of bubble that keeps me safe."

I let out a little cough and said, "So time stops, and you are in a bubble, and you can see that everything around you is not moving, correct?"

"That's what I said," my grandfather said, sounding a little agitated now.

"So what happens then?" I asked him.

"Well, after a few minutes, everything returns to normal."

"That's it?" I asked. "Nothing happens, except time stops for a few minutes, and you are not affected, and then time starts up again, and everything is back to normal."

"That's what I said," my grandfather replied. "Now you know what it is and what it can do, so when you get back to the house, destroy it and all the documents, like you said you would."

"I agreed to destroy it," I said, "that's true, but I didn't say when."

"Don't do this, Doug." My grandfather's voice echoed loudly in my head as I watched his faint outline dissolve away, and with it went the smell of cigar smoke.

I turned around to face the front of the vehicle, opened the windows wide, and took in a fresh breath of air. I put the car into drive and raced through town to get home quickly. I wanted to do a few tests myself on the recorder before I destroyed it. My curiosity was taking over my rational thinking. What was it that my grandfather said, he didn't want me to get into trouble? What kind of trouble could I get into by playing with a tape recorder? I pulled the car over to the curb in front of my house and practically ran inside the rear door. I couldn't wait to get my hands on the thing to see what stopped time looks like.

I jumped out of my clothes, washed up quickly, and put on something comfortable. After pulling on a sweatshirt and a pair of ripped sweatpants, I took the recorder and plugged it into the wall outlet in the kitchen. I decided to just leave it plugged in for a while before engaging in another test. I lay down on my bed and put my head, intending to just rest for a minute. I was awakened by the phone on my nightstand and its annoying ring.

I fumbled for the thing, knocking the receiver to the floor. I heard a woman's voice and started to wake up. I gave my head a quick shake to snap me back to the land of the alert, reached over, and put the phone to my ear.

"Hello?" I said.

"Hey."

"Oh, hey, Marie."

"Whatcha doin'?"

"I was just taking a quick nap. Still feeling a little drowsy," I said. "Can you come over right away? There's something I want to show you."

"Are you hungry?" Marie asked.

"I'm not hungry now, but later I may get the munchies, why?"

"I'm bringing over something, okay?"

"Sure, okay."

It wasn't long before I heard the sound of knocking at my kitchen door. I pulled myself out of bed, walked over to the door, and opened the curtain. The first thing I saw was Marie's smiling face, looking at me. One thing I could say about her: No matter what was going on in her life, she always had a smile for me.

I opened the door, and she stepped inside.

"I brought some leftovers from dinner at my aunt's house tonight," she said, placing a bowl on the kitchen table.

"Thanks," I replied.

"What the heck is that?" she asked, pointing to the cassette recorder on the table.

"It's a tape recorder."

"I know it's a tape recorder, but what happened to it?"

"What do you mean?"

"It looks like it's been through a war," she said.

"Yeah, it's a little beat up, I know."

"So do you feel like eating, or should I put this in the fridge for tomorrow?"

"I'll have it for lunch tomorrow," I replied and gave Marie a kiss on her cheek.

Marie opened the heavy door on the old fridge and placed the bowl inside. She slammed the door closed, took my hand, and led me into the bedroom.

"You look tired, rough day at the office, dear?" she asked, while running her fingers through my hair.

"Not really, just the usual day at work, but there is something else I wanted to tell you."

"Can it wait until morning?" Marie asked, positioning herself directly in front of me and planting a warm, soft kiss on my lips.

"I really want to tell you what happened on the way home from work."

"Oh?" Marie pulled back with a concerned look on her face. "Everything all right?" she asked.

"I'm not entirely sure about that," I said. "I ran into one of my old relatives tonight."

"Anyone I know?"

"I don't think you ever met my grandfather, did you?"

Marie looked at me with confusion and asked, "Didn't your grandfather pass away not long ago?"

"Yes, he did."

"So how did you meet up with him?"

I stood up and started pacing back and forth in front of Marie, who seemed to be anxiously awaiting my response. "He, um, just appeared in the back seat of my car, right after I got a flat tire. I almost ran off the road."

"Oh, my gosh," Marie said with a start. "You were in an accident?"

"No, I was not in an accident, but I did have a conversation with my dead grandfather."

Marie put her hand to my forehead and checked the temperature.

"No, you don't have a fever," she said with a smile.

"I can't explain it, but I did speak with him, and what made it even more realistic was that he was smoking his smelly cigars. The smoke made my eyes tear."

"I'm not sure I understand what you're trying to tell me."

"I'm going to have to start from the beginning."

"Okay, then, start from the beginning."

I walked over to the box of pictures, pulled out the old photo of my grandmother and the tape recorder, and handed it to Marie.

"Who's this, your grandmother?"

"Yes, it is. Can you see what she is holding?"

Marie looked carefully at the picture and then at me and then again at the picture and asked, "Is this date correct?" She looked at me again, now realizing that a mystery was brewing.

"Yes, it's from the 1930s, that's for sure. You see how old it is? Look at the tape holding it together, how yellowed it is."

"Doug, this is impossible. Someone is playing a joke, I think," Marie said, giving me a wink.

I just shook my head and said, "No, it's not a joke."

"So you're trying to tell me that the beat-up tape recorder on your kitchen table is the same one in this picture with your grandmother from the 1930s."

I took the picture from Marie and returned it back to the box, and then I pulled out some of the other documents and pictures and handed them to her.

"Oh, you have got to be kidding me," she said. "This can't be; I mean, they didn't have tape recorders back then, did they?"

"I researched that, and no, tape recorders were not around until the late sixties, early seventies, at least this type of cassette recorder."

"Then how is that your grandmother had one back in the thirties?"

I picked up my grandfather's journal and handed it to her.

"What's this, now?"

"It's my grandfather's journal; he writes about the tape recorder, and get this, according to my grandfather, it's not just a recorder, it's a, well, some type of time-stopping thingy."

"Time-stopping thingy?" Marie repeated, with a bit of humor in her voice. "What the heck is a time-stopping thingy?"

"Keep reading and see what he has to say about it. In the meantime, I'm going to unplug the tape recorder and bring it here for us to try something."

Marie buried her face in the journal and continued reading; from time to time, she raised her head and gave me a look that seemed to say "You've got to be kidding me."

After a while, she laughed and said, "There is no way this is true; someone is pulling your leg."

"That's what I thought, until I reviewed every single document in the box. There are even doctor's evaluation reports concerning my grandmother and her quote 'mental state,' unquote." I handed a few of the reports to Marie.

"I can tell you one thing," she said. "These reports look genuine."

I sat back and watched as Marie read through the documents. I pulled the tape recorder over and placed it on my lap. As Marie continued to read, I moved next to her and told her to stop for a second.

"What do you have in mind?" she asked with a smile.

"I want to try this tape recorder and see if anything happens."

Marie put down the papers and gave me her full attention.

"The recorder has been plugged into the wall outlet for hours, so it should be ready."

"Go ahead and push your buttons," she replied. "I'm sure nothing is going to happen."

I put one arm around Marie and pushed the Rewind button with my other hand. We sat on the edge of my bed and watched as the lights in the room began to darken, and at the same time, a bluish bubble formed around us.

"This is weird," Marie said as she gripped my thigh with her one hand and squeezed tightly. "What's supposed to happen now?"

"I don't really know," I said. "This is more than I have been able to get it to do before." Speaking in a whisper, as if someone would overhear us, I explained, "According to my grandfather, time itself is supposed to stop."

"How can we tell if time stopped or not?" Marie asked.

"You're wearing a watch," I said. "Look at the second hand; is it moving?"

"Yes."

"Then I don't get it; nothing has stopped."

"Wait, look at that," Marie said, pointing to the clock on the nightstand. "It's not moving!"

I asked her to stand up, and we moved toward the living room window. I opened the curtain, and we both looked outside. Nothing was moving, not even the leaves on the trees or the constantly blinking streetlight.

"This is the coolest thing I've ever seen," Marie said, with excitement in her voice.

"Who would have believed that this tape recorder could stop time?"

"Now that you know what it can do, what are you going to do with it?"

"I have no idea," I replied and started to move toward my bedroom, with Marie close behind. "I just wanted to make sure I was not going crazy."

We walked back into my bedroom and sat back down on the bed, with the recorder in my lap; to our amazement, we noticed that sound also had stopped as well.

"Freaky," Marie said.

"Yeah freaky, that's for sure."

As we continued to sit, we noticed that the lights in the room were beginning to return back to normal, and the second hand on the clock on the nightstand began to move. The sounds all around us returned slowly, as if someone started up an old-fashioned record player. Soon, everything was back to normal.

We sat on the edge of the bed for several more minutes, waiting to see if anything else would happen, but nothing did. We let go of each other when we were sure it was safe to do so. Excited, I stood up quickly, forgetting that the tape recorder was still in my lap. With a crash, if fell to the floor and shattered.

Both Marie and I stood, motionless, staring at the tape recorder, with hundreds of pieces now scattered across the floor.

"What the hell?" Marie said. "You think you can fix it?"

I gave her a silly look and shrugged my shoulders in response.

"I don't think so," I replied, and as I said the words, I remembered promising my grandfather that I would destroy the device after seeing what it could do.

I said aloud, and in a clear voice, "It is done, Gramps."

"What's done?" Marie asked.

"I promised him I would destroy the tape recorder after I saw what it can do. Well, we saw what it can do, and now it's destroyed."

"You can say that again," Marie said with a chuckle.

I bent down, gathered the pieces together, and noticed a small piece of metal, about one inch by three inches; it had numbers etched in it. Then I noticed a name etched into the piece of metal; it read "Doug." I showed it to Marie, and she looked at me with disbelief.

"You said you didn't know where this came from."

"I don't know, and I can't explain why my name is on this thing."

Marie gave me another look and said, "If not for the demonstration, I would think you were definitely pulling my leg. So what are you going to do now?"

"I'll keep a piece for a souvenir and discard the rest."

"It's a shame you can't fix it."

"I don't know if I want to even try; just holding it rattles my nerves."

Marie leaned over to me and said, in her sexy bedroom voice, "You really know how to show a girl a good time."

"What do you mean by that?"

"Your little tape recorder stopped time for us; how many girls can say they have done that with their boyfriend?"

"I guess you have a point about that. We will never be able to tell anybody about it," I added. "Who would believe us, anyway?"

"I saw it for myself, and I don't even know if I believe it."

"We did see it happen, didn't we?"

"We did."

I leaned down, gathered the remaining pieces, and put them into the box, along with all the documents and photos. "Tomorrow, I'm going to burn everything outside in the yard."

"You're not keeping anything?"

"Just this little piece of metal with my name on it," I said. "Everything else goes."

After cleaning up the mess, Marie and I settled in for what we hoped to be a quiet night. She went off to the bathroom to freshen up, and I put the box out on the kitchen table so I would remember to take care of the disposal first thing after breakfast. I walked back into the bedroom and threw myself down on the bed. The day's events were replaying in my head, over and over again. I felt dizzy from the influx of data just smashing into my brain. It wasn't long before Marie returned and joined me on the bed.

She immediately snuggled up alongside of me and put her head on my chest. I felt all my worries and concerns melt away until I was completely relaxed.

"Awww," Marie said, rubbing her hand on my chest. "Is my little mad scientist feeling better?"

I took a deep breath, and as I exhaled, I released the last of my troubles. A warm and cozy feeling washed over me as I inhaled the fragrance of Marie's body.

I moved down lower in the bed and joined her face-to-face. "Thanks for coming over tonight."

"My pleasure, sir," Marie replied.

I reached over and turned out the light on the nightstand. I felt my body began to respond to Marie's, as we slipped our arms around each other and drifted off to another place where time was not an issue.

The morning came in like a lion, as the sound of heavy rain and wind blowing against the old windows announced itself. They rattled when the wind was heavy, acting like an alarm clock sometimes. I had become used to the noise they made, but this was something new to Marie. I leaned over to see if she was sleeping and noticed that her eyes were wide open, with a look on her face that said "What the hell was that?"

I gave her a kiss on her neck, and she let out a comfortable sigh. She turned and faced me, and we kissed good morning.

"Hungry?" I asked.

"I guess I could eat something," she said, yawning. "Do you have any coffee or tea?"

"I have tea, but I'm not sure about the coffee. Would you care for some tea with your breakfast?"

"Yes, I would, but let me help you." With that, Marie sprang out of bed, grabbed her clothes, and darted into the bathroom.

I put on my sweats and went into the kitchen to put some water on the stove to boil. I pulled out some eggs and bacon from the fridge and laid out Wonder Bread for toast. I didn't have a toaster the worked, so I made my toast on the hot frying pan.

"One thing I gotta say," Marie commented as she came out of the bathroom, "your hot water is always very hot." She dried her hands and moved over to the stove, where I was starting breakfast. "You gonna brush your teeth, lover?" she asked me with a devilish smile.

"I'm going right now," I said. "Can you get this started for me? I put the water on for the tea already."

"I got this, don't you worry," she said, and with that, she began preparing the meal.

I went into the bathroom to wash up and brush my teeth. I emerged refreshed and feeling great, and then I stood there, watching my barefoot Marie cook our breakfast. The clouds parted, the rain stopped, and the morning sunlight was hitting her in a way that made her look almost angelic. I sighed, walked over to her, and kissed her.

Marie responded with a hug and kiss as well. "Can you set the table? I got this over here."

"Sure, no problem."

I moved the box containing the documents and the fragments of the tape recorder off the table and placed it on the floor. I set the table, and soon we were both seated, having our breakfast.

"What a night last night," Marie said with a huge smile.

"Yes, I was quite the stud, wasn't I?"

"I'm not talking about that; I'm talking about the time-thingy thing."

"Oh that; yeah, that was really something," I said, "strangest thing I ever saw. Too bad we can't do it again."

"Why would you want to do it again?"

"I was thinking that it would be really cool to just walk right into a bank, take the money, and walk right out again, without anyone seeing anything."

Marie froze in her seat, and her mouth dropped open. "I'm surprised you would even consider such an act," she said. "That's not the guy I thought I knew."

"I'm not saying I would really do it, just pointing out the possibilities of what it could be used for."

"Hmmm," was Marie's reply.

"What's hmmm?"

"You and your time-thingy got me thinking."

"What about me and my time-thingy?"

"It seems to me that this was a good thing, that it broke on the floor in a million pieces."

"Hey, I said that I was only pointing out the possibilities."

"You're a nice guy, Doug. I want you to stay that way."

I sat still for a moment and let Marie's words soak into my thoughts.

"You're right," I said, "this really was a good thing to happen. Oh, that reminds me, I have some burning to do."

"Let's do it together," Marie replied.

"Yes, let's do it together."

After breakfast, Marie and I cleaned up quickly, threw on some clothes, and took the box outside to the back yard. I placed it inside of my homemade barbecue and soaked it with charcoal lighter fluid. I used the entire bottle and made sure every inch of the box was covered. I struck a match and threw it into the box, and it immediately caught fire. The roar of the flames and the crackling of the contents drew some attention from my neighbor, who poked his head out the window for a quick look-see. I waved at him and gave him a reassuring nod that everything was okay.

"Just me starting a fire, nothing to worry about," I joked.

After a few minutes, he pulled his head back in and closed the window.

"I know this was not easy for you to do," Marie said, holding onto my arm and placing her head on my shoulder.

"Actually, it wasn't as hard as I thought it would be."

"I'm glad." Just then, she excused herself to go back to the bathroom. "I'll be right back, nature calls."

"I'll be right here."

Marie walked into the house, and I stared at the flames licking up the sides of the box, causing black and white smoke to rise swiftly into the air. As I stood there, staring into the flames, I began to smell my grandfather's cigars again. The smell was overpowering, and my eyes began to water.

Just then, I saw his face inside the smoke from the box. "I'm proud of you, my grandson."

"Thanks, Gramps," I replied.

"Did you get everything?"

"Yes, I put everything into the box, including the documents, pictures, and the tape recorder."

"So everything is in there? Everything?"

"Well, I still have this," I said, pulling the small piece of metal from my pocket.

"I want you to destroy everything, every single piece, including that," he said, while puffing out large amounts of smoke.

"But Gramps, this is all I have to remember you with. What can I do with this tiny little piece of metal? The tape recorder is destroyed, so what would be the harm in keeping it?"

"Listen to me, I'm going to tell you a little secret," my grandfather whispered. "Come a little closer, I don't want anyone to overhear me."

I moved a little closer but kept my eyes on the flames, which were now shooting up into the air.

"Are you listening?" my grandfather asked quietly.

"Yes, you have my full attention, Gramps."

"First of all, nobody can hear me but you, right?"

"Right."

"Second, burn that piece of metal." His voice rang in my ears like standing next to a cannon blast.

"Gramps, let me keep it," I said. "What can I possibly use it for?"

"That little piece of metal is the time machine, not the tape recorder."

"What?"

"I should have told you before, but I thought that too much information would be dangerous."

"It would be dangerous to whom, Gramps?"

"Dangerous to you and everyone you know."

"But I don't even know how to make it work without the recorder."

"Yes, you do," he replied. "Somewhere inside of you, you know."

"How do you know this piece of metal is the time thingy? Did you make it?"

"Me? I could not even imagine creating such a thing."

"Then who did?"

"You did!" my grandfather exclaimed.

"Come on, I never made anything like that in my life."

"Not yet, but you will, and only if you hold onto that piece of metal."

"I still don't get it."

"Close your eyes," my grandfather said.

"Why?"

"Just close them; I want to show you something."

I complied and closed my eyes.

"Now empty your head."

I cleared my thoughts as best as I could and waited for something to happen. The smell of that cigar was irritating me to the point of vomiting.

"I'm going to show you what happens in the future if you hold onto that piece of metal."

"I'm ready, Gramps; go ahead," I said, not thinking that he was going to show me anything I didn't already know.

My grandfather blew a puff of his cigar smoke directly into my face, and I instantly began to see images forming in my mind. "I'm taking you backward from the time you dissolved in my kitchen with Marie, all the way back to the first thought of a time machine."

My head began to fill with images of the history of my time machine. I saw Marie and me as older people, still together, and then we weren't together. I saw many sad and lonely people, their faces passing my thoughts in a flash. I saw myself as an old man, tormented by a lost love. I saw Marie die over and over again, and I saw myself suffer in the same way. I saw a boy named Robert, who was somehow attached to Marie and me at some point in time. I saw myself tormented at losing Marie to another guy. Wait, losing Marie to another guy? When did this happen?

"Concentrate," came my grandfather's voice.

I watched myself build the contraption that would become the time machine. I saw blueprints and schematics race by in a blur. I watched as Marie and I made a life together and raised our children. I saw many years pass by, one after the other, until ending up at this exact moment in time.

The images stopped, and I opened my eyes. My grandfather's face was still hovered inside the burning box. My expression changed from confusion to deep concentration. This exact moment in time, while I stood in front of a box burning in my homemade barbecue, I had my very first thought of constructing a machine to manipulate time itself.

"Yes, that's right," my grandfather said. "Today is the day when everything changed in your life going forward, not just your life but everyone you ever knew and will know in the future, as well."

My grandfather paused, and then his image began to rise out of the smoky box and float toward me. He stopped just an inch or so in front of me.

"I know you will do the right thing this time, my grandson," he said in a comforting tone. He raised his hand and put it on my shoulder. "I can't visit you anymore; they are calling me back. You take care of that girlfriend of yours. She's the best thing that will ever happen to you. Good-bye, Doug." His words drifted away, as if coming from someone on a passing train.

I felt a hand on my shoulder, as I realized that I was not alone. Marie had returned from her bathroom break.

"Who were you talking to?" she asked quietly.

"I was just having a conversation with my dead grandfather's ghost."

"Oh, is he still here? I want to say hello," Marie laughed.

"I know, it's crazy, right?"

"I'm kidding you," she said and rubbed my back with her hand. "Are you okay? You look different."

"Different how?" I asked.

"I don't know, your face just seems very intense."

I told Marie what my grandfather showed me with the images in my head and said that the one thing that troubled me was when he said I had lost you to another man.

"What man?" she asked.

"I don't really know, but supposedly this guy took you away from me. I didn't like that one bit."

"Well, I'm here with you now, no other guy in sight."

Marie reached around me and planted a kiss squarely on my lips.

"How's that?" she asked.

"Wonderful," I replied. "I can't imagine not having your lips touch mine anymore."

"They are just for you, honey."

I pulled Marie close to me and hugged her tight.

"Are you okay?" she asked.

"I will be in a second."

Still holding onto the little piece of metal, I pulled away from Marie and stepped over to the flaming box. I looked down at the seemingly insignificant thing in my hand for several minutes and watched as it caught the sun's light, and the glint of it washed over my face. I thought about the possibilities of what a time machine might be used for. I saw visions of plans and schematics and working models of a device.

I saw myself working for years, obsessing over its construction. I saw how that obsession pushed Marie away. I saw my life pass by without her by my side. I saw many years of misery and frustration.

There was torment as payment for poor decisions and lost love. I felt lost and completely alone, with only the thought of the time machine to keep me company.

Then without hesitating further, I tossed the last small piece of metal into the fire and watched as the heat began to distort it. Its edges began to turn red, and then it began to melt away. Seconds later, a gust of cool breeze blew past us, and we felt completely rejuvenated.

"Wow, what was that?" Marie asked.

"Whatever it was, it's better than coffee."

"I know," I said. "I feel great, like I don't have a care in the world."

As we stood there, watching the box continue to burn, our memories of the entire day slipped away, one after another. Every single thought of a time machine disappeared forever from our minds. Soon, all that was left were the happy thoughts of us together. The terrible memories were being replaced by happy ones. Marie and I stood silent next to the ashes and watched as the last glint of red disappeared from the embers.

"The box and all its contents burned down into ash," I mumbled, "taking with it all the remaining remnants of the um, what was I saying?"

"You talking to me?" Marie asked.

"I was just saying something, but I forgot what it was I was thinking about."

"Are you happy now that you had your little fire?" she asked.

"I guess so, just wanted to try out my homemade barbecue."

"Let's go inside and watch some TV."

"Sounds good," I replied.

We started to walk back into the house.

"The *TV Guide* said there is a movie on later called *The Time Machine*."

"I know that movie," I said. "It's really cool, because this guy invents a time machine, and then he goes into the future and …"

Printed in the United States
By Bookmasters